PASSION'S SPLENDOR

CARLA SIMPSON

OLIVERHEBERBOOKS

1

MAY 1892

Late morning sun spilled into the second floor of the women's academy, washing the pale walls with sunlight as the half dozen young women crowded around the narrow gap in the floorboards and peered into the office of the head mistress below.

"If you get caught, I'll be to blame," Laine pointed out.

"Oh, Lainey, you're just afraid that you'll get another mark on your evaluation when you know that Miss Carter won't dare expel you. She likes the tuition she receives from your guardian."

It was true, and possibly the reason she'd escaped so far. The headmistress of the academy was like a warden at a prison. Or it was possible that she'd outgrown most of the escapades, such as the current one, that her younger schoolmates were prone too.

There was, of course, no way of knowing exactly how old she was as she had no idea when she was born. Her birthdate on her records at the prestigious private academy was the date she had gone to live with Elizabeth Ralston after she was orphaned.

The great mystery remained just who her parents were. It was something that Laine Dalton struggled with—no true family, no history other than the one Katherine Ralston had given her, no way of knowing who she was. There had been only that note, pinned to her dress when she arrived—*'Please take care of this child. Her name is Laine.* It was signed, *A. Dalton*

Since she had no other name, Laine Dalton became her name on official records of adoption. There had been attempts to find who her family might have been by Mrs. Ralston. She'd even had a private detective investigate. But he was never able to learn anything about a small child that arrived with other children and was taken in by Mrs. Ralston.

"Aren't you the least bit curious?"

"No!"

But she was. She crossed the room and dropped down beside the other *'young ladies'* of Miss Carter's exclusive academy.

"Who is it?" one of the girls asked, trying to get a better view into the office below as they all crouched over the planked flooring, and peered through the crack between the boards into the room below.

"Can you see anything?"

"There's a man sitting in front of Miss Carter's desk. I can't see his face," Laine's best friend Ellie Morgan, groaned as she crawled around on the floor to gain a better view.

"It must be Mr. Ambrose from the bank, his carriage is in front," Melissa answered from the window where she had kept watch since the carriage had been discovered in the circular drive below.

Laine frowned. He had been there just last month to discuss the arrangements for her to attend college in the fall. What could have brought him back again so soon?

"Someone's coming!" Dotty Adams warned from her lookout place at the door.

"It's Miss Mayhew!" She closed the door and joined the others as they all scrambled to pull the rug back into place over the gap in the floorboards.

There was hardly time for more, as there was a light knock at the door. Without waiting for a response, the academy's head matron, Elvira Mayhew, entered the room.

She surveyed the room with sharp dark eyes, her gaze also flitting over the half dozen young woman who stood before her. More than just the head matron, she also taught English literature, specifically the sonnets of Shelly and Byron, much to her *'ladies'* amusement.

As far as anyone knew she had never been married, which explained her preference for Shelly and Byron. Of course, it might also have been due to her disposition. Years before, she had been nicknamed, the old crow, by some brave young woman. She dressed in black with her hair pulled back severely, and there was an uncanny resemblance to that pesky bird.

Nothing escaped those sharp eyes now. Her thin lips were pursed as she gazed at her *'young ladies'*, and her brows pinched together as she wondered at the sudden silence in the room.

Unquestionably, her most effective weapon against the young girls at Clairmont was intimidation. It failed miserably and no doubt accounted a great deal for her waspish attitude towards all of the girls at Clairmont.

Laine glanced down at the floor, her gaze landing on a conspicuous wrinkle in the rug and she smoothed it with the toe of her shoe. She exchanged a look with Ellie, hoping the head matron hadn't seen it.

She looked directly at Laine. "Miss Carter wants to see you in her office," she informed her as those eyes slowly scanned the room.

"Yes, ma'am," she replied and held her breath as the woman

passed behind them, then rounded to the front of the room once more.

"I am certain the rest of you have studies to attend to," she reminded the rest of them.

"Yes, Miss Mayhew," they responded in unison. As the teacher left, they made faces at her back.

"Prune-faced old witch!" Ellie Morgan muttered, then asked the others, "Did you see anything?"

"There wasn't enough time. It has to be Mr. Ambrose from the bank. Who else could it possibly be?" Laine replied. She squeezed her friend's hand. "If I'm not back in an hour, send in the troops."

At the ground floor landing she found Miss Mayhew waiting for her. There was nothing in the woman's expression to give any indication what Miss Carter, headmistress of Clairmont, wanted to see her about, or who her guest might be.

Laine smoothed her hands down over her skirt and followed Miss Mayhew to the headmistress' office. At a knock on the door, the headmistress rose from her chair behind a desk to greet her with a friendly smile.

"Please join us, my dear. Mr. Ambrose has come to speak with you about a matter of some importance that has been brought to his attention."

As she crossed the office and took a chair across the desk from the head mistress, she caught a glimpse of someone else in the room, a figure half-hidden in the shadows at the other side of the office.

She nodded politely at Malcolm Ambrose, even as she angled a glance toward the other side of the office. A man sat there, that much she was able to determine but not anything more as Mr. Ambrose greeted her.

"It is good to see you, although I had not thought we would be meeting again quite so soon," he said politely.

He reminded her of a scrawny, gray mouse with his thin,

straggly mustache that twitched from side to side as he leafed through a stack of papers he had placed at the edge of the desk.

She folded her hands in her lap as she waited for him to collect his papers as well as his composure. She almost expected him to jump up at any minute and scurry across the room, squeaking.

"I do apologize for this, but certain matters have just been brought to my attention, and to the attention of Mr. Harold Patterson, the president of the bank. He has asked me to come here today, so that these matters may be cleared up."

She wished that he would get on with the matter. He finally seemed to find the paper he was looking for.

"Yes, here it is." He cleared his throat again. "You have been at Clairmont Academy for several years. You were brought here at the age of four as the ward of Mrs. Althea Ralston, distinguished philanthropist of our fair city."

He smiled in that way that Laine always noticed when he spoke of her guardian, careful of his words lest they be overheard by someone who might mention them to Mrs. Ralston.

He smiled again, and Laine caught the slight movement of the man across the room. As he shifted in the chair, she caught the slightest impression—he was tall, with long legs and he wore boots. Through the shadows there she glimpsed the wide shoulders beneath a jacket and longish hair but was unable to see anything of his features.

Had he come there with Mr. Ambrose, or was he there for another reason? What was the reason that he held back, watching, listening? What did that have to do with her as the banker continued?

"At that time, a trust was set up for you by Mrs. Ralston for the purposes of your education. And you are also the beneficiary of funds held for you until your twenty-first birthday." He looked up then, and the '*mouse*' smiled.

"By the records that we have, that would be in two months."

When she didn't respond but continued to listen, he continued. "As you well know, an extensive effort was made at the time of your arrival to locate your family... "

He flipped nervously through the paperwork and Miss Carter came to his rescue.

"What Mr. Ambrose is trying to explain, my dear, is that after all these years, certain... information has been made available which may lead to the identity of your real family."

Her family? Laine looked over at the banker. After all this time? Was it possible?

All these years she had hoped there might be some word of them, what had happened to then, through connections of Mrs. Ralston, some way to learn who she was.

She had always been keenly aware that she was different than the other girls, who had families they spent the holidays with, or traveled with when school was closed for a month each summer. Not that she wasn't grateful for the care she had received from Mrs. Ralston, but there was always that reminder that she had no family, had no idea who she really was...

As the years passed, hope of learning anything about her past, faded. There was only the future and she had forced herself to face it. Now, U.S Federal Marshal, Ranse McCandliss, had appeared and insisted on questioning her.

For what? The only answer was that it had to be about the reward money. If that handbill he'd now shown them was correct, five thousand dollars was offered just to know the whereabouts of the Dalton Gang. How much more might have already been offered for finding and arresting them?

She didn't know anything and if he thought she would be a pawn in some game he was playing, he was wrong. And as for Mr. Ambrose, he could take his ledger and leave. Unless he knew something that he wasn't telling her.

"If you have information about my family, then please tell me," she insisted.

"Yes, well," the mousy little man twitched. "I suppose introductions would be in order."

With that, he rose from the chair and turned to the back of the office.

"There is a gentleman who might perhaps better explain."

It was then that the man seated at the back of the office slowly stood. He emerged from the late morning shadows there, and slowly and walked toward them.

Her initial impressions had been correct. He was tall, dressed in a black coat and pants, with black boots. The hat he carried was a Stetson with a wide brim in the style only occasionally seen on the streets of Philadelphia.

On those rare occasions, it was more to draw attention, the one wearing it hardly the sort stories were heard about from the western states and territories that were still considered primitive and dangerous.

This man didn't need to draw attention to himself, it would have naturally found him with that lean intensity as he crossed the office toward her, the handsome angled features, dark hair that was in need of a trim but she sensed he wasn't the least concerned about. And those green eyes that fastened on her.

Miss Carter made the introductions. "This is Marshal McCandliss. He's here on official business and would like to ask you some questions."

Impressions, clues, a look or a gesture—Ranse McCandliss, U.S. Federal Marshal, slowly crossed the office. In his line of work, it was important to pay attention to details—the way a person moved, a sudden shift of uneasiness, an expression, facial features, a resemblance to someone, or an inflection in someone's speech, a laugh that came too easily.

He had deliberately waited in the shadows at the edge of the office so that he could study the young woman he had spent the better part of a year tracking down. But if he hoped for any hint of recognition in the features of her heart-shaped face or

those incredible eyes that watched him with what could only
be described as mild curiosity, he was disappointed. That, or
she was very good at concealing any sort of reaction.

On the surface, she was hardly what he'd expected. She was
more mature, quiet, thoughtful even. But he was willing to
admit that money and the proper environment could transform
anyone into a proper, young lady. Even the daughter of a notorious outlaw family. And there was the slight physical resemblance—the dark hair with a hint of red even if her eyes were
darker blue that any of those others he was looking for.

"This won't take long."

Marshal Ranse McCandliss, the head mistress had introduced him, a federal marshal in Philadelphia, a law man who
could have stepped from the front cover of one of those dime
novels the other girls devoured with avid curiosity and no small
amount of swooning.

What was he doing here? And what did it have to do with
her? Laine thought, as he pulled a packet of papers from inside
his coat that included a photograph, the edges frayed and worn,
and handed it to her.

He watched her face for any hint of recognition of those in
the photograph. "Do you recognize any of those men?"

She looked at them, then shook her head. "No."

He handed her the faded handbill with the image of three
men, and the notation of a reward that was offered—five thousand dollars for the Dalton gang!

The Dalton gang? A name that was the same as hers!

"Do you recognize anyone there?" he again asked.

It took her a moment to recover from the surprise of the
same names, obviously a coincidence.

"No," she replied, slightly shaken and more than a little
confused. Was that the reason he was there? A coincidence of a
name that had to be very common?

"Look at both very carefully," he told her, convinced that he had seen something in her slight hesitation.

She glanced at both once more and felt a faint prickling at the back of her neck. The girls had read about the Dalton Gang in one of those dime novels. Even Ellie had commented on the coincidence of her name—*'Wouldn't that be amazing if you were related to them— outlaws!'*

She had brushed it off at the time. Her friend was a romantic. There was certainly nothing romantic about the men in that photograph or the coincidence of the name that had been pinned to her clothes when she arrived all those years before with other orphans sent east, hopefully to find new families.

Some of them had lost their families to fever, others to the lawlessness in the territories, some were simply abandoned. She was around three or four years old at the time and had no memory of her family other than vague images of a pretty young woman that had faded over time.

"Do you recognize any of those men?" Marshal McCandliss again asked, his green eyes narrowed as he watched her.

"I've already told you," she replied, short-tempered at his insistence. "I don't recognize any of them."

"Do the names Bob, Emmett, or Grat mean anything to you?" He continued to watch her for any sign of recognition. There was only the slight angle of a dark eyebrow.

"Those are the men in the photograph?" she asked.

He nodded. "Bob, Emmett, and Grat Dalton."

She had willingly answered his questions, but sensed that he had wanted different answers, answers she didn't have. Other than the coincidence of the last name, she didn't understand what this had to do with her.

She shook her head again. "You've come on a fool's errand. I don't know those names or any of those men. You thought because of my name that I might know something about them?

I assure you, marshal, I know nothing of those people. I arrived in Philadelphia as an orphan. I had no family except for Mrs. Althea Ralston, after she became my legal guardian."

"Do you remember anything before you arrived in Philadelphia?"

"This is ridiculous!" Laine responded with growing irritation. "Do you make it your business to question everyone with the last name of Dalton? I have no way of knowing if that is even my real name. There is nothing I can tell you."

Ranse watched her. "If there was nothing more than the name, I might have to agree with you. There is, however, the matter of the deposit of twenty-five thousand dollars in your name at the National Bank made within two months after your arrival in Philadelphia. Mr. Ambrose has checked the bank's records, and can verify the deposit."

She stared at him. "I have no idea what you are talking about. I told you, that I came to Philadelphia as an orphan. Perhaps Mrs. Ralston placed the money in that account."

"I'm afraid that is not the case," Malcolm Ambrose spoke up in his squeaky voice. "I researched those records very carefully. Indeed, Mrs. Ralston's funds at the bank were always carefully recorded so there would be no mistakes as her holdings were quite substantial.

"There is no record of any transfers or withdrawals from any of her accounts, in this amount at that time. At Marshal McCandliss' request I have brought the ledger of your account with me today."

He placed it in front of her. "This entry was made within two weeks after your arrival in Philadelphia. The amount is exactly twenty-five thousand dollars. It was a bank draft deposited with the First National Bank in Coffeyville, Kansas."

Kansas?

Laine looked at Marshal McCandliss as the banker continued his explanation.

"You can see here, where the entry was made," Mr. Ambrose indicated.

"I don't understand any of this. The only funds I have, are those that were specifically set aside by Mrs. Ralston for my education." It was something that always bothered her, being dependent on her guardian's generosity. But it was something she was determined to change when she started college in the fall.

Once she had her degree, she would be able to find a teaching position and begin paying back Mrs. Ralston for her generosity. Even if it took the rest of her life.

It was a conversation they had often, with Mrs. Ralston insisting that it wasn't necessary, but it was necessary for her. It was a way of reclaiming herself, who she was, even if she had no memory of her family.

"Are you certain there isn't something you're leaving out?" Ranse persisted. "It's possible that you've forgotten something important from your childhood," he continued. "Something that you might remember now?"

She suddenly felt as if everyone in the room was watching her, waiting for her answer, as if they didn't believe her and it was difficult to breathe.

"I've already told you that I don't remember anything, and I don't know those people," Laine repeated.

Miss Carter rose abruptly from behind the desk. "Miss Dalton has answered all of your questions. I must insist that this meeting is ended."

Ranse nodded, still not convinced. "I apologize for any inconvenience I might have caused." He handed the photograph and the handbill to her. "Look them over again. Maybe you'll remember something. I will be staying at the Barclay Hotel."

"As I've already explained, I don't know anyone in those photographs. I hope you find the person you're looking for."

It was a lie. She didn't like him or his questions. Whoever the poor woman was that he was looking for, she hoped Ranse McCandliss never found her.

"I intend to, Miss Dalton."

2

Laine stepped down from the streetcar as she and the other girls returned from the afternoon concert in the park.

A young man waited as they approached the front gate of the school. He leaned against the stone gatepost and straightened as they approached.

"I am looking for Miss Laine Dalton," he greeted them.

She nodded as the other girls gathered round with curiosity.

"I am a reporter with the Philadelphia Gazette. You're quite a celebrity, Miss Dalton. We're running a series of articles about outlaws of the West, and we are doing a special edition about the Dalton Gang. We want your side of the story about your brothers."

Here it was, again, and just after that meeting with Marshal McCandliss. How had this man learned about all of this?

"I don't know anything about the Dalton Gang," she replied. "I've explained all of this before. It's a mistake."

"Come now, Miss Dalton," he said congenially. "We have information that indicates you may be related to the Dalton brothers. My source is reliable. It will make a sensational story —'*Young Society Woman Part of Notorious Outlaw gang.*'"

She stared incredulously at him.

"I don't know the source of your information, but this is all a mistake. I have nothing more to say to you or anyone else about this."

She pushed past him, only to find her way blocked as he stepped in front of her.

"There is nothing to tell you," she repeated with far less patience now. "I don't know anything about any of this.

Miss Carter came out the front entrance of the school. She motioned to the other girls to enter the building, then came down the steps.

"There will be no further questions, sir," she announced firmly. Then motioned for Laine to follow her.

A slow smile spread across the reporter's face, as he watched the young women, and one in particular disappear inside the school.

"What are you going to do?" Ellie Morgan asked as she lay across the width of her bed, elbows bent, chin propped on her hands.

Laine sighed heavily. "I don't know. Two days ago, I had never heard of the Dalton Gang. Now, I hear nothing else."

"Do you think the marshal gave the information to that young man from the newspaper?"

"It seems odd that the paper shows up the very next day," Laine admitted. "I have to put an end to this. If I don't, everyone will think I'm part of the Dalton family. Somehow, I've got to prove that I'm not related to them."

"What about Gerald Ralston? Maybe he knows of some papers or letters that his aunt might have kept that explain who you were," Ellie suggested hopefully.

Laine frowned. "Whenever I asked her, she always said

there were no records, nothing to indicate who my family was."
She sighed with frustration.

"I've had very little contact with Gerald since her funeral
two years ago. I think he resented her taking me in. But maybe
now he would be willing to help me. I need to see him and find
out if he knows anything about my background."

Ellie smiled as she swung her legs over the side of the bed.
"I'll go with you. I can't let you face that weasel alone. And don't
worry," she assured her. "I'm certain you'll find the answer to all
of this, and then we can get on with more important things,
such as the Spring Cotillion."

Laine nodded, wishing she felt the same enthusiasm.

THE LIBRARY DOOR slammed behind Laine with a cold finality.

She' d been humiliated and embarrassed in her meeting
with Gerald Ralston. Now she smiled shakily as Ellie rose to
join her.

"What happened?" Ellie whispered. "Was he able to tell you
anything?"

"You might say that he was less than cooperative." That was
an understatement, she thought.

"He refused to help?" Ellie's voice rose above a whisper as they
reached the horse-drawn coach they had taken from the school.

"Much more than that. He wasn't at all surprised to see me.
It seems the reporter from the newspaper has already been
here asking for information for his story. He's furious about the
publicity this has caused."

"Really?" Ellie replied. "From the stories I've heard, he's
done quite well on his own destroying his public image. It's
public all right—all over Broadway Street." She leaned in. "Red-
light district. Whatever respect he has is because of Althea

Ralston's social status in Philadelphia, certainly not because of anything he can boast about."

Laine stared at her friend as they climbed into the carriage. "What do you know about that sort of thing?"

Ellie shrugged. "It's common knowledge. Dottie's brother has seen him there several times. He's made quite a reputation for himself... if you know what I mean."

They burst out laughing. It somehow helped to lift her spirits after her meeting with him.

"Just think, if all of this had never happened, you might have been forced to defend *your reputation* because of him," Ellie observed.

"That may be, but I certainly won't get any help from him."

Ellie gave the driver instructions to return to the school.

"I had forgotten how awful Gerald can be. I appreciate your company," she told her friend. "But Mrs. Mayhew will be furious that you've been gone this long."

"You're not coming back with me?"

"There's someone else who may be able to help me. I have a terrible feeling that newspaper reporter is going to be more determined than ever about this after meeting with Gerald."

Ellie nodded sympathetically. "Papa has always said the press is like a weapon. Best to use it to your advantage, than to have someone use it against you."

Laine nodded. "Gerald threatened to press charges if anything else was printed in the papers. I'm afraid all I can hope for is to get the truth, before some newspaper prints the story. He did give me this." She showed Ellie the pack of letters neatly tied with a string.

"Letters?"

"I wrote them over the years to my family. I gave them to Mrs. Ralston to mail even though I had no idea where to send them. She kept all of them."

Ellie laid a hand over hers. "You were trying to find your family all this time."

She nodded. "I hoped someone might come someday and tell me about them, or possibly someone from my family. But they never did."

"And after all these years, someone has," Ellie replied. "What are you going to do?"

"I need to know more about all of this first."

"Are you going to meet with Marshal McCandliss again?" Ellie sighed. "He certainly is handsome. He's by far the best looking man I've ever seen. I wonder if he knows how to use that gun he was wearing."

"You were eavesdropping!"

"If you remember, we were all eavesdropping. We simply continued after you had gone downstairs. After all it isn't every day that we have a U.S. Marshal at the academy," Ellie explained nonchalantly. "And are you going to tell me you didn't notice how dark his eyes or how handsome he is?"

She ignored any further attempt on her friend's part to discuss Marshal Ranse McCandliss as they arrived back at the school.

"So, where are you going?"

"I'm going to see Mrs. Ralston's housekeeper who was with her before Gerald came back to Philadelphia," she replied. "She might remember something from when I first came to live with her. I should be back in a couple of hours. But if I'm not you'll have to make an excuse to Mrs. Mayhew. Tell her that I've gone shopping or something. You're very good at that."

Ellie smiled as she stepped away from the carriage as they arrived back at the academy and waved.

"I can handle that old warhorse any day of the week. When you get back you have to tell me everything you find out."

. . .

LAINE SHIELDED her eyes against the heat of the late morning sun as she gazed down the street of small cottages. Most had fallen into disrepair from neglect, except for one at the far end. It had been painted, with a small patch of neatly manicured lawn in front protected by a picket fence.

She closed the gate carefully behind her, remembering the last time she had seen Miss Jane after Mrs. Ralston's funeral three years earlier. She knocked lightly at the door. She was about to knock again when the door was opened by a tall, lanky young man.

"What do you want?" he asked.

"I've come to see Miss Jane," she replied, taken back by the blunt question and concern that the woman who had been both friend and confident to her as a child might have passed away.

Mrs. Ralston's housekeeper had been the constant in her life for as long as she could remember, a comforting hand and gentle voice in a world that often seemed confusing to an orphan in the household of a woman who was old enough to be her grandmother but who bore no relation to her.

Outcast, unwanted—words she had learned at a young age from other children who knew no better according to Miss Jane, who had comforted her with gentle words, encouragement, and praise.

"There's no one smarter or finer, and don't you ever forget it. It's not where you come from, child, but where you're going that matters."

She had stayed in contact with Miss Jane and called on her often, even as Miss Mayhew disapproved. There were several things the old biddy disapproved of, including her plans for college.

"College is for men. You need to look to making a suitable marriage."

That conversation, if a one-sided comment could be called

a conversation, had been brief, as if the matter was decided... as if that was her only option, being an orphan. Fortunately, Mrs. Ralston had provided an endowment that included her college education. She had been very supportive of her continuing her education.

"You must be your own person, Laine. Not what someone expects you to be. It is my hope that you will find a suitable vocation for that keen mind of yours." She had smiled at her that day, not long before she passed away.

"Don't let anyone stand in your way, my dear."

Gerald Ralston was another matter. He had been furious when he learned of her plans for college, even going so far as to 'suggest' to the university board that the endowment for her education would be better served if made available for some young man.

However, Mrs. Ralston's instructions in the matter were specific and iron-clad according to her lawyer, and Laine had made plans to attend college after leaving the academy at the end of spring.

"Who's at the door, Mason?" came that faint voice from inside the cottage.

Small and thin, Miss Jane appeared beside the young man. She peered at Laine through rimmed glasses as she leaned on a cane.

"Good heavens. It's Miss Lainey," she announced. "Come in, child."

Miss Jane stood inside the doorway of the small house, gently prodding Mason towards the back of the house, as she reached for Laine's hand.

She followed the old woman into the parlor. All about the room was evidence of the woman's great skill with a needle. Miss Jane had always taken great pride in her fine stitchery.

"Mason is my grandson, come to live with me a few months back when his mama died. He's good boy and company for an old woman who doesn't get around so good anymore.

"He takes care of the work around the house when he's not working at the mill. Now, dear, what brings you here?"

Laine took the old woman's hands in her own and smiled as she remembered all the times those same hands had comforted some childhood misery, or eased the sort of pain known only to an orphan.

When the estate was settled after Mrs. Ralston's death, Gerald had dismissed her without explanation. But there was nothing he could do to change the provisions of his aunt's will that had provided amply for Miss Jane. She had made certain that she would always have a home of her own. The cottage had been given to her along with a trust fund to cover her living expenses for as long as she lived.

"Are they treatin' you all right at that school?"

"Everything is fine. This is my last term, and then I hope to attend college in the fall. I've already put in my application in Boston."

"College, imagine that. Mrs. Ralston would be proud of you. That's somethin' special for a young woman." Miss Jane stroked her hand as she had when Laine was a child.

"Now, when are you going to tell me what brought you here today, when you were just here a few weeks ago? I always knew when something was troubling you."

"Something has happened. I need to know more about how I came to live with Mrs. Ralston."

"I suppose this has to do with that lawman who came here yesterday—a federal marshal."

"He was here? He questioned you?" She was incredulous. Then came the anger. She felt as if her life was being turned upside down.

"Stay for lunch," Miss Jane said as she stood. "We'll talk."

When she returned, she helped her with the plate that

contained small sandwiches. They sat across from each other at the small table in the parlor.

"He had no right to come here," Laine pushed back the anger that he seemed to be taking over her life, intruding where he had no right to be.

"No harm, dear. There's nothin' to be concerned about. He asked a lot of questions, but he didn't get any answers. I didn't tell him anything. Now, I want *you* to tell me what this is all about."

Laine told her everything, including the visit by the newspaper reporter at the school. She waited for what Miss Jane could tell her about that time all those years ago.

"There's not much to tell. Mrs. Ralston was already a widow for a long time, and never had any children of her own. Over the years she kept bringin' home first one child and then another, from that orphanage.

"She had all that money and nothin' else to do with it. I remember the first child she brought home, and all them little girls that came after. She made sure they all had a good education and became proper young ladies, so they could make a good life for themselves. Those girls mostly came from around here, except for one."

Laine met the old woman's gaze evenly. "I didn't come from Philadelphia."

Miss Jane smiled. "You were brought to Mrs. Ralston by a church lady who travelled a long way. She had relations in the East and brought you with her."

"Do you remember where she was from?" Laine asked.

Miss Jane shook her head. "The two of you had been travelling for days and nearly froze to death when that train was stopped on account of snow. The only thing you that told anything about you was that note pinned to your coat and a cloth doll."

"I must have said something about where I came from, or mentioned a name even that young?"

"You didn't say anything, and Mrs. Ralston feared you couldn't speak at all for a long time. Not one word, for days. You were just closed off inside yerself, like something dreadful had happened. Keep in mind, you were just a little thing, not more than three or four years old."

Laine frowned. "What about my name?"

"That church woman didn't know anything about that, just that note that came with you. It was almost like you didn't have any life before Mrs. Ralston took you in. I suppose that was why you was so extra special to her, like you were her very own child, with no other memory of anyone else for your family. I think that's why Gerald turned so angry and hateful," she continued.

"I do have something she gave me for you before she died. She said that I would know the right time to give it to you. I had thought to give it to you when you graduated from that academy, but I suppose now is good time."

She went to a small table beside the hearth. She opened the single drawer and removed a small box.

"Besides that doll, you had this," she handed her the box.

Carefully wrapped in a small square of blue velvet, Laine found the treasure that Miss Jane had kept for her. It was a perfect teardrop crystal. Nestled in the palm of Laine's hand, the precisely cut crystal caught the sunlight that poured in through the window and created a prism of colors on the wall behind her.

"That was the only thing you had when you came to us. It must have meant a great deal to you. Mrs. Ralston told me to keep it for you. She said you might want it someday. I'm sorry there isn't more."

Laine leaned over and kissed her on the cheek.

"Thank you."

3

L aine sat back in the carriage thinking back over what she
had learned from Miss Jane.

She rubbed the crystal between her fingers, wondering
what it might have meant to an abandoned child so many years
before. But she remembered nothing more than what she had
always known of the train ride and the snow, sitting beside a
sad-faced woman.

She couldn't even be certain that these were her own
memories or merely details retold over the years about when
she arrived. Everything else was blank—who she was, where
she came from, her family, what had happened to them.

The carriage stopped. She gathered the folds of her skirt to
keep it from underfoot as she stepped down. Her head immediately came up at the hand that closed around her arm,
steadying her.

The smile on her face quickly faded as she stared into the
dark gaze beneath the wide brim of a black felt hat. Then came
the anger at the man who wore that hat, Marshal Ranse
McCandliss.

She had two choices—she could retreat back inside to the carriage, or she could leave him standing there as she entered the school hall. She did neither.

She pulled her arm free, but in the process lost her hold on the wooden box. It slipped from her hand and fell to the pavement. The wrapped crystal rolled under the carriage.

Laine swore as she bent to retrieve it, a hand closing over her arm as Marshal McCandliss retrieved it for her.

"You dropped this."

He held on to the velvet wrapped crystal for just a moment, then handed it to her.

"Do you always make a habit of interfering where you're not needed?" she demanded.

"It seemed the thing to do, unless you wanted to crawl under the carriage,"

he replied. "It could be dangerous."

"Rescue me?" she flung back at him. The idea was so completely preposterous when everything he'd done was completely upending her life. Which raised the questions—What was he doing there?

"I don't need your help," she said.

She wanted no more of Ranse McCandliss or his ridiculous story about the Daltons. The entire story was impossible to believe. But her greatest concern was the increasing number of people who were willing to believe it. With sudden determination, Laine snatched the crystal from his grasp and whirled about towards the gates of Clairmont Hall.

"Gerald Ralston supplied me with some very interesting information. I wanted to talk to you about it," McCandliss called after her.

Laine halted as she reached the gate. Feeling that dark gaze at her back, she turned around slowly.

"Gerald Ralston is hardly qualified as a reliable source of information."

"He seemed more than eager for me to believe that he had some proof of your connection with the Dalton family. I found it hard to believe until I visited the Mrs. Ralston's lawyer this morning."

"What about her lawyers?"

"It seems Gerald Ralston is only the temporary custodian of the Ralston house. Mrs. Ralston executed a codicil to her will several years ago naming you as the main beneficiary of her estate, which includes the house, which you can't inherit until your twenty-first birthday.

"However, you stand to receive a substantial amount of wealth, cutting Gerald Ralston completely out of her will. That might be reason enough for a man in his position to try to convince me that you are related to the Dalton family.

"With you out of the way, he could have the will set aside. As Althea Ralston's only surviving, blood relative, he would be in a good position to inherit the entire estate. That made me question his eagerness to cooperate.

"Please continue, Marshal McCandliss."

"Gerald Ralston is the sort of person who takes advantage of whatever will benefit him. He claims he has proof you are related to the Daltons. I have a meeting with him in the morning at the bank."

"If he has proof then why has he kept it a secret until now?"

Not only beautiful but she was also smart, along with the anger.

"My guess is that Mrs. Ralston was able to control her nephew while she was alive. She obviously wanted to protect you. But with her gone and the terms of the will made public naming you as beneficiary, he's willing to do whatever is necessary to claim her estate for himself.

"It's obvious that she cared about you," he continued. "She may have prevented you from knowing the truth about your family, afraid someone would try to take you away from her."

"That is ridiculous!" Laine replied. "You didn't know her. She was not capable of lying," her voice softened, as she recalled the tall, imposing woman who had been her guardian and the only family she had ever known.

He heard the way her voice changed, saw the sadness in her eyes.

"I want you to know that I don't enjoy any of this," he said.

"Is that some sort of apology for all of this?" She wanted to be angry with him. She had every right to be angry for the trouble he had caused her.

"I never apologize unless I'm wrong. I won't know if I'm wrong until tomorrow."

"I wouldn't have accepted it anyway!" She turned and left him there as she closed the gate behind her.

He watched as she walked down the driveway then climbed the steps into the front entrance of the school. He should have been relieved that his search of the last months would soon be ended.

It had seemed simple in the beginning—find a young woman who had that same last name, who had mysteriously appeared almost twenty years ago and had been living in Philadelphia, the daughter Adeline Dalton had given up years before, and who might know where to find the Daltons.

It was anything but simple.

He knew men like Gerald Ralston; arrogant, with that superior attitude, and out for himself. In a way, he hoped the man didn't have any evidence of her relationship to the Daltons. That would be the end of it and Miss Laine Dalton, or whatever her name was, could go back to her privileged life.

"Please translate the text for us, Miss Dalton."

Laine suddenly looked up as she realized that Madame Delacroix had called on her.

"Madame?" she asked as the classroom had fallen silent. Several pairs of eyes were turned in her direction. Everyone waited expectantly.

She glanced beside her to where Ellie sat. Her friend pointed to the page of the book indicating the paragraph that their teacher wanted translated. She proceeded to translate it.

"Merci, mademoiselle," Madame thanked her. "Perhaps next time you should pay more attention."

When class was finally dismissed, she and Ellie quickly escaped the classroom.

"What time is it now?" she asked again as they crossed the hall, French lessons forgotten. Ellie glanced down at the small watch pinned to her blouse as she ran to keep up.

"Eleven thirty. When did Marshal McCandliss say he would let you know what he found out?"

They rounded the corner of the main hall and suddenly halted at the sight of Elvira Mayhew coming towards them.

Laine realized retreat was impossible as the woman descended on them. Surely it was too soon for her to have heard from Madame Delacroix of her lack of attention in class. Laine sighed expectantly as the woman approached.

"Miss Carter would like to speak with you. She is in her office now." The woman cast a disparaging glance over Laine's shoulder as Ellie listened attentively.

"And you, Miss Morgan, need to apply yourself to your studies. Your marks are not the best."

"I swear the woman rides a broom. Someone needs to knock her off it."

It wasn't the first confrontation or the last, Laine thought.

"Go on. I'll find you after I meet with Miss Carter."

"My father could buy and sell this school ten times over and put her out on the street where she belongs," Ellie commented as she turned towards the wide stairway that led to the second-floor rooms.

Laine sighed with relief as she turned towards Mrs. Carter's office.

Within a very few moments her meeting with the headmistress of Clairmont School was over.

The entire wall shook from the force of the door being slammed, the small, watercolor print on the wall of the room tilting crazily as it threatened to tumble to the floor. Startled, Ellie Morgan looked up.

"What happened?"

Laine leaned against the firm frame of the closed door, struggling to put her jumbled thoughts to some order.

Ellie crossed the room and seized her by the shoulders. "What is it?"

"I have been asked to leave Clairmont."

"What?" Ellie gasped.

Laine sat wearily on the nearest bed. "The bank has been instructed not to release any further funds from my trust account until this matter has been cleared up completely.

"Gerald?"

Laine nodded. He's informed Miss Carter and the trustees that he will not be giving me any financial assistance. Not only that, he has insisted that I be dismissed immediately, or he will make certain the school never receives any more funds from the endowment Mrs. Ralston set up for the school years ago," she laughed, a small, broken sound.

"And there is the matter of unwanted publicity by the parents of the other girls."

"You didn't tell the reporter anything!" Ellie exclaimed.

"No, but someone did." She handed Ellie a rolled copy of the morning edition of the *Philadelphia Gazette.*

In bold print across the front page were the glaring headlines of the presence of a member of the notorious Dalton family at the prestigious school, mingling with the daughters of mainline Philadelphia society.

Ellie slowly sank down on the bed beside her.

"So, Gerald controls everything, even though you were named beneficiary in Mrs. Ralston's will. What a greedy snake," Ellie added with disgust.

"Do you think he gave the information to the newspaper?"

"As much as I dislike Gerald, I think Marshal McCandliss might be responsible for this. It's the only explanation. And I was willing to wait until his meeting this morning with Gerald. All I did was give him time to have this story published. Now it will be impossible to prove that I'm *not* part of the Dalton family," she admitted miserably.

"There must be something you can do. This is your final term. If you don't complete it, you won't be able to attend college in the fall."

"Without the money from the trust for my tuition, I won't be able to attend anyway." She rose from the edge of the bed.

"There is one person who can straighten all this out." She seized her reticule from the top drawer of the dressing table.

"Where are you going?"

"To the Barclay Hotel. Marshal McCandliss is responsible for this, and he is going to give me some answers."

"Going to a man's hotel? That's absolutely scandalous." Ellie giggled with delight. "I'm going with you."

"No," Laine told her. "Considering everything that's happened, I won't be missed at all. But I don't want any of this to fall on you. I shouldn't be gone long."

Ellie sighed. "I've always wanted to see the inside of the Barclay Hotel. It's supposed to be quite grand. Supposedly the Governor keeps a very special *'lady friend'* there."

Laine smiled at her friend. "I won't have time to check up on the Governor."

"Good luck," Ellie called after her.

· · ·

ELLIE'S PARTING words echoed through Laine's thoughts as she caught the cable car at the end of Haverford Street very near the school and took the seat at the far end of the car.

She knew very little about her background. She had a feeling it was going to take more than luck.

Reaching the center of the city, she asked directions and walked the three short blocks to the Barclay Hotel.

She hesitated as guests entered and left the grand hotel that rose six stories above the street entrance. In stark contrast to the silks and satins worn by the fashionable ladies she glimpsed, she was aware that she was conspicuously out of place in the dark-green skirt and starched cotton blouse that was the uniform at Clairmont School.

Laine caught her reflection in the large glass windows that fronted the street and frowned at her schoolgirl appearance. Inside the hotel's front entrance, she stepped into an alcove with a writing desk.

She searched her reticule for pins for her hair. She found several then twisted her hair into a knot and secured it at the back of her head. Stepping once more before the large, glass windows of the hotel, she caught her reflection. It would have to do. She crossed the lobby to the main desk.

The manager tried to ignore her presence as he spoke with an assistant clerk. He finally looked up.

"Is there something I can assist you with, miss?"

It was impossible to ignore the look he gave her from head to toe, or the disapproval.

"I was told that Mr. McCandliss is staying here. If you could please provide his room number."

He regarded her with faintly bemused expression that she chose to ignore.

"We don't provide that information regarding our guests," he politely informed her. "Their privacy is important to the staff."

"It's an important matter. I need to speak with him. I would like to send a message to his room."

The clerk, looked from her to the manager, then back again.

"Mr. McCandliss checked out late this morning," he replied in spite of the glare from the manager.

Checked out?

"Surely there's some mistake. He had an important meeting this morning. Could you please check his room?" Laine asked.

The young clerk glanced hesitantly at the manager.

"He left early this morning, returned about an hour ago, then checked out."

"Did he say where he was going?"

"I'm sorry, miss," he replied.

"Is there something else?" the manager then asked. "We do have other guests who need our assistance."

It was obvious he didn't intend to assist her further as he turned and greeted another guest.

What was she going to do now?

Gerald had taken steps to have her inheritance and funds for college set aside. Without that she had no prospects, no way of furthering her education. All she had was a small amount of money in her bank account that Mrs. Ralston insisted she keep for emergencies. Everything else was always taken care of by Mrs. Ralston's attorney.

Anger mixed with uncertainty. All of this was because of Ranse McCandliss and his claim that she might be related to the notorious Dalton Gang!

"Miss?" the young clerk had followed her from the front desk. "I don't know if it's any help and I probably shouldn't say anything, but Mr. McCandliss received a telegram from Washington last night. When he checked out this morning, he asked that any messages be forwarded to him at the National Hotel. He had the driver take him to the train station."

The National Hotel in Washington.

She thanked him.

ELLIE MORGAN STOOD in the center of their room as Laine pulled clothes from the closet.

"What were you able to find out?" Ellie asked.

"Marshal McCandliss was already gone by the time I reached the hotel."

A disappointed look crossed Ellie's face.

"I did get to see the inside of the hotel," Laine teased her friend. "It's quite grand once you get past management."

She pushed back her irritation at that particular encounter.

"Why are you packing?" her friend asked.

"I've been dismissed. Remember?"

"Of course I remember, but that will all be straightened out. All I have to do is wire my father. You know how fond he is of you. He credits you completely with salvaging my education.

"I'm certain he'll be able to straighten everything out. If the President of the United States takes the advice of a Morgan, I don't think Miss Carter will ignore it. My grandfather and father have donated a fortune to this school. Just give me a few days to get word to them."

Laine folded the last gown, then crossed the room.

"You've been the best friend anyone could ask for. But I don't think Miss Carter will allow me the time to wait for your father to help. Gerald has too much influence over her and the trustees. Yesterday he was talking about having the police look into the matter. He even spoke of the possibility of having me held in custody until it could be straightened out."

Ellie stared at her. "You can't be serious!"

"The longer I remain in Philadelphia, the harder Gerald is going to work at having me discredited completely unless I have proof that I'm not involved in any of this. I can't find that here in Philadelphia," Laine added.

Ellie glanced at the suitcase. "Where are you going?"

"The only person who can help me now is Marshal McCandliss."

"What if he's convinced that you're related to these other Daltons? What if he is responsible for your dismissal from Clairmont?"

"I have to know the truth. If I am related to the Daltons, then I have to find a way to establish my innocence. If I'm not related to them, I have to clear my name if I'm ever to have a normal life."

Tears welled in Ellie Morgan's eyes. "Where are you going?"

"The desk clerk at the Barclay Hotel told me where Marshal McCandliss is staying in Washington. There is a train to Washington in the morning."

Ellie sniffled indignantly as she wiped her nose in very unladylike fashion. "You're going to need money. How much do you have?"

"I have almost fifty dollars remaining from our shopping trip to buy the new gowns for the cotillion."

"It will take at least half that much for your train fare to Washington," Ellie informed her.

"The fare is thirty-three dollars," Laine told her, realizing the amount left her very little funds once she reached the capital other than what as in her personal account.

Ellie crossed the room to the closet, emerging a moment later with a hat box. She removed the lid and retrieved a silk purse.

"There's two hundred dollars." Ellie tossed the small purse onto the bed.

"I can't take that from you," Laine protested.

"Sure you can. You are my best friend, don't you know. If I can't help you, then who can I to help?" Ellie declared passionately.

"I don't know when I will be able to repay it."

Ellie shook her head. "Consider it an investment in your future." She smiled at a sudden thought.

"Considering his financial empire, my father would appreciate such an arrangement. As for the train fare, I'll see that it's taken care of. The Morgan name carries very heavy weight in railroading circles. If I can't go along with you, at least I can help you get started."

She crossed the room and hugged Ellie. "I don't know what I'll find in Washington. You may have made a very bad investment."

Ellie pulled back to smile mischievously at her. "You could always rob a train," she teased lightheartedly.

VERY EARLY THE next morning they both slipped silently through the staff entrance at the back of Clairmont Hall. At least Miss Carter had allowed her to remain one more night instead of throwing her out on the street.

They took the early morning cable car to the center of town and then transferred to a horse-drawn carriage for the ride to the train station. Her friend kept up a constant line of chatter about Washington, D.C., a place she had visited often with her father.

Arriving a full hour before the departure time, Ellie disappeared into the ticket office, emerging barely ten minutes later triumphantly waving a ticket jacket in her hand.

"How did you do that?"

Ellie smiled smugly. "Didn't I say the Morgan name could strike fear into the hearts of mortal men? Actually, the station-master is well acquainted with my father. He sees him every time Father comes to visit me at school. I merely told him I was planning a surprise visit to Father in the capital. He was more than happy to provide the ticket."

"And he believed you?"

"I have a feeling that he was more concerned that my father owns the railroad." Ellie dissolved into fits of laughter. Then, her expression changed.

"It's a round-trip ticket. I'm hoping you'll be back in no time."

Laine smiled gratefully as they walked arm-in-arm towards platform. "I don't know how to repay you."

"You can repay me by telling me all about it when you return, and... all about Marshal McCandliss."

She gave her friend a narrow look. "I can already tell you that he's despicable, arrogant, and doesn't care if he ruins my life."

Ellie hooked an arm through hers. "You have to admit that he is quite handsome, in a rugged sort of way. Those dark eyes... And don't tell me that you didn't notice."

She had but that wasn't the point.

"All I know is that he's responsible for all of this," she replied as her train rolled into the station.

"I wish that I was going with you," Ellie told her.

"You need to stay here and make certain that you complete the term," she reminded her.

Her carpet bag had been checked with the attendant. Meeting Ellie's somber gaze, she realized it was time for them to part.

"Send me a telegram and let me know that you're all right," Ellie insisted.

She promised and thanked her again.

"I told the stationmaster that you were my cousin, recently widowed, and still mourning the loss of your husband. He said he would let the conductor know."

"Whatever for? I hardly look like a widow." She smoothed her hand down the skirt of her gray traveling costume.

"You are a young woman travelling alone. According to Miss Carter, that is hardly a suitable arrangement. This is much more acceptable. At any rate, the conductor said he would make certain you arrived safely in Washington. And just in case anyone bothers you, I want you to have this." Taking Laine's hand, she wrapped her fingers around a gold ring.

"Unless, of course, the man is tall, handsome and very wealthy."

Laine stared at her. "I can't take this."

Her friend stubbornly refused. "You're to wear it on the third finger of your left hand, like all respectable married women, or newly widowed young ladies."

"Your father gave this to you on your last birthday."

"And I'm confident you'll return it. You can hardly board a train as a widow with no ring. Besides, it'll keep unsavory characters from bothering you. Although sometimes I wish an unsavory character would bother me," Ellie added. "Every man my father picks is so boring."

"All right," she agreed. "But you'll have it back as soon as I return from Washington."

Both girls glanced up as the conductor reminded her that it was time to board the train.

She waved to Ellie through the windows as she moved through the car to her assigned compartment. It was comfortable and private with long velvet seats that were turned to face one another across a wide expanse of space.

Her friend certainly took advantage of her father's connections.

She had always envied Ellie, never having any family of her own. At least she would have known who she was. As it was, she had no idea who Laine Dalton was. Just another orphan with no past, or the sister of notorious outlaws?

The train lurched, hesitated, then lurched again, left the station and slowly gathered speed.

Laine watched as the city passed by, leaving behind everything she had ever known with no way of knowing what lay ahead.

4

Laine stood on the sidewalk in front of the stately hotel and gazed about her in silent awe of Washington.

In the distance, looming above a majestic line of trees in a nearby park, stood the capital buildings.

"Is this the right place, miss?" the driver asked.

"Yes, thank you." She paid him the fare from the train station. Then he was gone.

It was nearly suppertime and there was a great deal of activity at the hotel. Several other carriages arrived, and young boys employed by the hotel, as well as the doorman carried baggage and escorted the newly arrived guests inside the hotel.

Feeling conspicuous for arriving without an escort, Laine picked up the carpet bag and followed them through the heavily paned doors of the National Hotel.

Laine waited patiently as several guests before her gave their names and were then escorted to the elevator on the far side of the lobby. According to Ellie, the National was one of the oldest and most prestigious hotels in Washington, often accommodating congressmen and visiting dignitaries. She listened discreetly as the manager of the hotel greeted the distinguished gentleman in front of her.

"Good afternoon, Mr. Travis. You have the good fortune to have the last available room in the hotel, perhaps in all of Washington. Everyone has come to the capital for the Governor's meetings. I doubt there is an empty bed in the entire city."

The gentleman before her smiled as he took the quill pen and signed the guest register. Laine felt a wave of panic stealing over her. She hadn't considered that she might not be able to find a room at the hotel. Now, it seemed she might not find a room anywhere.

She forced herself to remember her purpose in visiting Washington. If she were able to meet with Ranse McCandliss that very afternoon it would not be necessary for her to remain in Washington. She would simply return to Philadelphia that evening. If all went well, she would be on that train. She met the manager's polite gaze evenly.

"May I help you?"

"I would like to see Mr. Ranse McCandliss. I was told that he is staying here."

"Mr. McCandliss is a guest of the hotel. But you have just missed him."

There it was again, that condescending way of addressing her.

"He left on a matter of business. You may leave a message if you wish."

Her thoughts raced. She could hardly wait for him in the lobby of the hotel. And there was every possibility that the manager might have her removed.

A faint smile returned as an idea formed. It was insanity, and yet it might work. It was something Ellie would have laughed hysterically over. She had begun her journey as a widow. She quickly decided she could allow herself one more small deception.

"Oh dear, I wanted to surprise my *husband*, but the train was delayed nearly two hours." She imitated her friend with the slight pout of disappointment, as she plunged ahead with her charade. Desperate circumstances sometimes called for desperate measures.

"Your husband?" the manager inquired uncertainly.

"Yes, he wanted me to join him for the trip, but my aunt was quite ill. She recovered quite nicely over the last few days and insisted that I join him here in Washington. I'm certain you can understand how dreadful it is to be separated from someone you love?" Laine continued, practically choking over the last words, as vivid memories of her last meeting with Ranse McCandliss came to mind.

She seized upon the manager's momentary uncertainty.

"If you would please show me to his room, I would like to freshen up before joining him. Oh dear, I've quite forgotten where he was to be dining this evening," she continued the charade.

"He was to attend the dinner being given in honor of the visiting governors," the manager offered solicitously.

"Yes, of course. He did mention that to me. You have been so kind. Ranse will be so pleased to learn how you have helped me." She smiled again.

He coughed to hide his discomfort as he reached for the correct key. At that moment, it was completely beyond the poor man's grasp that Laine might be anything other than what she told him.

She breathed a small sigh of relief as she accepted the key. She would decide what her next move would be once she reached the room and had time to collect her thoughts.

"Perhaps I can be of assistance, Mrs. McCandliss."

Laine looked up at the gentleman who had stood before her at the front desk. She had completely forgotten him during her little performance.

"I was not aware Ranse had married. May I say this is, indeed, a great pleasure."

What was she to do now?

In for a penny, in for a pound as the saying went. She forced herself to remain calm as she returned Mr. Travis' smile.

"Do you know my husband?"

"I've known Ranse most of my life. I thought I knew him pretty well. It seems he's full of surprises. And, may I say, a very pleasant surprise. Please accept my congratulations on your marriage."

"Thank you," she replied.

If he saw through her little deception, he gave no outward sign. Her confidence gradually returned on the slow ride in the small, enclosed elevator. If it had been some time since he had last seen Ranse, then he would have no reason to doubt her story.

The bellboy took the key from Laine and opened the door to the suite of rooms, setting her carpet bag inside. Before Laine could reach inside her purse to give the boy a coin for his assistance, Mr. Travis had generously tipped him. He smiled down at her.

"Allow me the pleasure of escorting you to the Governor's dinner. I couldn't allow you to travel there alone. Ranse would hardly approve of it. It will be a surprise for him that you were able to make the journey after all."

Surprise didn't begin to describe what it would be.

He tipped his hat politely. "I'll call for you and escort you to the dinner."

"That's not necessary. I can easily wait for his return," she hastily explained.

The last thing she wanted was to meet with Ranse McCandliss at some public gathering. Certainly not something known as the Governor's dinner where she could only guess there would be many people.

She forced a polite smile. "I couldn't possibly impose on you. And I am quite tired after the trip."

"Nonsense! We still have a couple of hours before the dinner. You'll have time to rest and refresh yourself. Ranse would never forgive me if I allowed you to remain here at the hotel," Mr. Travis offered kindly.

He would not likely forgive him for bringing her!

Laine inwardly groaned. She could hardly afford for Mr. Travis to go alone and inform Ranse McCandliss that his *wife* was waiting at the hotel for him. She slowly nodded.

"I will call for you at seven o'clock, and again it's a pleasure meeting you Mrs. McCandliss." He turned and followed the bellboy down the carpeted hallway to his own room at the far end of the hall.

She quickly closed the door to the room and collapsed back against the it.

Oh, what dangerous web we weave when first we pratice to deceive.

That saying somehow seemed appropriate.

She could imagine what Ellie's reaction might have been to the lies she had told. Her friend would have been thoroughly entertained. She could just hear her: *'I wish I could have been there!'*

She was beginning to wish that she was anywhere but there in spite of the fact that it really was quite amazing that one of Miss Carter's very proper young ladies had just sneaked into a man's hotel room.

Scandalous, she would have said while Gerald Ralston would have flown into his usual tirade at such behavior. Not that he would ever admit that his threats had driven her to do just that, she thought as she removed her gray silk jacket and laid it across a nearby chair.

The last daylight streamed in through the double, glass paned doors of the room that opened out onto a small veranda over the street below. Over the street noise Laine could hear the faint chiming of church bells marking the hour. She had only two hours before Mr. Travis would be calling to escort her to the Governor's dinner.

Laine looked about the spacious suite, noticing for the first time, the brush and razor that lay on top of the dressing table beside a wash basin.

Clothes she had previously seen Marshal McCandliss wearing, that included that black coat, pants, and boots, had been set aside, obviously for something more formal for the Governor's supper.

She turned at the sound of a knock at the door, her heart in her throat. Common sense told her that Marshal McCandliss wouldn't knock on his own hotel room door. She answered it and let out a slow breath of relief at the hotel maid with an armful of fresh towels.

"I was told to bring these, and to ask if you needed anything ironed for this evening."

"Yes, of course." She crossed the room and opened her bag. Ellie had possessed far more insight than she in the choice of her clothes for the trip. Though she had laughed at the idea, Ellie had insisted that she take the gown other than her traveling costume. She removed the gown and handed it to the maid and she promised to have it back within the hour.

A tour of the suite revealed a porcelain tub with clawed feet and a shower over in the adjoining room. The water closet was hidden behind a wood partition with a basin.

She was not about to take a bath in a stranger's hotel room, however after spending most of the day on the train and considering she was to attend a formal dinner escorted by Mr. Travis, she made use of the wash basin, soap, and one of the towels the maid had brought.

If all went well, she could be on her way back to Philadelphia that night or first thing in the morning. There was still the matter of accommodations for the night if she was forced to remain longer but that was a problem that would have to be solved later.

Surely, when Marshal McCandliss knew her dilemma some other arrangement could be made with the hotel manager. If necessary, she would sleep in the lobby. It would only be a matter of a few hours.

The maid returned with her freshly pressed gown. She accepted the young woman's offer to assist dressing her, quickly buttoning the tiny row of buttons that she would never have been able to reach.

"Great balls of fire!" she whispered at her reflection.

The gown was in a shade of deep blue that molded her waist then flared to the floor, with small seed pearls at the neckline that hadn't seemed quite so low when she tried it on at the seamstress' shop.

She tugged at the neckline that barely covered the top of her breasts in an attempt to force it higher to cover more but was forced to give up at the knock at the door as Tom Travis arrived to escort her to the Governor's dinner.

"You'll make all the women in Washington jealous, and all the men will envy Ranse. He'll be pleased that you're here," Tom greeted her.

Somehow, she doubted that, and had considered the possibility that he might have her arrested. Although for what? Impersonating someone who didn't exist? Following him? The remote possibility that she might be related to the Dalton family and the Dalton brothers?

Common sense told her that if he was going to have her arrested for something, he would have already done it. And in spite of their notorious reputation, as far as she knew, it wasn't a crime to be related to criminals.

No, but he might have information that would help her find

out the truth about her real family, and that was the entire reason for making the trip. She needed to know.

Tom Travis wrapped the matching shawl around her shoulders, then escorted her to the main floor of the hotel and a waiting carriage.

Gas lights lined the streets of Washington, casting a soft glow upon the carriages and teams of horses. Laine listened attentively as Tom Travis pointed out the various buildings along the thoroughfare.

A short while later they turned down Pennsylvania Avenue. In the distance loomed the White House.

"Great balls of fire," she whispered. She hadn't realized this is where the dinner was being held, and swallowed her panic as she stepped down from the carriage at the entrance.

"Is something wrong?" Tom asked.

"It's very impressive," she replied over what she would liked to have said—something that would have gotten her discipline marks if it was overheard at the academy.

After all, proper young ladies did not swear. Her friend, Ellie, had never paid much attention to that rule and had expanded Laine's education on that topic considerably.

Every window in the magnificent house blazed with light as they walked up the steps. Several uniformed men stood at attention at the entrance, their gleaming brass buttons, and sabers glowing in the night.

In spite of the warm, evening air, Laine was seized with a sudden chill as Tom Travis tucked her arm through his and escorted her up the steps at the East entrance.

She told herself this was no different than the cotillion or any of the society parties she and Ellie had attended the past two years. She just wished it was one of those boring events instead of a formal dinner at the Executive Mansion and her upcoming meeting with Marshal McCandliss.

Her little deception had gotten her this far, but what would happen when Tom Travis, assuming she was Ranse's wife, appeared with her. She hadn't precisely thought that part of it through considering she wasn't aware at the time that she would be meeting with him again under such circumstances.

She smiled the polite expression that she had been taught was expected of a young lady of society as she and Mr. Travis entered the foyer of the mansion and then followed the other guests through a reception line.

'*Damn the torpedoes, full speed ahead*', she thought as Tom Travis introduced both of them.

"Mr. Tom Travis and Mrs. Ranse McCandliss."

To her relief the only response was a polite smile as they made their way through the receiving line. Only when Tom escorted her to the edge of the salon did she finally draw a deep breath.

"I'm not certain where Ranse might be," Tom commented. "However, I intend to take full advantage of his absence. I insist on the first waltz."

An orchestra was at the far end of the salon and couples already filled the dance floor.

Thank heaven for the lessons at Clairmont Academy for Young Women that included learning how to dance, something that was expected of all young ladies as they approached their '*season*'.

She had always found it quite boring even though the different moves came naturally to her. Unfortunately, that was not the case with Ellie who ironically wanted very much to attend the next cotillion while she couldn't have cared less.

"*How else will you find a husband?*" Ellie had demanded.

"*I suppose the old-fashioned way. I'll meet someone, or not,*" she added at the time, thinking the entire process seemed quite embarrassing being paraded about like a horse at an exclusive auction.

She much preferred to concentrate on her studies and then

attend college. She wasn't fooled that her status as an orphan presented certain obstacles particularly for families in mainline Philadelphia.

It was a fact she could never overcome, and she had experienced that cool appraisal and dismissal more than once at a social function. Except where her friend, Ellie was concerned.

"They're just jealous," Ellie insisted of the other young women at the school. *"They'll probably all end up old spinsters,"* she had added, taking another puff on one of the cigarettes she had smuggled into their room.

"And you're prettier than any of them. Look at horse-faced Amelia Longstreet. If it weren't for her father's money, she'd never find a husband. That's why they ignore you."

"You don't ignore me," she had pointed out.

"Pretty as you are, I figure that I'll be able to catch some young man as he passes by when a friend trips over his own feet at the sight of you, and certainly not Andrew Peabody."

Ellie's father already had her future husband selected for her from the time she was twelve years old.

"Besides, who else would put up with my bad habits and cover for me when I sneak out at night. By the way, you're coming with me the next time."

That time never came, unless she counted her current circumstance.

Now those lessons were put to good use—the last opportunity she would probably ever have, as Tom extended his arm to her and swept her out onto the floor.

"I'm not very good at this," he explained. "My mother tried to teach me but decided I had two left feet. I'll try to keep both of them off of yours."

She laughed in spite of everything. "I'll never tell."

He was actually an excellent partner, leading her through the steps with great ease, and never once endangered her toes. It would have been easy to forget the reason she was there, but she couldn't help scanning the guests as they swept around the salon with the other couples. Somewhere among them was Marshal McCandliss and she needed to be prepared for the encounter.

She was breathless as the next waltz ended and used the excuse to ask for a moment of rest, realizing if she remained on the dance floor there was every chance that Marshal McCandliss might see her first—an advantage she didn't want him to have. Tom escorted her to the edge of the dance floor and went to find refreshment for them.

When Tom had disappeared in the crowd, Laine slowly moved around the crowded room, seizing her opportunity to look for Ranse McCandliss.

Her wandering had brought her very near the refreshment tables, where attendants in finely starched uniforms carefully poured champagne or provided punch from silver bowls.

Tom Travis stood only a few feet away talking to a group of elegantly dressed ladies and their escorts. Before Laine could retreat through the crowd of people, he glanced up, a smile spreading across his face as he came towards her, his hand closing about her elbow.

Laine smiled at him when there was no escape, but her smile faded as her gaze fastened on Ranse McCandliss only a few feet away. She had hoped to meet with him in private but that was now gone.

"Here is the surprise I was telling you about," Tom told those gathered. "Everyone, I have the pleasure of introducing Mrs. Ranse McCandliss who graciously allowed me to escort her here this evening."

He continued on with other comments that were lost as she felt the full weight of her deception crashing down around her.

This was all wrong! This wasn't at all what she had hoped for as she saw first surprise, then the way that Ranse McCandliss' dark gaze narrowed as he stared back at her with an expression what could only be described as surprise.

However, it was no greater than the surprise of the elegantly gowned woman beside him. Her gray eyes widened at the announcement that was obviously an equal shock to her.

"Your wife?" she exclaimed as she turned to Ranse McCandliss with an amused expression.

If Laine thought speaking with him might be awkward or even difficult, this had all the signs of a disaster. Tom's little announcement, as well intentioned as it was, had obviously interrupted a very private moment between them.

Her thoughts scrambled as she tried to think how to explain everything, then changed her mind as she realized there was no easy explanation for the lies she had told. Her biggest regret was her deception of Tom Travis. She liked him and felt terribly guilty that she had used him as part of her scheme.

He glanced from her to Ranse, and then back again.

"You shouldn't keep such things a secret," Tom told him with a good-natured slap on the back.

"No, you shouldn't," the woman beside Ranse commented. "Unless this is a joke, I think an explanation is in order," she added with delicate raised brow.

Laine had suddenly become the center of several conversations among the guests around them.

Seizing upon the surprised silence that had descended upon them all, an amply- endowed woman moved towards Laine with deliberate purpose, linking her well-rounded arm through Laine's in an attempt to draw her away from the disaster.

"Since the gentlemen present are lacking in manners, allow me to introduce myself. I am Madeleine Delaney. I assisted in the planning of this grand affair. But, my dear, I can hardly match the entrance you have made."

"And you are?" The question hung in the air as the woman waited.

Laine felt the heat that spread across her cheeks as several pairs of eyes glanced from her to Ranse McCandliss, then back again.

She could almost hear her friend, Ellie, snorting with laughter.

"Give them and their society manners hell!" she would have told her.

It was one thing for Ellie Morgan to thumb her nose at society matrons in the privacy of their shared room at school. It was quite another to be confronted with several ladies of Washington society and the lie she had told to get there. If there had been a loose floorboard in the ballroom, she would have gladly crawled under it. But it didn't appear that she was going to be able to find one.

"I would like an explanation," the woman with Ranse McCandliss insisted.

"I would also like an explanation," Ranse commented.

"Damn the torpedoes, " Laine thought, as she tilted her chin.

"It's really quite simple... "

Everyone waited expectantly. Simple, and not at all simple.

"You'll have to excuse us." He took hold of her by the arm, gently but forcefully and pulled her away from the doyenne of Washington society, not to mention the woman he had been with.

He escorted her across the crowded room and out through a set of glass doors and onto a veranda, his hand still locked around her arm.

"Now, do you mind explaining to me just what you are doing here?" he demanded. "Posing as my... wife?"

"I am perfectly willing to apologize, but it's important that I speak with you."

"Apologize?"

"Yes, to your wife. I didn't realize... that is I didn't know that you are married, and it was the only way that I was able to get into the hotel."

She knew she was rattling on, but she needed to get it all out since she didn't know if there would be another opportunity.

"After you met with Gerald Ralston, he has taken steps to have me discredited and disinherited. After your visit, the headmistress of the academy asked me to leave. Mrs. Ralston's attorney has frozen my inheritance that would have meant I could attend college in the coming term.

"I have a limited amount of funds to support myself and those will soon be gone. And all of this is because of your inquiries about my background and your claim that I might be related to the Dalton gang." She finally took a breath.

"I believe you can understand that it was important for me to find you and try to straighten all of this out. You have created a very difficult situation for me, Marshal McCandliss and I didn't know any other way to reach you except to... "

"... follow me here."

"Yes," she replied. "I know that it's not proper but under the circumstances, I think we're past that. I need answers. It's the only way I can clear my name and continue with my life.

"I realize something like that might not seem important to you. But it's extremely important for someone who has no family."

Ranse watched the expressions that crossed her face— embarrassment, then determination in the set of her chin and the way those blue eyes flashed, and something else that had her standing there ready to do battle if necessary.

He had almost recovered from his first surprise at seeing her there, and that ridiculous announcement. He heartily doubted that Elizabeth had recovered yet. But then Elizabeth was resourceful and he was confident that she was already flirting with Tom Travis or some other acquaintance. The questions would come later.

"For your information, she is not my wife which might have created a problem. Can you tell me what you have planned next, *Mrs. McCandliss*? By the way, you look considerably stronger than a few minutes ago. I thought for a moment that you might faint."

"You need have no concern, Marshal. I am very strong. I have never fainted in my life. As for what comes next... I was hoping that we might talk, that there might be a way for me to convince you that I'm not who you think I am."

"I'll get you a glass of champagne while we discuss this, Mrs. McCandliss," he replied.

"You don't have to call me that."

"What am I supposed to call you?"

"By my name... " Which of course was the reason that she was there, her name, and the fact that he believed she was somehow related to the Dalton Gang.

She waited on the veranda where the air was cool and there were no questions she couldn't answer, or prying eyes. But more than once she glanced through those double doors.

Considering the lies she'd told and what he must think of her, she half expected him to leave her there and return to his friends, including the woman he had been with. Just when she was certain that he had done exactly that, he returned with a glass of champagne and another glass in his other hand. He handed her the champagne and downed the contents of the other glass.

"It'll help calm you."

She accepted the champagne glass then set it aside, when what she wanted was to throw it in his face.

"I don't want champagne. What I need is your help."

He watched her, trying to see the real person past the polite manners and speech. He had to admit that the young woman with him now bore little resemblance to the schoolgirl he had met only two days earlier with her hair neatly pulled back in a braid, her pristine shirt and skirt, a uniform worn by all the other girls at the school.

But her eyes were the same—that shade of dark blue with questions behind them, more than a little anger, and surprising boldness in posing as his wife in order to find him.

"Why should I help you?"

"Because you're to blame for what's happened, and... " This was the hard part. "... You want answers, too."

"Even if it turns out that you *are* related to the Daltons?"

"I'll face that when it happens."

Intelligence and courage. Whether or not she was related to the Daltons, she had enough of both. She was going to need it.

He reached inside his coat and retrieved a cigarette. He lit it, watching her through the fragrant smoke that wrapped around them.

"I'm sorry about Gerald Ralston." He could at least give her that.

She hadn't expected an apology.

"It doesn't change anything as far as he or the bank are concerned," she replied. "Was he able to tell you anything?"

"All he has is a poorly written letter from the woman who brought you to Philadelphia nearly almost twenty years ago. There was nothing in that letter that proves you are related to the men I'm after."

"And nothing that proves that I am not," Laine concluded. "Now that the story has been printed in the newspapers, everyone believes that I am part of the Dalton family. Unless I can prove otherwise, it doesn't matter what I tell them."

"I don't control what's printed in the paper."

"That's all you have to say for the situation you created?"

"I've already told you that I gave nothing to the newspaper or the banker," he replied.

"That's not good enough! I have tried to explain to the bank and the newspaper that this entire matter is a coincidence. But there's nothing I can say that will convince them I am not one of the Daltons unless I have proof.

"This is my life! You'll go on with yours, but I can't go back until my name is cleared! I hoped you might understand that. I see that I was wrong."

She wanted to throw the champagne in his face. Instead, she turned and left him standing there.

"You really know how to treat a lady," Tom Travis announced from where he had witnessed the last part of their conversation. "I always did say you had a way with women. But it seems that you may have met your match. I'll say one thing for sure. She is the prettiest one I've ever seen and if you don't take care, someone is going to steal her away from you."

Ranse cursed him. "You talk too much."

Laine barely stopped long enough to retrieve her shawl from one of the attendants, then ran out the main entrance of the White House.

Damn Ranse McCandliss, she thought. She should have known that he wouldn't help her.

"May I call you a carriage, miss?" the attendant at the front entrance politely asked.

She nodded. When a driver arrived, she gave him the name of the National Hotel. She needed to retrieve her things from the hotel. And then?

She needed to have time to think, to figure out what to do next. Ranse McCandliss had been her best hope for straightening all of this out, but she could hardly have called their meeting amicable.

When the carriage stopped, she stepped down in front of the National Hotel, and counted out the necessary fare for the driver. She turned back towards the entrance of the hotel, the key to Ranse McCandliss' room in her hand.

She crossed the foyer of the hotel, mostly empty that time of the night, and stepped inside one of the lifts. The gate was closed and it slowly rose to the third floor.

Inside the room, she leaned back against the closed door and gave in to tears of frustration.

RANSE PUSHED past Tom Travis as he tried to follow her. By the time he reached the front entrance, her carriage had already disappeared down the circular drive and out onto the thoroughfare.

A second carriage was quickly summoned, and Ranse thrust several gold coins into the driver's hands.

After two hours of searching the surrounding streets, he had no interest in returning to the White House where there were too many people and too many questions they would undoubtedly ask about his '*wife*'. And the first one to ask would be Elizabeth Summers.

Laine stared about her. A single gas lantern beside the door had been lit and turned low to give the faintest light when entering the room. Evidently the maid had left the light burning.

She crossed the room to the double glass doors that led out onto a balcony that overlooked the street below. She leaned heavily against the window frame. Somewhere across the city, a clock chimed the hour—eleven o'clock. She needed to leave before Ranse McCandliss returned.

She turned back to the room, changed into her travel costume, then folded the blue gown and packed it with her other things in the carpet bag. She left the key to the room on the dressing table, and left.

She had no idea where she was going and didn't have enough money for a hotel room even if one was available. She returned to the main floor.

The lobby was now completely empty this time of the night, as well as the adjacent dining room with only a handful of candles still burning on the tables that had been cleared with new table linens laid out for breakfast the following morning.

She found an alcove near the entrance of the restaurant and decided that it was probably better and safer than wandering the streets of Washington. She would leave unnoticed when morning came and make her way to the train station.

Ranse inserted his key into the lock and let himself into his hotel room. Tom had mentioned she was there earlier and he could smell that faint sweet scent that he'd caught out on veranda at the White House. But she wasn't there.

She had very little money and even he knew there was probably not a hotel room to be had in the capital. Where would she go?

He returned downstairs. The night manager hadn't seen her return.

"Is there something else, sir?"

He shook his head as he turned from the front desk. It was after midnight. Other guests hadn't yet returned.

Damn little fool! Where would she go? His eyes narrowed on the door to the restaurant. The door stood ajar.

It was long past the supper hour and the restaurant was dark inside except for a handful of candles that burned low on the tables.

He found her in the alcove near the entrance, her head propped on her arm along the back of a chair. Damn little fool, he thought again as he gently woke her.

He saw the confusion in her blue eyes, then the anger as she recognized him.

"Were you planning on spending the night here?"

"That's none of your business."

He smiled at that. "Since everyone at the hotel thinks that you're my wife, it is my business for the moment."

"You made it very clear that you won't help me. So, please go away."

'Please', go away? He'd never been asked to leave with *'please'* in front of it.

"I came to offer you the use of my room for the night."

She blinked. That was the last thing she expected.

"I don't understand. Why would you do that?"

"You're right that I'm responsible for your being here. It's the least I can do."

She looked at him suspiciously. "Where will you be?"

"In spite of what you think of me, I do have friends."

"Mr. Travis?" She knew that he had a room at the hotel.

"Possibly not what he had planned for the evening, but I'll manage. And I'll make certain that you have the only key."

She reluctantly accepted. The offer to sleep in a bed as opposed to the chair she occupied seemed reasonable.

She stood in the middle of the room she had left only a few hours earlier. She should probably feel guilt that he'd given up his room, but under the circumstances...

"The manager told me earlier that you're leaving Washington in the morning."

"That's right."

"You'll be returning to the Oklahoma Territory."

"That's where my work takes me."

"I will be on the same train," she informed him. If he thought the use of his room changed anything, he was sadly mistaken.

"The Territory is no place for a schoolgirl."

Schoolgirl?

"This is a free country, Marshal McCandliss. I may go where I please. I have no doubt that you'll continue your search for the Daltons. Whether you allow it or not, I'm also going to try to find them."

5

Laine set the carpet bag down at the platform of the train station. Waiting patiently behind the elderly couple in front of her, she recounted the paper bills clutched tightly in her hand.

She had earlier sent off a hastily worded telegram to Ellie, explaining she would not be returning to Philadelphia right away, and that she would write more later. She desperately hoped the stationmaster would allow her credit for her unused return passage to Philadelphia, against the cost of the train fare to the Oklahoma Territory.

She was aware of the mixed expression that crossed the ticket master's face when she asked the cost of the fare. It was obvious that he didn't often have young, unescorted ladies purchase tickets for such a long trip. She leaned across the counter as she tried to hear over the shouts that grew more persistent from behind her.

"There you are. I'm certainly glad I was able to find you."

The voice was oddly familiar, but before Laine could turn around to see who called out, she was gently seized by the arm and drawn aside by Tom Travis.

The ticket master had opened the small glass window and peered impatiently out at her across the counter.

"Miss, do you still want that single fare to Guthrie, Oklahoma?"

"Yes, of course. Can you tell me how much that would be with this ticket in exchange?" Laine smiled faintly at Tom as she leaned toward the ticket window.

Tom Travis looked at her with surprise.

"You don't need to purchase a ticket. Ranse has the use of a private car at the end of the train. The Governor of Oklahoma provides it for official business. There's more than enough room for all of us. I suppose he didn't have time to explain last night."

He leaned around her and thanked the ticket master for his help.

All of them? What else could he possibly mean after last night, except that she planned to travel with Ranse to the Oklahoma Territory.

"I appreciate your concern, but you don't understand..."

The last thing she wanted was to be in the company of Marshal McCandliss, particularly after last night and then again this morning when he had made it perfectly clear what he thought of her.

"I understand that Ranse can be bull-headed at times, but I'm certain he wouldn't want to leave you stranded here."

She was certain that is exactly what Marshal McCandliss intended but before she could explain further, Tom pulled her arm through his, and guided her along the platform to where the passengers waited to board the next train.

All her objections and any excuse she might have been able to come up with froze as her gaze locked with that of Ranse McCandliss, as he also approached the train escorting the woman from the night before.

She pulled back. At that moment, Ranse McCandliss was the last person she wanted to see or be with.

Tom laid his hand over hers and squeezed it encouragingly.

"It's all right. Things will smooth out between you. I know you and Ranse haven't known each other very long. But give him a chance. Beneath that hard exterior beats the heart of a real, live, human being." He winked at her.

She sincerely doubted that and could only imagine what he had told Tom Travis of the evening before. Obviously, he hadn't told him the truth.

She forced a smile. She'd be damned if she would let Ranse McCandliss embarrass her in front of him. Tom had been kind to her and offered her help. Somehow she would find the right time to tell him the truth herself. But for the moment, it seemed that lie had trapped her again.

"Remember, if you need a friend, I'm here. Besides," he lowered his voice as if sharing a secret.

"He snores."

She almost burst out laughing. She didn't yet know Ranse McCandliss well enough to know if that was the truth or just something to make her feel more at ease. And she probably never would. Elizabeth Summers, however, made no attempt to disguise her contempt behind her forced smile.

"Ranse, you really must keep better track of this young lady, or someone will try to steal her away from you; especially in the Territory." Tom teased.

"We thought you might not be ready to make such the trip, Elizabeth commented. "It is a quite long. Are you certain you are up to it, my dear?"

We? Laine had no idea what the woman's relationship was with Ranse McCandliss and didn't care. Once she reached Guthrie, she would continue on her own.

"Of course she's up to it," Tom commented. "Anyone who can wade into the thick of Washington society and survive is ready to face the Territory. My concern is whether or not it's ready for her," he added with a good-natured smile.

Ranse pulled her aside. "I thought we'd settled this last night. The Oklahoma Territory is dangerous and no place for... "

Laine pulled her arm free. "Just what is my place?" she whispered, aware of the two who watched their exchange.

"The only hope I have of clearing my name is to find the truth, and that is not in Philadelphia. And quite honestly," she added. "I don't give a damn what you think." She braced herself for his reply. It wasn't what she expected.

"All right, if you're so determined to see this through, then it's none of my business, but you'll find you've made a big mistake. You have no idea what you're getting yourself into. This isn't exactly an afternoon social event in the park."

The warning whistle of the train sounded, reminding them that the time for departure drew near.

She seized the handle of her carpet bag.

"We need to board," Tom announced as he tucked her arm through his.

Ranse frowned as he watched them join other passengers to board the train.

"I don't understand any of this. How could you have married that girl? You were only in Philadelphia a few days! Surely you weren't indiscreet enough as to get yourself caught with her," Elizabeth confronted him.

"For heaven's sake, Ranse, she's not with child is she?" her voice rose.

He eased the long rifle under one arm and took hold of her arm.

"Even if that were the case, it doesn't concern you. We better board now, the train won't wait. Not even for you."

The final whistle sounded and the conductor checked his

watch one last time before departure. Elizabeth leaned against him, laying her hands against the front of his coat.

"I have no intention of giving up this easily."

"We'll talk about this later," Ranse replied.

As she boarded the train, Laine reminded herself that Ranse McCandliss' feelings for Elizabeth Summers hardly mattered.

She was grateful when Tom Travis guided her through the next two cars. She looked at him as he opened the door to the private car.

"I don't think my ticket includes a private car," she commented.

"Ranse has the use of it for this trip courtesy of the territorial governor," he replied.

"I don't need this..." she fumbled for an excuse. "A seat in one of the other cars is fine." More than fine under the circumstances, she thought.

"I know things are difficult right now," Tom replied. "But I know Ranse and no matter what's going on, he wouldn't want you to spend the next four days in a passenger car."

"You don't understand... "

"You're going to have to settle your differences with Ranse sooner or later," he continued. "The Oklahoma Territory can be hard on a woman, and the Governor has made the Daltons top priority for every lawman in the Territory. It'll require a lot of time away until they're brought in.

"You 're going to be alone a lot of the time. That can wear on a woman out in the Territory, especially one who is used to the finer things in life. But unless I miss my guess, Ranse will find a way to wrap all this up quickly so he can get back to you.

"If you were my bride, I sure wouldn't stay away any longer than was absolutely necessary." He smiled kindly as he held on to her hand.

She knew it was hopeless to argue. As far as Ranse McCandliss was concerned, she would deal with that when she saw him.

"Is there someone special waiting for you when you return?" she asked.

"I'm still looking for the right woman. I'm not lucky like Ranse. Seems when I find her, she's already spoken for." He winked at her.

He opened the door to the private car for her.

"You should be comfortable in here. I hope to see you for supper."

Then he was gone.

The car was incredibly luxurious. The walls were covered with gleaming dark wood. Windows lined both sides of the car, each draped with green velvet drapes and fringed with gold-satin tassels. Between each of the windows were oil lamps affixed on the wall.

A carved mahogany table sat beneath one set of windows with chairs upholstered in that same green velvet. Matching loveseats sat across the aisle. Overhead, the wood-paneled ceiling of the private car was set with a carved wood frieze and crown cornice.

The centerpiece was a six-lamp, gasolier with etched-glass shades that swung sharply at the sudden motion of the train as it pulled out of the station, with what appeared to be a separate room at the far end of the car.

She set the carpet bag on the floor of the car as she braced herself against the motion of the train.

She took off her jacket and settled into one of the uphol-stered chairs by the window. She watched as the capital slipped past, across the Potomac River, giving way to square, flat-topped buildings, and streets lined with trees and houses, then picking up speed as it turned southwest.

How long would it be before Ranse McCandliss arrived, possibly with Elizabeth Summers?

It was several hours later that she heard the latch click at the door and Ranse McCandliss stepped into the car. That dark gaze met hers, then took in her unpacked bag on the floor.

What did she see there? More objections? Another argument?

There was no surprise and she could only assume that Tom had told him where he'd left her. His mouth thinned. Whatever he might have said he seemed to decide against, she thought; short of physically throwing her off the train.

"I apologize," she said, bracing herself once more as she stood. "This was not my idea; I didn't know that this was your car. I can easily go to another."

That gaze came back to hers. He shook his head.

"It's probably best that you stay in here until we reach the next station, then transfer to another train. It's more private than the other compartments."

And further away from Elizabeth Summers, he thought, as he turned back to the door.

"I'm not going back," she told him so there would be no misunderstanding.

He turned and saw the way her shoulders straightened, that slight angle of her chin. He had to give her credit, she'd met Elizabeth Summers and survived to tell about it. Not the usual outcome.

He admired strength and courage. As for her determination to continue on to the Territory...?

"You *will be* on a train back to Philadelphia as soon as it can be arranged."

The door to the car slammed behind him.

She knew that he thought her foolish, even reckless, he had made that perfectly clear. But she had no choice if she was to get her life back. And she wasn't about to let Marshal Ranse McCandliss stand in her way.

It was noon when Tom knocked on the door of the car and

invited her to join him for lunch. She begged off. The last thing she wanted was another confrontation with Marshal McCandliss or his companion.

"I understand, but you can't stay here for four days. I'll be back to escort you to supper."

True to his word, he returned as evening approached and an attendant arrived to turn up the lights of the oil lamps.

"You can't hide in here forever," Tom told her when the attendant left.

"I'm not hiding. I simply don't want..." How to explain, she thought.

"Confrontations with Elizabeth Summers?" he guessed.

She nodded in response. Elizabeth Summers and... others."

"The best defense is a good offense," he added. "And I think you're up to it."

She was hungry. That stale breakfast roll she'd brought with her had worn off hours ago.

"And you have Ranse to back you up."

"Somehow, I doubt that."

He smiled. "The first call to dinner was half an hour ago. I would consider it a pleasure if you would join me," Tom offered sincerely. "Besides, he's in another car with..." he hesitated at something he obviously hadn't intended to say. "He doesn't usually eat this early," he coughed, uncomfortable, and made the excuse.

He had no way of knowing that the fact Marshal McCandliss wouldn't be there suited her perfectly, and she was starving.

"I accept."

When they arrived in the dining car, there was no sign of Ranse McCandliss or Elizabeth Summers.

After dinner, Laine gave the excuse of being tired and returned to the private car. It was much safer to remain there than risk another confrontation with Ranse McCandliss.

The last purplish-blue streaks of light in the sky had faded into early twilight when the attendant knocked on the door. He smiled congenially and informed her that the gentleman had asked him to see to her needs. She could only assume that request had come from Tom Travis.

He laid out towels and fresh bars of soap at the wash basin, then entered the compartment at the other end of the car and turned back the linens on the bed. He then politely asked if there was anything else she needed.

"Thank you, no," she told him.

She smiled at the thought that at least she had found one friend. Come morning, she was certain she would need all the help she could get if she was to convince him against sending her hack to Philadelphia.

As darkness fell beyond the car, she pulled the heavy shades down at the window in the bedroom and turned up the gas lamp. She removed her walking skirt and then unbuttoned her shirtwaist.

She washed, then removed the pins from her hair. Wearing her chemise and underdrawers, she crawled under the covers on the bed, but it was several hours before she slept.

SHE AWAKENED JUST before sunup at the sudden change in the motion of the train. She quickly dressed and made her way from the private car as the train gradually slowed.

"Good morning, ma'am," an attendant greeted her as she stepped into the next car.

"How long will we be stopping?"

"Just enough to take on more water, and passengers. Seems there are more of those Pinkerton men getting on board." He smiled again as the train lurched then came to a full stop.

"Will you be leaving the train, ma'am?"

"No, I'm going all the way to the Territory. But I need to send a telegram."

"The stationmaster inside can send that for you. We'll be here about a half hour."

She thanked him as she went down the steps from the train, and the thought occurred to her that if Ranse McCandliss had plans to put her on a train returning to Philadelphia, he would be hard pressed to do so if he wasn't able to find her.

Her best plan was to avoid contact with him as much as possible. At least Tom Travis was on her side, even if he didn't know everything about the reason she was there or the deception.

She found the stationmaster and quickly sent her telegram, informing Ellie that she would contact her when she reached the Oklahoma Territory. She could imagine her reaction when she received it.

She paid for the telegram, then turned back toward the train, and immediately glimpsed that tall, lean figure that stepped down onto the platform.

Ranse McCandliss stopped to look first in one direction and then the other. The conductor standing on the platform at the front of the train caught his attention. Several men joined them and then boarded the train and she could only assume they were the Pinkerton agents the attendant had mentioned.

She had read about the agency in the newspapers that had earned a reputation for hunting down criminals no one else seemed to be able to find. The cases they solved and the people they apprehended had been publicized in the newspapers.

Who were they after now? The Dalton brothers? She quickly crossed the platform and climbed the steps into the train. The Pinkerton Agency might be willing to help her if Ranse McCandliss still refused.

She moved quickly through the dining car and took a table

at the far end, so that he wouldn't easily see her when he boarded the train once more.

"Breakfast isn't quite ready yet, ma'am," the attendant informed her. "May I get you coffee?"

She thanked him and continued to watch through the train windows that faced the station and smiled to herself that she had been able to avoid Ranse McCandliss when she felt the gentle lurching of the train as it pulled out of the station.

That hope died as he entered the dining car, saw her, and then slowly walked toward her table. He asked the attendant to bring him coffee as well.

"You're up early," Ranse commented as he took a chair opposite her without waiting for an invitation which he was pretty certain she wouldn't have offered.

"I had business to attend to at the station," she replied, not that she owed him an explanation.

She felt that dark gaze on her as the attendant returned with coffee for both of them.

"Thank you for the use of the private car," she said, at least being grateful. "It wasn't necessary," she added.

"I thought it might be best for your safety."

"My safety?" That he would be concerned at all was surprising.

"Your arrival was a surprise." That was an understatement, he thought, considering Elizabeth Summers' reaction.

Was that a trace of humor at his mouth, she thought? Who knew that Ranse McCandliss was capable of anything but that frown, the way one corner of his mouth lifted in an almost smile?

She set her cup down on the table. She wasn't naive enough to think they'd reached a truce, but the least she could do was apologize for the lie she'd told about being his wife.

"I never intended for anyone else to think that we were..." How did one explain the circumstances?

"Married?"

"Yes, and I apologize. It was the only way I could think of to see you at the hotel. Unfortunately Mr. Travis overheard, and everything became very complicated after that. I'll apologize to him, and Miss Summers as well."

That faint smile deepened. "Don't worry about Tom, and a far as Elizabeth is concerned..."

"You obviously have an understanding, and my presence has caused difficulty."

There was a full smile now that reached those dark eyes and she wondered if some other man had taken Marshal McCandliss' place for she hardly recognized the handsome man who sat across from her.

"Elizabeth is strong-willed, stubborn..." That steady gaze fastened on her.

Was he comparing them with that comment? She wondered.

"There is no *'understanding'*," he continued. "She says and does as she pleases."

"I noticed."

That smile returned. "You'll have an opportunity to return when we reach Abilene. There's a direct line from there."

So, they were back to that, she thought, in spite of the fact that she had made herself perfectly clear about it.

"You need to reconsider going all the way to the Territory. It's not the sort of place... "

"... For someone like me?" she finished the thought. "I believe Elizabeth Summers called me naive and foolish. "

She pushed the cup of coffee back onto the table and stood.

"I am neither of those, Marshal McCandliss. There's nothing to prevent me from continuing on—not even you. And I won't go back... can't go back to Philadelphia until I'm able to clear my name. You're to blame for that."

Ranse watched as she turned and left the dining car, back

straight, slender shoulders squared. Strong-willed and stubborn.

She would need both if he couldn't persuade her once they arrived in the Territory, he thought with more than a little admiration.

There was more to Laine Dalton than he first assumed when he took the assignment to track her down. Then it was just another assignment not all that different from delivering prisoners to another town, or tracking down stolen cattle. Find the girl, find out what she knew about the Daltons, and whether or not she'd had any contact with any of them.

The polish from the proper upbringing and private school education were there, but beneath the cool gaze in those dark blue eyes and the finishing school polish there was also fire and grit. He'd glimpsed both briefly the night before, and just again now.

Was it Dalton blood? The reckless way the boys had that he knew all too well? He hoped not, for her sake.

Halfway down the passage, Laine slowed at the sight of Elizabeth Summers leaving her own compartment. Her surprise was obvious as well in the sudden arch of a brow.

"What have we here? My dear, I really had hoped you possessed more sense than this. You should have taken the opportunity to return to Philadelphia. You have no idea what you're getting into," she sneered.

She tried to brush past but found her way blocked, as Elizabeth stepped into her path. "You little fool, do you really think I'll give him up that easily?"

She'd had enough of Marshal McCandliss with those dark eyes and slow look, and more than enough of someone who reminded her too much of some of the women she'd been forced to meet in Philadelphia, the ones that her friend Ellie Morgan referred to as pampered cows that no man in his right mind would want.

"I don't give a damn what you do." Laine pushed past, flattening her against the wall of the passage.

Once inside the private car, she collapsed back against the door. It was several moments before she trusted her unsteady knees to the lurch of the train. She had to admit that Ellie was right.

She didn't know if Elizabeth Summers was pampered, although by the cut of her clothes it seemed that she was of some means. As for being a cow that no man in his right mind would want?

That was Ranse McCandliss' business and none of her own. Her business was to stay away from the woman as much as possible until they reached Guthrie in the Oklahoma Territory and continue on her own to try to solve the mystery of the Daltons and her own last name.

At least for today, she had met the enemy and won. Well, if she hadn't won, at least she was still on her way to the Territory, and for all she cared Elizabeth Summers was welcome to Ranse McCandliss. They suited each other.

Over the next two days as they continued farther south and then west, she politely refused Tom Travis' invitations to leave the car. If she stayed there, she wouldn't be likely to encounter Elizabeth Summers or Ranse McCandliss.

Only when they left late the third day and she was confident that he wouldn't have her physically put off the train, she agreed to join Tom Travis for dinner in the dining car.

He'd been more than kind and she had to find some way to explain everything to him. Her one disappointment was catching sight of Elizabeth Summers seated with Marshal McCandliss at the only places still available

She thought of turning back and returning to the private car, but Ranse McCandliss had already seen them and stood as they approached. A gentleman? Who would have thought that?

"I'll kick Elizabeth under the table if she starts to get out of line," Tom whispered over her shoulder as they reached the table.

She couldn't help but smile at that. "I might be tempted to do the same."

Tom pulled out the chair next to the window, across from Ranse Morgan, then took the chair across from Elizabeth Summers.

That, Laine silently thought, might prevent a well aimed foot at the marshal's companion.

Tom kept up pleasant conversation that immediately drew her attention away from the others at the table and most of the dinner passed with only angled glances from Elizabeth. She wondered if Ranse McCandliss had spoken to her. Only when dessert was served did the woman attempt to engage her in conversation.

"Tell me, my dear, where did you and Ranse meet?" she inquired casually.

"We met through my work," Ranse replied.

That was true as far as it went and saved her from needing to reply.

"I wasn't aware that you had acquaintances in Philadelphia," Elizabeth commented. "You shouldn't keep so many secrets." She then turned to her.

"It's fortunate that you didn't get yourself 'caught,' as so many naive young girls seem to do through their own ignorance," she continued.

Which answered the question about what he had told her. And hadn't...

"That's none of your business," he surprised everyone at the table with the remark.

"The poor child will have enough adjustments ahead of her travelling to the Territory. God knows you won't be able to spend any time in Guthrie when we arrive. The Governor will undoubtedly send you off on a new assignment."

The *'poor child'*, as she so deliberately pointed out was tired of being talked around, as if she weren't there, which she was fully aware was exactly what Elizabeth Summers intended.

"You need have no concern," she told her. "I am capable of taking care of myself."

"Of course, you are," Elizabeth sarcastically replied, then turned to Ranse McCandliss.

"More wine perhaps? To celebrate your marriage?" she suggested. "Ah, there is the attendant now."

The woman really was loathsome, Laine thought. More wine was served all around, even though she had no desire for more. She was about to excuse herself with a look at Tom Travis.

"I must say," Elizabeth continued. "I have always felt well protected." She laid her other hand over Ranse McCandliss' arm as she reached for her glass of wine.

Her hand bumped the goblet, knocking it over. Red wine splattered across the table and onto the front of Laine's gown.

"Oh, dear, that was so clumsy of me. Look what a mess I've made. I do apologize," Elizabeth exclaimed. She stood then.

"If we don't get that stain out right away, I'm afraid your clothes will be ruined. You must let me help you."

Laine pushed back from the table, attempting to soak up as much of the wine as possible with her dinner napkin. Ranse McCandliss cursed under his breath, waving down the attendant as she suddenly stood.

She'd had more than enough of Elizabeth Summers. The last thing she wanted was her offer of help.

"I'll take care of it myself, if you all will excuse me."

Tom Travis came out of his chair abruptly.

"I'll see you to your compartment."

She shook her head. "I don't want to interrupt the conversation. Good evening." With that, she threw down the napkin and left the table.

"Oh, dear, she is quite upset. Understandable, as she undoubtedly brought few things with her in the one bag she brought aboard the train," Elizabeth commented. "I really must see if there's anything I can do to help. Women understand these things so much better than men."

Ranse rose from the table. He threw down his napkin, then left the car.

When she would have protested and followed him, Tom Travis lightly kicked her under the table.

"Sit down," he told Elizabeth Summers. "After all, she is his wife."

"There are times you interfere too much," she spat at him.

"The same might be said of you." He tipped his wineglass in a mock toast, thoroughly enjoying himself.

6

Ranse followed her to the private car.

Since boarding the train in D.C. he'd been working with the Pinkertons who had been hired by the railroad as part of a plan to put a stop to a series of train robberies that the railroad had over the past year.

It was no coincidence that his effort to find the Daltons was part of that plan. He'd been assigned to the Pinkertons by the Governor with specific instructions to do whatever was necessary to put an end to the robberies. But that plan didn't include Elizabeth Summers attack on Laine Dalton whether or not she was involved with the Dalton brothers.

If she was, he would find out soon enough. If not, then she was another victim caught up in all of this.

Unfortunately, victims were a sad and unpleasant part of his work. They were usually cared for by family or friends.

She'd been raised as an orphan, taken in by a woman who had been kind enough and wealthy enough. The friends she had were those left behind in Philadelphia. A person needed both in order to survive. She had neither one as far as he'd been able to find out.

That might have been the reason he followed her, to apologize for Elizabeth Summers. Over the past few days, he'd seen too much of her ability to be hateful and spiteful, and that was his fault—something that he *would* take care of.

Or maybe it was the look in Laine Dalton's eyes as she stood to leave—that flash of anger then the strength, and her refusal to lash out in return. He reached the private car, knocked at the door—he didn't expect her to invite him in, then opened the door that stood ajar.

She looked up with more than a little surprise, then that mask that he'd seen in the dining car was firmly back in place.

"Please, leave. I've had enough for one night." She didn't want any more confrontations or arguments.

One more day according to Tom Travis, she told herself, just one more day and they would be in the Territory and she would be rid of Ranse McCandliss and Elizabeth Summers.

'Please'. She had manners, which was more than he could say for Elizabeth Summers after the way she had treated her.

"I came to apologize. Elizabeth had no right to say the things she said. She can be..." He shook his head, not used to making excuses for other people's comments and actions.

"How about spiteful?" Laine suggested.

"I was thinking that she can be cruel," Ranse replied.

"She has that one down perfect!"

There it was again. Strength and something else... grit.

"I should have explained to her about that night in Washington and how you managed to get inside the Governor's supper. That's my fault."

"Yes, you should have," Laine replied.

"Then I apologize for myself."

"Apology accepted."

The stain on her skirt was still wet. She took the saltshaker from the small dining table in the private car and rubbed some into the stain.

"What are you doing?"

"Salt removes wine stains," she explained. "It's one of the things we were taught in classes about manners and deportment; something every lady must know and most of it useless." She looked up.

The train suddenly lurched, slowed, and then lurched again. She stumbled and would have fallen if he hadn't caught her.

"Is there another stop tonight?" she asked.

Ranse shook his head. Something was wrong. There were no stops scheduled. Then, they heard another sound over the grind of the wheels on steel tracks as the brakes engaged again.

Her gaze locked with his as gunfire cracked outside the car and shattered one of the windows.

He forced her to the floor of the car, protecting her as glass showered down around them. Then there was more gunfire.

"Stay down," he told her as he pulled the Colt from his holster and checked it.

He counted the seconds between rounds of shots and listened. There was the distinctive sound of the thirty-eight caliber that the Pinkerton agents carried, followed by the sound of forty-four caliber shots from outside the train.

"What is it?" she asked as more shots were fired.

"Train robbers most likely after the mining company payroll we took on board at the last stop," he replied. "It's also the reason we took on extra agents."

That dark gaze met hers as he pushed into a crouched position. He knew what she was thinking. He shook his head.

"I doubt it's the Daltons. The last we heard they were in the Territory, not around here." But he also knew that they could have left the Territory for a bigger take, and the mining payroll was substantial.

He stayed low and moved to one of those shattered windows, then looked out the edge of the window shade. There was another round of gunfire farther up the train toward the baggage car.

"Stay here." He turned toward the door.

He didn't like leaving her alone, but at the moment it was the safest place for her.

"I need to find out what's happening, and I want to find Tom," he explained. "Lock the door behind me." He saw the questions and the fear in her eyes, but there was also strength.

She nodded.

He stepped out onto the deck that connected to the next car, waited for the sound of the lock, then made his way forward into the next car.

She stayed low inside the car at the sound of more gunfire. Then there was a lull.

Was it over? Had Ranse and the Pinkertons been able to stop the robbers? It was frighteningly quiet. Then she heard the sound of someone outside the door followed by frantic pounding.

"Open the door!"

Elizabeth Summers. Dear God what was she doing here?

Ranse had told her not to open the door for anyone but him or Tom, but she couldn't leave her out there when there was no way of knowing if the danger had passed.

"Let me in!" Elizabeth frantically demanded.

Laine made her way to the front of the car as more shots were fired. She threw the latch and opened the door. Elizabeth pushed her way in.

"This is the only safe place! Lock the damn door!" she demanded, then screamed as more shots were fired just outside the car.

"Get down!" Laine shouted and made a grab to push her down from the line of windows at the car.

Shots exploded inside the car, shattering lamps on the tables and splintering the elegant carved wood of the walls.

Pain tore through her shoulder as she was thrown back against the wall of the car. Then she was falling.

Elizabeth screamed something, then it slipped away as darkness swept over her with her last thought that she had been shot.

"WHAT THE HELL HAPPENED?" Ranse demanded as he reached the car with Tom Travis right behind him.

His first thought—What was Elizabeth doing there?

She was going on and on, prattling and carrying on about the attack.

"My God, we could have been killed! Is it over...?" she came out from behind one of the settees.

"Please tell me it's over! I've never been so frightened in my life...!"

"Where's Laine?" he demanded. Then he saw her slumped on the floor a few feet away, a stain at her shoulder on the back of the shirtwaist she'd worn with the skirt when he'd left her there.

"What the hell happened?"

"I came to warn her," Elizabeth replied. "There was more gunfire. I don't know what happened... she got in the way. We could have both been killed!"

He had a pretty good idea what had happened and it didn't match up with what she was telling them. He knew Elizabeth pretty well, and the past few days had only reinforced what he already knew.

Got in the way? The little he knew Laine Dalton, she was smart and she had grit. She wouldn't have gotten in the way. There was another possibility that he didn't have time to argue about with Elizabeth, she had already made herself clear toward the young woman on the floor in front of him.

"You have to believe me, Ranse..." she continued.

He'd heard enough. He jerked his head in Tom's direction.

"Get her out of here, and see how soon we can get back underway."

When Travis had managed to pull Elizabeth from the car, he returned to Laine, slipped an arm under her, then lifted her and carried her into the nearest stateroom. He gently laid her on the bed. The sleeve of his coat was stained with blood. He took it off and threw it aside.

He'd seen more than his share of bullet wounds, a couple of them his own. But a woman with a gunshot wound was something different. He felt anger all over again at Elizabeth's foolishness. He didn't believe her story for a minute, but this wasn't the time to set the record straight.

He heard the door of the car open then shut.

"How bad is it?"

"Bad enough." He looked over at Tom. The question was answered in the sudden lurch of the train, the grind of wheels under the car, then the slow gathering of speed.

"Three dead and the Pinkertons have two others under guard in the baggage car."

Ranse nodded as he gently felt the pulse at her throat. "She's alive, but she's lost a lot of blood."

Tom caught sight of his coat and nodded. "You need to get the bleeding stopped. Her shirt is going to have to come off and we'll get cloths for bandages. I'll get my bag... "

"No." Ranse shook his head. "I'll do it. The bullet went through. I need to find out how bad it is, then bandage her shoulder."

Tom nodded. "With four other staterooms, I'm pretty certain I can find some linens to cut up and something to cut them with. I'm pretty sure the Governor won't mind."

Ranse didn't give a damn about the Governor or anything else at the moment as he bent over the bed and slowly unbuttoned the row of buttons on her shirtwaist.

Wounds didn't usually bother him. Out here there were all kinds of things that happened that people who lived in Boston, New York, or Philadelphia never saw much less experienced. But out here it was still the frontier, for now. And it came with all sorts of injuries and wounds, and deaths.

As much as he'd seen and experienced, the sight of the bullet wound in her shoulder stopped him. Then he eased her onto her side and cut away the rest of her shirt. The wound was smaller at the back of her shoulder, larger where the bullet had come out at the front—both good and bad news.

The good news was he didn't need to go digging around for the bullet to get it out. The bad news was she had bled a long time and she was going to have one helluva a scar.

Blood had soaked the camisole she wore under her shirt. He cut that too, lowering it just enough so that he could bandage the wound.

She stirred as he gently washed around the wound with a wet towel. He saw the confusion in her eyes, then the way they widened as she became aware of the pain.

"Don't try to talk," he told her when he saw the question in her eyes. "You got in the way of one of those bullets, but it passed through. I need to get the bleeding stopped and then I'm going to bandage your shoulder." It was about this time that he expected some protest or righteous indignation. There was neither as her gaze fastened on his.

"Elizabeth?" she whispered.

"You got the worst of it." The rest of it would wait until later. "I'd like to tell you this won't hurt, but it would be a lie. The bullet went in the back of your shoulder and came out the front. I'll have to roll you onto your side to bandage both wounds."

He would have preferred if she cursed or cried, he could handle that. She did neither, but simply nodded. Grit, he thought and more damn honesty and courage than someone else who came to mind.

"Easy," he told her as he gently rolled her onto her left side toward him, exposing the wound at the back of her right shoulder.

"Hold on to me." He gave her his hand. "Squeeze as hard as you like."

Her hand clutched his, but she didn't make a sound as he wiped away the blood at the back of her shoulder.

"She's conscious. That's a good sign," Tom commented as he returned with strips of linen that he'd cut from sheets pulled from one of the beds. He made a thick pad of one of the strips of linen and handed it to him.

"Do you want me to check the wound?"

Ranse shook his head. Tom Travis, ever the physician.

"It's clean. The bullet passed through," he replied as he pressed the pad against the wound. "I'll take care of it."

Tom handed him another folded piece of linen that he pressed against the wound at the front of her shoulder and then bound both with strips of the sheet.

"Where's Elizabeth?" he asked. He didn't want any more confrontations.

"In her own compartment and full of excuses," Tom replied.

"What about the payroll shipment?"

"Safe and under guard by our friends with the Pinkerton Agency."

Having made the trip just the week before and now this unexpected stop, Ranse knew they wouldn't reach Guthrie until late the following morning.

"Make certain there are guards posted in all the cars and with the engineer."

"Anything else?" Tom asked.

He shook his head. He was responsible for her being there, and for what had happened.

"I'll move my things in here, so that I can make certain there isn't more bleeding through the night. Have the deck between the cars guarded. I don't want any more surprise visitors."

Tom nodded. "I'll take care of it. If you need anything else..."

"I know who to ask."

A SUDDEN LURCH WAKENED HER. There was the confusion of waking in a strange place, followed by another lurch and the clatter of steel wheels. She was on a train.

There was confusion, then everything slowly came back through the shadows in the car with only a sliver of light at the door from outside the compartment.

They'd been attacked by train robbers. There was gunfire, the windows in the car shattered and Elizabeth Summers...

She tried to push herself up off the bed, then fell back, gasping at the pain as another memory slipped through the darkness in the compartment.

"The bullet went in the back of your shoulder and came out the front."

She'd been shot?

"Take it easy." The words found her, that voice slipping back through the shadows along with vague memory.

"Hold on to me..."

A light on the wall of the compartment winked on.

The edge of the bed dipped under his weight as Ranse brushed back her hair and laid a hand against her cheek.

She was warm, but that was expected. He saw the confusion at her eyes, the questions, then the way she tried to cover herself and winced at the pain that caused.

"The bullet went through," he told her. "It will take a while and I know it hurts, but you'll be all right."

"Tom...?" It was barely a whisper, her throat dry.

"He checked the bandages, said that you'd live," he added.
"He should know."

At her look of confusion, he explained, "He's a doctor."

She nodded. "Elizabeth?"

He frowned, surprised that she would ask when Elizabeth had deliberately been cruel to her told him more about her, the sort of person she was.

"She's all right," he replied.

There was something in his voice, something almost angry, but she might have been mistaken. The next words softened.

"You got the worst of it."

When she tried to sit up, he placed another pillow behind her, then poured water into a glass.

"Drink this."

Her hand shook as she reached for it. He held it for her, then set the glass aside when she finished. She closed her eyes as she laid back on her side. He pulled the blanket up over her.

"How long...?"

"You've been asleep for hours."

"Was it the Daltons?" She had to know.

"No."

He didn't tell her that he'd recognized two of the dead men after it was over who had once ridden with the Daltons.

She looked over at the chair beside the bed.

"You've been here all night?"

Ranse, not Tom Travis? The thought came then slipped away as she felt a cool cloth on her forehead and drifted off again.

Unable to sleep, Ranse listened for her breathing through the sound of the train as the hours passed. When the cloth dried, he replaced it. When she stirred, restless, no doubt because of the pain at her shoulder, he pulled the blanket back up over her.

She was alone with no family except the woman who

became her guardian; luckier than most orphans left on their own or those who ended up in the factories in the East, or worse.

She had survived, but even with a benefactor, it took strength and courage when someone was on their own, never fitting in with others, and now to come to a place where she didn't know anyone, trying to find the pieces of the past no matter what it meant in the end.

He knew about that sort of thing; painful loss, the emptiness inside where memories of family should have been that was never filled up, to go to a dangerous place that might get you killed.

He knew a lot about that. It took courage, strength you didn't know you had, and grit to face things you didn't know were out there. She had it.

She stirred again and made a painful sound but didn't waken. It was a sound he knew well enough. He wrapped his fingers around her hand where it lay at the bed beside her.

"Hold on," he told her, even though she was already asleep again.

Ranse came out of sleep that way that was instinct from too many places, too many hard lessons, and reached for the rifle.

He listened for a change in the movement of the train as first daylight streaked through the shattered window at the far side of the car and fell through the opening of the compartment, then relaxed as Tom Travis poked his head into the compartment.

"The engineer says we'll make Guthrie by late afternoon. How is she?" he asked.

"Slept most of the night."

Tom approached the bed and felt her forehead, then lifted the edge of the blanket to check the bandages.

"Bleeding stopped and she doesn't seem to have a fever now. You would have made a good doctor."

Ranse shook his head. "That's yours."

"What about when we arrive in Guthrie?" Tom asked. "She'll need to take it easy for a few days."

Ranse nodded. "I'll take her out to the ranch."

"What about Elizabeth?"

"That's another reason it would be best for her to be at the ranch."

"When are you going to tell Elizabeth the truth?" Tom asked.

Ranse's eyes narrowed on his friend.

"You barely spoke to her in Washington, and you don't share the same bed," Tom pointed out. "It doesn't take a genius to see that it's not much of a marriage if one at all. Not to mention, no one even knew about her before your trip to Philadelphia."

"I don't owe you any explanation," Ranse told him.

Tom nodded. "It's your business, but it might take the venom out of the fangs of a snake we both know. And this young woman doesn't deserve to get bit."

"I'll handle it," Ranse replied as he lit a cigarette and inhaled the smoke that helped push back the last hours with no sleep.

"Best handle it as soon as we get back home," Tom added. "It's no secret that Elizabeth and her father have plans for you. Summers is a powerful man and he doesn't like to be disappointed. And he doesn't like his daughter to be unhappy."

Ranse shook his head. "There's a lot that has to happen before Oklahoma becomes a state, and I have no intention of being the first governor no matter what Summers wants."

"Like bringing in the Daltons?" Tom asked.

"Them and others like them."

He liked Tom, he wasn't going to discuss it further. He looked over at the bed.

"Like I said, I'll handle it."

7

L ight slanted across the bed from the edge of the window shade, waking her. She winced as she moved and the fog of sleep cleared.

She slowly sat up and discovered that she was wearing only her petticoat and what was left of her camisole that had been cut away, a thick bandage at her shoulder. She held on to the bed's side-rail as an urgent need made itself known and moved to the end of the bed.

She took a deep breath, then slowly stood, bracing herself at the wall of the compartment against the motion of the train and slowly made her way to the bathing closet next to the compartment.

A stained cloth at the metal wash basin explained the condition of her camisole. She refused to think about that now as she made her way across the chamber to the adjoining toilet room.

If Ellie could see her now, she thought. Nothing at the academy included lessons in the use of the toilet on a moving train and more than once she was afraid she was going to end up on the floor, then slowly, painstakingly made the return trip.

"What the hell...?" Ranse demanded as he found her leaning against the wall of the sleeping compartment.

Aware that she was almost naked except for her petticoat and the remnants of her camisole, she tried to cover herself.

"It's a little late for that," he told as he brushed her hands aside and picked her up. He gently set her at the edge of the bed.

She was pale and there was a sheen on her forehead even thought it was cool.

"What were you thinking?" he demanded even though it was obvious that she no longer had a fever, as if she were a child that needed watching. But the young woman who glared up at him was no child. He'd discovered that the night before.

"I needed to use the toilet," she replied with more than a little attitude for someone who had been shot.

"Not that it's any business of yours." Except that it was. If she remembered correctly, and most of it was there. He was the one who had bandaged her shoulder and sat in that chair most of the night.

He shook his head. It appeared that she would live. And as far as finding her out of the bed, he understood that more than she knew.

"It's going to take a while for you to get your strength back," he told her as she pulled up the bedcovers.

"I suppose you know a lot about that," she replied.

"Some, and food will help. I'll have the attendant bring breakfast."

Breakfast? The next day? They hadn't arrived in Guthrie yet.

She glanced at the chair as he moved it out of the way.

"You stayed here last night?" She should have been embarrassed, a man in her bedchamber. Oddly enough, she wasn't. And under the circumstances she wasn't in any condition to protest.

"It seemed the best thing to do, to prevent your hurting yourself if you woke and tried to wander about," he added and made his point.

"I have you to thank for this?" She indicated her bandaged shoulder.

"I've had some experience with that sort of thing. I apologize for ruining your clothes. It was necessary at the time."

There it was again, the way he could surprise her when she wanted very much to dislike him.

"It can be replaced."

That simple, and a far cry from someone else he knew who would have pitched a fit at the loss.

"I'll have the attendant bring something for you to eat." He looked back over his shoulder at her.

Her hair was down around her shoulders, the blanket pulled up to her neck. There were dark circles under her eyes, and she was pale but there was strength and more than a little sass in her this morning.

Grit. The word came again.

"We'll be in Guthrie in a few hours. No more wandering about on your own. Push that button for the attendant if you need something." He indicated the button on the wall beside the bed.

Push the button? Easier said than done, the pain at her shoulder a reminder that she'd been shot.

"Damn!" she said as she leaned back against the headboard, eyes closed to stop the room from spinning. The spirit was willing, but the body very definitely was not.

She had no idea what time it was when she heard the outer door of the car open and there was a knock at the door to her compartment.

It took some effort but she was determined and slowly managed to dress herself. She wore her walking skirt and a clean camisole. It was impossible to pull the other shirtwaist over the bulky bandages. The jacket that matched the walking skirt would have to do. Her boots were another matter.

She fully expected that Ranse McCandliss had returned, and was surprised when Tom—Dr. Travis, pushed open the door and looked in on her. His surprise was obvious as he saw that she had dressed.

"Up and about when you should be resting?"

Wearing only the camisole with the skirt, she pulled on the jacket.

"No need to be embarassed," he told her. "I am a doctor. Even though I'm not practicing at the moment, I've seen my fair share of naked bodies."

"So I hear." She replied as she finally pulled it on.

"We'll be arriving in Guthrie shortly. I thought I would check and see if you needed anything."

"The name of a good hotel," she replied fighting the exhaustion and the pain.

"That's already taken care of," Tom replied as he tugged the jacket away and examined the bandages.

"Taken care of?" She should have been embarrassed, but she was too tired and hurt too much.

"Ranse is going to arrange for you to go to the ranch where you can rest up."

Ranch? At her confused look, Tom explained.

"Addison Stanton's place outside of town. Ranse stays there when he's home."

As if that explained everything. She realized that she knew almost nothing about Ranse McCandliss.

"His family?"

"His family is dead. Addison took him in a long time ago after his father was killed in the outlet out in the territory—a wasteland of desert, little water, and outlaws. He raised him and sent him back East to school; one of those law schools."

Law? She very definitely didn't know anything about him.

"He's a lawyer?"

"He could be one helluva lawyer if he had a mind to, but there have been other things."

"Hunting down the Dalton gang?"

"That and other things, other people. But I think I'd better let him tell you what he chooses, Miss Dalton."

Her gaze fastened on his. "He told you."

"I may not be a lawyer, but it wasn't too hard to figure out that you're not married. We talked and he told me about Philadelphia and how you met."

"It was the only way I could get into see him in Washington. I didn't think... "

"That you'd end up on a train in the Territory with a bullet wound?"

She managed a small smile. "I thought that I might be able to learn something about my family even if... "

"Even if it's the Daltons? Your secret is safe with me. But I'm glad."

She didn't ask the reason behind that.

"I tried to tell him that I didn't know anything about them. My guardian was always very secretive about how I arrived in Philadelphia. She said that the past didn't matter, only the future. And she was determined to give me a good future. Without her..." she hesitated. "I was an orphan when I came to her. There was only a note that was pinned to my clothes."

She didn't bother to mention the crystal. It probably didn't mean anything beyond what a child might have picked up.

"You feel that you owe her a great deal."

"Yes, at the same time I need to know the truth, and the only way I could to that was to come here."

Tom nodded. "Not much different than Ranse. He came up the hard way after his father and mother were gone. He might have ended up like the Daltons if it hadn't been for Addison Stanton." He smiled then.

"The old man is as hard as they come, especially after the loss of his son and his family. But he sets great store by Ranse, and you'll be more than welcome. It might just do the old man good to have a young woman around."

Somehow that was not very encouraging.

"I would prefer to stay in town."

"You can take that up with Ranse, and good luck with that."

He seemed to be satisfied that she didn't have a fever even though she could barely stand, she was so weak.

"Another reason that you won't win that argument," he told her. "He feels responsible for what happened."

"No one is responsible for me," she replied. He nodded and gave her instructions to rest.

Easier said than done, she thought, as she shifted against the pain at her shoulder. That was her last thought as he left and she laid back to rest; until she felt the bump of the car, heard the sound of the brakes as the train came to a stop.

She slowly sat up and managed to lift the window shade. She had lived most of her life in Philadelphia, traveled to Washington DC, and New York before that with Ellie and her parents. Those cities were modern with streetcars, electric lights, the theatre, museums, and art galleries. None of those prepared her for Guthrie, Oklahoma.

The town stretched beyond the train station to the flat plains. The buildings—the rail station, the row of businesses along a thoroughfare including a saloon, dry goods store and stables were no more than a single story compared to the high-rise buildings of New York.

The street was dirt, the congestion of carts and wagons churning up clouds of dust and could have been any one of the photographs in the dime novels that Ellie collected and they read at night after all the other girls had gone to bed.

"Isn't it exciting?" Ellie had exclaimed more than once. *"We should go!"* After they'd seen a Wild West Show.

"Cowboys and Indians!"

"Your father wouldn't approve."

"We won't tell anyone, we'll just go!"

Now she was here and there were cowboys riding through town, waiting at the train station, and cattle—hundreds of cattle in pens.

It was wild, primitive, and raw with a different sort of energy from the bustling streets of New York. It was a place of women in gingham dresses and sunbonnets, children following in a single line behind a young woman, the spire of a church in the distance.

And... outlaws? The truth was out there, and she wouldn't leave until she found it.

She closed her eyes as the pain at her shoulder reminded her that the town was a dangerous place.

She opened her eyes at a light knock at the door. The dizziness passed and she pushed herself to the end of the bed as the door of the compartment opened.

Ranse McCandliss—Marshal McCandliss now, that badge on his vest and the Colt revolver in the holster at his belt. Friend, or enemy?

By the look on his face, it was difficult to tell.

He took in the skirt, and the jacket wrapped around her shoulders over the camisole, and his earlier assessment came to mind—she had grit.

"You're dressed." He saw the way her blue gaze angled away from his. It had to have been painful to dress herself.

"More or less," she replied, trying to hold the front of the jacket together one handed. "I wasn't able to lace my boots."

He smiled at her admission as he entered the compartment. Then he knelt on the floor and took hold of an ankle, propping her boot on his knee. He tied off the laces, then reached for her other boot.

"You need to take it easy for the next few days."

"I didn't come here to take it easy."

The strength was there, for now. He reached out and retrieved the jacket from her shoulders. Her startled gaze met his.

"We'll do this nice and easy," he told her. "Unless you want everyone at the train station to see you like that." He glanced at the lacy camisole that barely covered her breasts as he gently took hold of her wrist with the injured shoulder.

She should have been embarrassed, but wasn't. It was obvious that he'd seen far more of her when he washed and bandaged her shoulder.

She winced but that was her only reaction to something that he knew all too well was painful as he pulled the sleeve up her arm then reached around so that she could insert her other arm into the other sleeve. Then, he pulled the front of it together and buttoned it. She slowly let out the breath she was holding. She was pale but didn't make a sound, braver than some men he knew.

"You've done this before." She caught the look in that dark gaze and realized how that sounded.

"I didn't mean... "

He shook his head. "Out here you learn to take care of things yourself. There are times it's the only way."

There was that look again.

"Do you think you can stand?"

"I made it to the toilet earlier." She would never have discussed that with any of the young men she knew in Phil-adelphia—proprieties. Somehow with him, proprieties seemed ridiculous.

That look was slightly amused.

"That could have been risky. You might have passed out."

"It was that or embarrass myself considering all the water you made me drink."

"It usually helps against the fever. Give me the hand of your good arm."

His hand was warm and strong.

"Hold on to me." The words came back from the night before, and she held on.

"Can you walk?"

She nodded and he led her out of the compartment, that dark gaze watching her. Once outside the room, he slipped his arm around her waist.

"Lean on me. Let me know if you feel faint."

"I don't faint..." she no sooner said it than it happened. She heard him curse as everything seemed to spin away.

She would have dropped to the floor if he hadn't swung her up into his arms.

He carried her from the car, Tom meeting them at the deck.

"What happened?" He laid a hand against her forehead. It was cool.

"She was determined to walk out of here."

"Strong-minded."

"Stubborn," Ranse replied. "I'll need a carriage."

"I saw Addison just outside the cattle yards. I'll let him know, and you should well know that Summers is here also. Elizabeth left the train a few minutes ago."

Ranse nodded. "I appreciate the warning. I'd just as soon leave without running into them."

"Good luck with that. I'll let Addison know that you need the carriage."

He caught sight of Addison and his ranch foreman Curry Parker. Both men looked his direction. Curry nodded and immediately left the two men, as Addison looked up and he felt that steely gaze that had a way of cutting through the bull and ending any argument.

Ranse had been raised by it, but knew that beneath that gaze and the tough exterior was a man who'd lived through hard times and come out on the other side, then opened his ranch and himself to a fifteen-year-old kid who could have ended up like the men he tracked down. It was a bond that connected the two men and that concern and kindness was there as Addison greeted him with a nod and then glanced at Laine Dalton.

"Good to have you home," Addison greeted him with another glance at her, still and silent in his arms.

"I'll explain later," he told him. "I want to get her to the ranch."

That's all that was needed. Addison nodded. "I sent Curry to livery stable to get a carriage after we spoke with Tom." He frowned as he glanced past him.

He nodded and excused himself. "I'll see to that carriage."

Ranse didn't need to be told who he had seen as Elizabeth swept toward him across the platform, with her father Daniel Summers.

"I was telling father about all the excitement," she commented with a glance down the platform at the Pinkerton Agents gathered there as two bodies were removed from the baggage car.

Daniel Summers nodded. "Good thing you were there." There was a brief glance at Laine Dalton and an uncomfortable moment, the look in Elizabeth's eyes enough to melt winter ice.

"An injured passenger?" Daniel commented. If Elizabeth had told him anything more, it wasn't mentioned.

Ranse nodded. "She was wounded protecting Elizabeth."

He'd come to that conclusion when he saw what had happened in the car that night. Anything else, Laine Dalton refused to tell him.

"Then I suppose we should be grateful. She'll be all right?" Daniel asked, ignoring his daughter's glare.

"She will be once I get her out to the ranch."

"The ranch?" Elizabeth exclaimed. "Surely it would be better for her to remain in town."

He wasn't going to get into this with her. Addison had returned and nodded again as he pushed past Elizabeth and greeted her father.

"Daniel."

"Ranse was just explaining to me about the attack on the train."

Addison nodded, then looked at Ranse. "Curry is bringing the carriage around now. You'll excuse us, Daniel, Elizabeth." Addison ignored both as he led the way down the steps from the platform as Curry arrived with the carriage.

"We need to get this young lady to the ranch," Addison told them. "Where she can be looked after." And ended any further conversation.

At the carriage, Curry helped Ranse lift her onto the seat, then eased her back against the cushioned seatback. That done, he rounded the carriage, climbed up next to her, and then picked up the team's reins.

"I'll finish up my business in town and be along," Addison told him, his mouth working with a grin.

"Hannah can take care of her when you get there." The grin deepened, curving the white mustache. He chuckled.

"You sure set off a firestorm. That won't be the end of it."

Tom had found them. Apparently Addison wasn't the only one enjoying himself.

"I'll bring her things round when I come to check on that shoulder," Tom told him.

"You have anything more to say?" Ranse asked.

"Not a thing, at the moment."

Ranse saw Elizabeth's furious expression as he swung the carriage about.

He glanced over at the young woman beside him. It wasn't over.

Guthrie, Oklahoma wasn't Philadelphia or Washington. By comparison it was still a small town and sooner or later the lie Laine Dalton had told to get there would come out and he would have to deal with that. But not today.

Elizabeth Summers and her father's ambitions weren't important.

8

She awakened slowly and stared at what appeared to be a cloud moving slowly overhead, then gradually became aware of other things.

She was lying on a bed in a room with the usual furnishings, pale yellow walls, and what she first thought was a cloud, she now realized was a curtain billowing gently on the breeze that came in through an open window.

When she tried to sit up, the pain at her shoulder was a reminder that brought back the memory of arriving in Guthrie, the train station, and Ranse McCandliss. Anything after that was missing, right up to the part about how she got into thisroom.

It took some effort, but she was able to swing her legs over the edge of the bed and discovered that her boots had been removed and set aside on the floor. Then another discovery, she was fully clothed more or less, but her jacket had been removed. She frowned. She had no memory of that either.

"I helped remove your jacket and shoes; thought you would be more comfortable that way."

Helped? That at least answered part of the question as she

looked around at the door and took in the sight of the stout, gray-haired woman standing there.

"Name's Hannah Bodine," she introduced herself. "I'm Mr. Stanton's housekeeper. Ranse brought you up here, checked your bandages, and said to just let you rest. You looked a mite done in." She'd planted a hand on one hip.

"Bad business, train robbery. He went back into town to make his report and meet up with them Pinkertons. Mr. Stanton followed from town. He's down at the cow pens with Curry, said I was to get you whatever you needed. Supper won't be till later when Ranse gets back."

"Thank you," she managed.

Hannah Bodine nodded. "There were supposed to be guests for supper, but that's been put off, giving you time to rest up and get yer strength back. Anything I can get you?"

"Maybe some water... I would like to wash. My clothes: I didn't bring much with me and my other things... "

"Bathing room is next door. Ranse's rooms are across the hall. We got our own boiler and hot water comes pretty quick once it gets fired up. You need any help, just call out. Annie usually works downstairs, but I told her you might need some help.

"We don't have electric all the way out here, but we do all right. And if you're up to it, you can come downstairs or have your supper here."

"But my clothes... " She would have pointed out that she wasn't exactly dressed for making an appearance even if she could make it downstairs.

Hannah brushed off her concern. "Don't worry about that. I think I can find you something to wear—Mr. Stanton did say that I was to see you had whatever you needed."

She smiled her gratitude. "I appreciate that."

"You just call out if you need help with yer bath and Annie will give a hand."

And with that, Hannah Bodine swept out of the room much like a large schooner under full sail, leaving her to take in the room that had been given her.

She would have preferred a hotel in town, but admittedly she had limited funds and no idea how long she would be there. Still, accepting hospitality from people she didn't know —or barely knew as she thought of Ranse McCandliss—made her uneasy.

Under any other circumstances she would have asked to return to town and made her way as best she could. She winced at the pain in her shoulder as she decided to try her legs, a circumstance that she hadn't counted on or could even have imagined.

"Hannah sent me up..." a young voice announced the arrival that could only be Annie. "Good heavens, miss! What are you trying to do?"

And that was her introduction to Annie, as she stood with a hand braced against the headboard of a finely carved bed with satin coverings as fine as any in Philadelphia or New York, feared her legs might go out from under her at any minute, and cursed her weakness.

"You'll fit in just fine around here with that," Annie told her. "Mr. Addison has a temper and I've never heard such words before. He's going to like you just fine."

That was the least of her concerns at the moment as she leaned against Annie and slowly made her way to the bathing room.

SHE SPENT the next two days limited to the four walls of the room, frustrated by her lack of strength and slow recovery. She had questions about the Daltons and no answers. The person who might have those answers was gone both days, returning late at night.

Tom called on her that second day, examined her shoulder and announced that it was healing fine, just to give it time and not to push herself.

There it was again—time.

That same day, Annie announced that the clothes she'd brought with her, few as they were, were washed and cleaned, when she brought supper to her. They were returned to her along with the dark blue gown she'd worn in Washington and two additional gowns—one for evening, the other for daytime compliments, she was told, of Mr. Stanton.

When she asked Hannah about the gowns, she learned they had once belonged to his son's wife, and he was pleased to have someone make use of them again. There were other things she needed but that would have to wait until she was able to go into town, and she was determined that would be soon.

As for Marshal McCandliss, he had been absent the past two days, attending business in town Hannah told her. But he would be there the following evening for supper with Mr. Stanton's guests. Annie was the one who informed her who those guests might be.

"Mr. Summers and his daughter will be there, along with some others. Let me know which gown you want to wear and I'll make sure to iron it for you. That is unless you don't feel up to it yet."

What she didn't care to experience was another confrontation with Elizabeth Summers, unless, of course, Ranse had already told her. Either way, she was a guest in Addison Stanton's home and the least she could do was make an appearance and then her arrangements to leave.

The third day, she'd had enough of confinement. She was considerably stronger. It was time to leave the room, possibly even leave the ranch and avoid Elizabeth altogether before the supper party that night.

With that in mind, she dressed herself, pulling on the shirtwaist and skirt. It took considerably longer to tie the laces of her boots.

"Good heavens! You dressed yourself," Annie exclaimed when she brought lunch.

Annie tied the laces of her boots for her. That done, Laine grabbed a sliced apple and headed for the stairs.

Going down was one thing. She quickly realized that coming back up the stairs was likely to require more strength, but she would worry about that later.

It was well into the afternoon, there was a breeze that came in through the glass doors of the living room and she was determined to make her way outside.

"He said you were stubborn, all right."

She recognized Addison Stanton's voice from that first day. Since then, he'd been gone from the house most of the time.

"A man his age should slow down, but you won't convince him of that," Hannah had shared with her.

"This is a big ranch and it requires constant work, and he's hellbent on working it himself then passing it on."

"You said that his son was dead," she had commented at the time.

"That's right. He's plannin' on turnin' it over to Ranse. And you bein' here makes that just about perfect for him. He's always wanted to see Ranse settled with his own family."

That had answered the question what had and hadn't Ranse told them about her. Now she turned as Addison left the dining room and crossed the room.

"Stubborn and with grit, as I recall," he commented. "It's good to see you up and about."

"Yes, I thought it was time... "

"Don't overdo it though. That kind of wound is serious even though Tom Travis says you'll be yerself again in a couple weeks. Until then you just rest, real pleased to have you here."

If Ranse hadn't told them, then she would have to do it.

"I want to thank you for your hospitality these past few days, I assure you... "

"Thank me?" He laughed, a hearty sound that filled the room.

"I should be thanking you. It's time Ranse settled down with a family."

Family? It appeared Ranse McCandliss had failed to explain the deception she'd used.

"That's what I wanted to tell you... "

That laugh came again. "You are more than welcome."

She would have told him if a man hadn't arrived. He slapped dust from his pants with his hat and dipped his head.

"Afternoon, ma'am. Beggin yer pardon."

She recalled that his name was Curry, the ranch manager.

He turned to Addison Stanton. "Them heifers got turned out in the wrong pasture with that bad weed we found. Ranse rode out with us, and we got most of them back, but there a dozen or so down in the ravine. I'm going to take two of the men and go after them."

"I'll go with you," Addison told him. He took hold of both her hands.

"It sure is a pleasure having you home."

And he and Curry were gone.

Home. So much for clearing up all those questions.

Ranse stepped down from the saddle, then removed it and carried it into the barn. He'd been out with Curry all morning, riding out with him and the other men, finding, then turning back over three hundred head of heifers that had gotten into an area where they'd found pigweed a couple weeks earlier before that could have ended up fatal and a huge loss for Addison Stanton.

He was hot, dirty, and in no mood for the supper that was planned for that evening.

"He's all lathered up, Mr. McCandliss. You musta rode him

hard," Seth, the young hand who took care of the horses, commented as he came out of the paddock where he'd been working one of the yearlings.

"It was a long ride. Cool him down slow."

"You gonna be leavin' again soon?" Seth asked.

"Not for a few more days. I saw your girl, Laurie, in town," Ranse added. "She asked me to give you this. She said something about a picnic coming up on the Fourth of July."

Seth reached to take the envelope, smiling sheepishly. He quickly stuffed the envelope into the pocket of his shirt.

"This boy sure has missed you, Mr. McCandliss. He gets downright ornery if he doesn't get run every day. With you gone all those weeks, and no one else bein' able to get near him, he gets just plain rank, so that Mr. Stanton threatened to take a board to him. He even took a nip at old Foley the other day at feedin' time.

"That old coot thinks he's part devil anyway. Now he's convinced. Just after you left for Philadelphia, that horse took that south fence sometime in the middle of the night. Then he shows up at the paddock next mornin' just as sweet as you please, waitin' for someone to let him in.

"Old Foley dang near jumped out of his skin when he came out of the bunkhouse and saw him just standin' there, like he was waitin' for him. He refused to go near him 'til you got home. Made me do it. This guy like to take a hunk outta me, but he seems okay now." Seth put a halter on him and led him out for that cool-down.

Ranse headed for the water tank. He needed to remove some of the dust and grime before going up to the big house.

LAINE LET herself out the side door of the great room. She stood there for several moments on the wide, sweeping front porch as her eyes adjusted to the brilliance of sunlight after the last few days confinement.

The air was warm and sweet in the late afternoon heat with a fragrance that drifted on the breeze, the ground that sloped away from the main house covered with a blanket of purple-blue flowers.

Raised in the city, the wide-open ranch with golden brown pastures, a huge barn and stables, white-faced cattle as far as the eye could see, and oak trees at the edge of a river, were things she had only imagined or glimpsed through grainy black and white photos in the newspapers or those dime novels. It was a world away from Philadelphia or New York, still wild and unsettled and she wanted to see all of it as she left the porch and followed the footpath.

The stables held different smells—of horses that she easily recognized but other scents from hay, the dirt floor and of old wood, with dust motes underfoot as she walked through to the far end and a new sound of water at one of the troughs.

She hesitated, then slowly approached the doors. The sound she'd heard was one of the men washing at a water tank. He'd stripped off his shirt, his back toward her, with one hand braced at the edge of the tank as he splashed water on his face and neck.

It wasn't the sight of a man without his shirt that stopped her, it was the scars on his back that stopped her—bullet wounds!

There were two of them, healed now and she remembered something Tom Travis had told her, that Ranse had been badly wounded going after outlaws in the outlet. The scars were pale against the skin at his shoulder and side.

"You feel strong enough to be out here?"

Startled that she'd been caught, she stared at Ranse McCandliss, water beaded across his shoulders and chest.

"I needed to get out. I wanted to get some fresh air... I didn't think anyone would be here."

She felt like she was babbling. It wasn't as if she had never seen a man with his shirt off, or as if she owed him an explanation, she thought. But the truth was, she did. He had saved her life after she was shot and then brought her here to recover.

"All you had to do was ask," he replied. That dark gaze watched her. "Anyone from the house would have come with you."

"I didn't want to bother anyone."

She knew the looks that men gave women, looks she'd seen before from young gentlemen, but not the way he was looking at her now, that dark, quiet way of his as if there was a great deal more going on behind that gaze.

"Please don't... I shouldn't have come out here." She turned and would have returned to the house.

"Don't *what*?" he asked, slowly walking toward her.

He didn't move like other men she knew, always in a hurry, self-conscious, hesitant. With him, each movement was deliberate, confident from the beginning when they first met, again in Washington, and on the train.

"THE WAY you're looking at me," she replied, feeling the heat of his dark gaze.

"How am I looking at you?"

He'd stayed away. There were things that had to be taken care of in town along with his work for Addison, reports to the local sheriff after the robbery attempt on the train, and the Daltons.

Who was she? The proper educated girl in Philadelphia? The determined headstrong young woman who'd lied so easily in Washington? Who was she now? An innocent victim, or a member of a notorious family who had terrorized, robbed, and murdered? All of those?

"As if... "

As if she should be afraid, she thought.

The sun angled off his strong features, glinted at his dark eyes that watched her with that same intensity. It was daylight, but there was something that pulled her toward him, something dark and powerful. It might have been the heat of the afternoon, the way he stood there without his shirt, or the heat that seemed to reach out from him to her.

She took a step back. This was crazy, she thought. It was as if she were the one standing there naked, the heat that seemed to reach out from him slipping inside her.

She took another step. Was she safe now?

"I should go back."

What did she see in that dark gaze now?

"I'll go with you," he replied. "I need to clean up before Addison's little get-together tonight."

There it was again—that quiet confidence as his hand wrapped around her other arm with that quiet strength, his shirt in the other and walked with her back to the house.

"Is there any word about the Dalton gang?" she asked, part of her wanting to know if there was anything new about them, at the same time she realized she might not want to know. He didn't reply.

He walked with her up the stairs to the bedroom she occupied for the past two days.

"I understand if you want to miss supper with everyone tonight." Including Elizabeth Summers? she thought.

"Everyone will understand. I'll have Hannah send up a tray."

He was offering her a way to avoid the evening, those present, and any questions. He opened the door for her, then turned toward the room across the hallway that Hannah had said was his room.

She thought about it. In the end, she refused to hide away just as she refused to quietly go about her life in Philadelphia while Ranse McCandliss continued to hunt down the Dalton gang.

And her? That thought came next. He'd said nothing more about the reason he'd gone to Philadelphia, but it was still there.

She knew he didn't believe that she knew nothing about the Daltons. It was the reason that had sent him to Philadelphia in the first place. And the doubt was still there no matter what she'd told him. She could see it in his face, in that quiet way he watched her.

In the end, she refused to hide in that upstairs bedroom. She had nothing to hide about and she certainly wasn't intimidated by Elizabeth Summers.

Annie helped her dress. She chose one of the gowns that Addison Summers had insisted on giving her. It seemed an appropriate way to thank him for his kindness and generosity.

Then she would simply return the gown along with the other one he had given her once she was able to return to town and purchase some clothes to replace the shirtwaist that was too badly stained with blood.

The gown she chose was a deep wine color with a low-cut bodice trimmed in tiny pearls. The neckline, both front and back, almost covered the bandages at her shoulder that were considerably smaller than when she first arrived. She had Tom Travis to thank for that. For shoes, she wore the formal shoes she'd worn in Washington.

Annie fastened her hair in thick coils at the back of her head with combs Hannah had provided, then stood back for final inspection as carriages arrived at the entrance to the house below. She turned the long tilted mirror so that Laine could see the final result.

"Oh, miss! You look just like one of those pictures in one of them catalogues I seen at the ladies' shop in town," Annie remarked. "And the gown hides most of the bandages. Mr. McCandliss will surely be pleased."

She didn't care what Ranse McCandliss thought, she had chosen the dress for Addison Stanton.

She thanked Annie.

"Are you sure you feel strong enough to go down by yourself?" the girl asked. "I'm certain Mr. McCandliss wouldn't mind."

She was fairly certain that he *would* mind.

"I can manage," she assured her.

"I better get back downstairs then to help Hannah."

The sound of conversations reached her as she stepped out onto the landing and slowly made her way down the stairs— Addison Stanton's boisterous comment, followed by Tom Travis' reply, emphasized by a woman's laughter. Elizabeth Summers, no doubt, as Ranse mentioned she would be there.

It would have been easy to simply turn around, return to her room, and avoid everything, but she hadn't come there to hide out at Addison Stanton's Ranch. She had come for answers, the same answers Ranse McCandliss was after and as soon as she could manage, she would go after those answers.

"Here she is!"

She heard Addison's booming voice as she hesitated in the entry to the great room. Escape was no longer an option.

"The evening is complete! Welcome, my dear!"

Addison's announcement caused all eyes to turn in her direction. That was another matter that needed to be taken care of as soon as possible, she thought.

It was Addison who met her at the opening and took her hand in his.

"One would never know that you've been injured, and you've worn one of the gowns." There was something in his voice and his eyes, something very emotional.

"You look beautiful."

He cleared his throat and then led her into the room.

"Ranse," he said. "Would you like to make introductions?"

"Certainly," he replied. "Everyone, this is Laine."

At least he left off the 'wife' part of the introduction as she was introduced to the half dozen men in the room. All of them were dressed in coats over pants, and boots, but of a style she had already seen with Tom Travis, and more casual than in Philadelphia or Washington.

She finally let out a sign of relief as Tom approached and offered her a drink. He returned with a glass of wine as Ranse was drawn aside by a somewhat older man who had been introduced as the sheriff of Guthrie.

"As your physician, I recommend you don't over-indulge," he commented with some amusement as he handed her the wine glass from the bar that had been set up with Curry pouring drinks.

"Do I have your permission to pour it over his head?" she asked with a look in Ranse's direction.

"A bit of a disagreement?" he asked with more than a little amusement.

It was complicated. She didn't know how much Tom knew. At least he knew that she wasn't Ranse's wife.

"He should have explained to Addison that I am not his wife."

"I've known Ranse a long time. I'm sure he has his reasons. You need to trust him."

She had trusted Gerald, someone she thought she knew. He had shown her what that was worth.

Trust Ranse McCandliss? A man she hardly knew? A man sworn to bring in the Daltons no matter what it took?

A man who had saved her life...

. . .

"I DON'T CARE what his reason is," she replied. "Addison has been kind to me and I don't want to continue the lie."

"You seem to be well on your way to recovery," Tom observed, attempting to hold back a grin. "I'll have to remember to stay out of the way of that temper of yours."

She smiled at that. At the academy, a show of temper, outbursts, most displays of emotion were frowned upon.

"I'll try to behave, for Addison's sake. I'm his guest. I wouldn't want to embarrass him."

"I think you'll find there's not anything that could embarrass him, or Ranse for that matter."

She had to admit that she had already discovered that on more than one occasion, particularly where it concerned Elizabeth Summers.

Laine caught sight of her, approaching with her father beside her.

"That temper will serve you well," Tom commented as he saw them as well.

She braced for another confrontation that was suddenly cut off as Addison announced the supper was ready in the dining room.

"You seem to have luck on your side this evening," Tom commented, angling his head in the direction of Elizabeth and her father.

"May I escort you to supper?" he added. "And may I prescribe a medicine? Avoid certain people at all cost, it will do wonders for your health."

Addison insisted that she be seated to his left, with Tom at the chair beside her while Ranse took the chair across from her to Addison's right. Protected by Addison at the head of the table and Tom beside her, she was able to enjoy supper and listened as a half dozen conversations were exchanged down the length of the table.

While the long table was set with the finest china and silver, she discovered that the fare was quite different from what would have been found at a table in Philadelphia or New York. Instead of lobster or the finest main course steeped in cream sauces, there was tender beef with roasted potatoes with cheese, assorted roasted vegetables, and a great deal of wine that was in constant supply.

Having eaten only sparingly the past two days, she as soon quite full. Or, it may have been the wine as she listened to the various conversations including an argument over the plans for the Territory to become the next state.

"I tell you Addison, it will happen, in less than a year and we have to be prepared with the right people to represent us," Daniel Summers announced his place at the middle of the table beside his daughter. He took another drink of wine.

"It's absolutely necessary that we have the right person who will represent our interests. You know it, as well as Ranse."

"I leave that for Ranse to explain," Addison replied with a look to the man at his right.

She caught the look Ranse gave him.

"We've had this conversation before," he replied. "My answer hasn't changed."

"Now is the time to set things in motion... "

The argument continued as she set her napkin aside.

"Are you all right?" Tom asked.

"Some fresh air," she replied. It was undoubtedly the wine, and the conversation.

Other guests had finished supper and rose from the table, including Ranse. The other men accepted Addison's invitation to join him in the library for after dinner cigars. Tom pulled her chair out for her.

He was slapped on the back by another man whose name she couldn't recall and quickly pulled in the direction of the library as she made her way to glass-paned doors that opened onto a stone terrace.

It was warm inside the house; the air was cooler outside and carried that faint sweet fragrance she'd discovered earlier. Everything here was bigger, bolder, and more beautiful, including the night sky with its streak of orange, red and purple as the sun went down.

What did this place hold for her, she wondered. Answers? Or more questions? Would she be forced to return to Philadelphia with no past? No future?

"Trying to escape?"

The question seemed filled with several meanings as Ranse joined her on the veranda. She had no patience for games and chose the easiest answer.

"It's cooler out here, the fragrance, and...

"No questions that you can't or won't answer?"

"You won't give up, will you." She turned and would have pushed past him and returned to the house.

"It's called lupine."

"I beg your pardon?"

He smiled at her response, the polished finish, the way she spoke, compliments of private school in the East. Was it all a carefully constructed facade to erase the past?

"The flowers you smell. It's called lupine, it grows wild." There was another he'd been told who was drawn to that fragrance—the young woman Addison's son had married and brought here.

"And no, I won't give up. It's my job." He watched her, that brief flash of anger, that moment when she would have gone back to the house, and now. The hesitation, the frown at her mouth and at the dark brows that drew together over eyes very near the color of those wildflowers.

"What will happen when you find them?" she asked, surprising him.

He pulled a cigarette from his pocket and lit it, the flare of the match in her eyes as she watched him. He lit the cigarette and snuffed out the match.

Those eyes, filled with questions. The anger was there, along with other emotions. Could he trust what he saw there?

He knew people, he'd learned to know them the last fifteen years; the lies they told, the way it was there in a too-quick glance that looked away, an uncomfortable shift of the body, words that came too easy, a sudden laugh. He'd looked for that in her, but all he'd found so far was the uncertainty, the determination with a fair amount of anger thrown in. And grit.

What could he tell her? Something that was sugar-coated when there was nothing sugar-coated about tracking down men who had chosen a path different from his own? That it was up to Bob, Grat, and Emmett Dalton? That it would be easier, safer for everyone if they were to turn themselves in, and come along peacefully? Or that it was just as likely to end bloody?

"Does it matter?"

They were strangers to her. She knew of them only through the newspapers and the dime novels. They were outlaws. It shouldn't matter. But it did.

He had come to Philadelphia tracking down an almost twenty-year-old rumor to find out what she knew about the Daltons, if there was a connection in the name, had possibly had any contact with them.

And so, he'd opened a door on the past, her past that might at last reveal who her family was, whether that was good or bad.

She had no reason to believe that she was part of the Dalton family, nothing except that note that had been pinned to her clothes when she was brought to Philadelphia all those years before. Once opened, she couldn't close that door.

The questions she'd had her entire life were there, and she wanted answers. He had done that.

"My whole life I've never known who I was. Just a name I

was given because of that note, and never allowed to forget that I was an orphan with no family. When the holidays came, the other girls went home to their families. My guardian sent a coach for me and I was taken to her home along with others she provided for." She shook her head.

"Don't think that I wasn't grateful. I was, even as I stared at all those strange faces and pretended to feel as if it was the same as a family. There was always this emptiness, as if there was this big hole in my life that should have been memories of my family. But there weren't any.

"And then you arrived in Philadelphia and for the first time that I could remember there was a possibility of a family; good or bad. At least it was better than never knowing and I couldn't just let that door close again." She looked at him then.

"Can you understand what it is like not knowing who you are?"

Light from the open doors of the house fell across the stones of the veranda where they stood. Her eyes were dark, filled with emotion as a tear slipped down her cheek. She brushed it away almost angrily.

He tossed the cigarette away and gently pulled her against him. He felt the resistance, then the way it slipped away.

He had lost both his parents by the time he was fifteen years old, first his mother, then his father. That long, lonely ride into the outlet to bring his father's body back had nearly killed him. He wouldn't have minded at the time. But it hadn't and he had found a way to go on even in those wild days when he rode with Frank Dalton.

At least he had always known who he was, who his parents were, and brief as their life together had been, knowing that had guided him and brought him to where he was now. But what about her? If, as she claimed, she knew nothing about the Daltons?

No family, no past except the one provided to an orphan through all the years since.

Nothing.

The word hung there between them in the faint light from the house.

He stroked her back, lightly brushing her shoulder with the thick bandage under the sleeve of her gown.

"I understand."

Two simple words but said with such heartfelt sincerity she realized that he did know, did understand as no one ever had, and she remembered what Tom Travis had told her about the loss of his father and that horrible long ride to bring him back —things that had changed him.

Was it any better she thought, her cheek resting against his shoulder, to have known and then lost your family, than to never know who they were?

"I'll help you find the answers."

It was more than anyone else had offered. In Philadelphia, it had simply been about the future, to make a good marriage, create her own family—an acceptable family that most certainly didn't include outlaws.

She thought of Addison and the kindness he had shown her.

"You need to tell Addison that we're not really married." She felt his cheek brush her forehead.

"He knows."

She looked at him then. "You told him?"

"I respect him too much not to." He brushed the tear from her cheek as she stared at him, trying to understand.

"He knows and still opened his home to me? The clothes he gave me? Why would he do that? A complete stranger?"

She caught a glimpse of his face as his expression changed, thoughtful along with a frown.

"This country is hard on people. It tests them. Sometimes

they fail and die because of it. He's been here a long time, helped settle this part of the country, and he knows what it is to lose people you love." He brushed the curve of her cheek with his fingers.

"And," he added. "It's a place where you're safe while you recover."

Or, a place where Ranse McCandliss could watch her?

She wanted to believe him. That was the irony in all of this. He made no secret that he was after the Daltons, and anyone connected to them. And yet she trusted him. She didn't want to, but she did.

"I have to find the truth. I can't stay here forever."

Strength, courage, grit.

She had it. It was what had sent her there. She wouldn't stop until she found it.

"For now, it's safer for you here."

"From what? From whom?"

"There's a man, Judge Parker," Ranse replied. "He's a close friend of Addison's. He's also earned the nickname of the 'Hanging Judge.' He earned it with a reputation for seeing criminals in the Territory brought to justice for their crimes.

"He thinks that all outlaws should he dealt with the same regardless of the crime. Some people think his judgment has been too harsh in the past.

"The laws aren't perfect, but they're all that separate us from all out war in this Territory. It'll take time, but the laws will be changed for the good of the people."

"In the meantime, you have Judge Parker."

"We have him and a few others like him. But Judge Parker has a deep, personal commitment to see the outlaw gangs brought to justice. He's vowed to see the Daltons hang for their crimes. He's even used me in an effort to get to them through their mother and sisters.

"If he thought for a minute that you were a Dalton, your life wouldn't be safe. He would use you to get to them." His voice was gentle as he spoke, trying to offer her some comfort.

"Even if I don't know anything?"

"It wouldn't matter."

The safest place for her was at the Oaks, where Hannah Bodine and Addison could keep an eye on her. As soon as he finished the inquiry on the robbery at Red Rock, he'd see about straightening all of this out. For now, she was going to have to be content with recovering from that gunshot wound there. Glancing at her, he saw the conflict of emotions.

"Here you are. How touching, the two love birds," Elizabeth Summers commented as she stepped out onto the veranda, her voice dripping with sarcasm. "Remarkable actually, considering you hardly ever spend time together, or know each other."

Laine caught the shift in his expression, the way his dark gaze closed to any emotion, except for the line that appeared at one corner of his mouth as she stepped away from him.

"I need to speak with Addison... " she made the excuse, then turned without looking at Elizabeth Summers.

Ranse watched her leave, the way she straightened her back and squared her shoulders even though it must have hurt, the angle of her chin, and the determination on her face.

"I'm glad I found you," Elizabeth continued. "A little bird told me something... well actually it was something that I overheard. She placed her hands on the front of his coat.

"Apparently the little schemer told everyone the lie that you were married. Very pathetic and a misunderstanding."

Ranse gently took hold of both her wrists and stepped away from her.

"The only misunderstanding is yours."

9

S he set aside the letter she had started to Ellie.

She had dined with Addison and Ranse earlier, the doors in the dining room left open against the heat as clouds rolled in. Afterward both Addison and Ranse left to check on the portion of the herd that had been brought in days earlier to be shipped north.

That was earlier. They hadn't returned yet, the silhouettes of riders in the distance appearing briefly with a slash of lightning, eventually followed by a rumble of thunder. And the wind had come up, gusting through the glass doors that opened out onto a balcony.

"Storms can be fierce," Annie commented as she came into the room with an armful of blankets.

"That wind comes up and then it starts swirling about. I've seen a tornado pick up cattle and toss them about. That's when Mr. Stanton has everyone head for the storm cellar out back. There's never been one close to the house, but you can never tell. That's the reason he has everyone including Mr. Curry and Seth head for cover."

Tornadoes. She'd heard of them, but had never seen one.

The weather in Philadelphia or New York usually just brought torrents of rain, being near the Atlantic according to Ellie's father.

As for lightning? It was something that appeared briefly over the rooftops of the high-rise buildings in the city, then quickly passed.

"I'll just close these doors," Annie said, after putting one of the blankets on the bed. "The temperature can drop like a rock, don't want you catching a chill."

"Leave them open," she told Annie, setting aside her pen and going to the opening with those glass doors on either side as lightning briefly appeared again in the distance and the wind came up, bringing an earthy smell that she'd smelled before but now with the scent of rain wrapped around it.

"I'll close them in a while."

This place, the Territory it was called, this land still wild, open as far as the eye could see, primitive. There were bands of Indians and outlaws that she'd only read about. Like the land—wild, dangerous.

Another shaft of lightning lit up the sky, closer now, momentarily blue-white against the night sky. She instinctively took a step back, something reaching out from the night, followed by a deep rumbling that reached deep inside.

Dressed only in her nightshift, she rubbed her hands down her arms as another bolt of lightning lit up the night sky over the barn, closer now, lighting up the paddock at the barn where Seth led a horse into the stables.

The wind had come up, suddenly sending the glass doors back hard against the walls as the storm hit, rain coming in waves as lightning sliced overhead followed by thunder that seemed to explode inside her—fascinating and terrifying at the same time... something remembered. She had to get away, to hide, her hands pressed against her ears. And ran into Ranse McCandliss.

She hadn't heard him come in, the sound of the storm breaking around them, the house shuddering.

"No!"

It came from inside her, screaming to get out as she tried to push past him... to get away.

He pulled her against him as the storm swept into the room. He had simply come check to on her, not prepared for the terrified young woman he found there.

She stared past him, her eyes wide, dark. She saw something...

"It's only a storm, it'll pass."

Only a storm... and a memory. Violent, dangerous, and someone was screaming as faces loomed before her and then disappeared.

"It's all right," he told her. "You're safe."

He saw something in her eyes as she tried to push him away, and it was like seeing himself—that fifteen-year-old boy as he tried to cross the river, the storm that night not unlike this one, the way the river rose, his father's body washing away as the horses panicked, someone shouting at him and a hand reaching out before he too washed away.

"I've got you," he told her, those same words from that long ago night.

"No," she whispered as he picked her up and carried her away from the storm that blew in through the doors and then laid her on the bed in the adjoining room.

When he returned after closing those doors, she had curled into a tight ball, arms wrapped around herself, her face pale and wet with tears. He grabbed the blanket from the end of the bed and wrapped her in it. Her hand closed over his.

"Stay," the word whispered through the tears and the shadows in the room as another round of lightning lit up the night sky and thunder rolled over them.

He sat on the bed and pulled her against him. She flinched

at another burst oflightning, her hands twisting in the front of his shirt, terrified, holding on.

He should have left. He didn't because he knew only too well what it was to be scared, alone.

He held her against him. "I've got you."

The fear was still there in her eyes, along with something else as she looked up at him. Something more than the fear. He brushed his fingers against her cheek, her lips. It was there, something inside him that recognized what that something '*more*' was. Need and want, and it at pulled him.

He had seen it on the train and again now, that something they'd both experienced, that was there now—naked and raw like a wound.

It was wrong, the need and want that sharpened deep inside. But those eyes... something he'd heard once that the eyes were the windows of the soul. It was there now, as if her soul were exposed, laid open as sure as the wound at her shoulder.

"Don't go..." a whisper through the shadows as the next flash of lightning splintered into the room.

His lips brushed hers... a question. And the answer as she reached up, fingertips against the faint stubble of beard at his chin... and the taste of him. It was wind, lightning, and rain on her lips then slipping inside her. It was dark and dangerous, as dangerous as an old memory, and she wanted...

Breathless and terrified all at once, with a heat that burned deep inside, she wanted more as her hand moved through the dark tangle of hair that spilled over the collar of his shirt, and she tasted the wind and rain, and him.

This was not for her, he thought, ending the kiss, pulling back. When this was over, when she had whatever answers were out there, she would go back to Philadelphia. This wasn't for either of them.

"So cold... touch me."

Two words—breathless, needy and those eyes—the color dark, reaching out through the shadows.

"You don't know," he warned her. Still innocent, raised with other rules for someone like her.

Her fingers brushed warm skin where his shirt lay open, wanting to touch more. His hand closed around her wrist, stopping her.

Did she know what passed between a man and a woman? Not just some fanciful, romantic idea, but the other part of it, afterward, the questions often with no answers, the way it was different for a woman than for a man, the leaving that came easy. Too easy, and for those like her—the consequences?

She reached up, those eyes fastened on him. It was there—the uncertainty, the need, and that something else that he'd glimpsed on the train. Strength.

"Make the cold go away..." as her lips parted beneath his.

The fear was there along with that strength, and the need. He tasted it as he kissed her again, the argument with himself, all the reasons against it slipping away as his hand closed over her breast.

He had seen that soft curve naked when he'd bandaged her shoulder. But that was then, this was now, and she was full and warm in his hand just there, beneath the sheer nightgown.

"Touch me."

A faint, breathless sound as his fingers brushed the nipple that tightened there.

"Has anyone ever touched you like this?"

He saw the answer in her eyes. No, then the sound she made—startled and a sharp intake of breath as he bent over her and flicked that hardened bit of flesh with his tongue. Her hand came up, but instead of pushing him away, her hand slipped behind his neck and held him against her.

More. That single word seemed to whisper between them as she pulled him closer.

"Ranse...?"

Did she understand that she was playing with fire? That he wasn't some over-educated Harvard school boy, that there were consequences for someone like her—the innocence tangled up with that taste of her mouth.

"This...?" he asked as he leaned her back on the bed, his teeth grazing her breast through the sheer silk.

The answer came in the sound at her throat and the way her hands clutched at him as he drew up the hem of her gown, stroked her knee just there at the top of her stocking, then discovered that tender soft entrance.

It would be now, he thought. Panic, at something she'd never experienced before, embarrassment. Then outrage?

He gently nudged her legs apart, that whorl of flesh that tightened against his thumb, as that nipple tightened for his lips.

Would she stop him? Could he stop?

The answer was instinctive, the need and want stripping away the fear as her legs moved restlessly. The need was there, hot, drenching him as he thrust his fingers inside her.

She gasped, a small, startled sound as lightning lit up the room. Her eyes were wide and dark, her expression stunned. Then her eyes closed, her head went back, her hair spread across the satin bedcover as he made love to her with his hands and mouth.

It built slowly; sensations she'd never experienced before, only whispered about among the girls at school. Heat, the tightness that coiled inside then tightened even more until it became a dull ache that reached out, wanting more, needing more...

Her hands clutched at the bedcovers and he felt innocence in the hesitant way her body moved, and an answer in the way her body drenched him, the look in her eyes and the silent question there, the way her breathing suddenly changed, turning wild, urgent and he could feel the contractions that squeezed at his fingers.

She was breathless, as if she'd been running. And he was there, gently stroking her, touching her in a way that no man had ever dared to touch her. And there was more, those whispers had told her. And she wanted more. Her hand closed over the sleeve of his shirt.

It was there in her eyes, then at her fingers as she pushed the leather vest from his shoulders, then unbuttoned the front of his shirt, the innocence and the need at war within her as his fingers stroked her cheek.

"Are you certain this is what you want?"

She looked at him. "All of it," she whispered.

Did she know that every time her fingers grazed bare skin that it was like someone breathing on a flame at a fire, just enough to send the flame higher, and hotter? Did she know that as she reached that last button and tugged the shirt from his pants that his belly tightened, that he needed to feel more? Did she know that the slightest touch of her hand hardened him? Did she? Did she know that it was dangerous for her?

Her breathing changed, deepened as she looked up at him.

It was there in her eyes, the expression on her face. That strength ... Her gaze locked with his.

"I don't know..."

The words whispered through the shadows.

He took her hand then and pressed it against his chest. She made a faint sound, suddenly pulling her hand away at the intimate contact. He waited, gave her that, the innocence in her eyes, then something more as she laid her hand there again, her fingers lightly stroking.

His skin was incredibly warm in the coolness of the room. He didn't move, didn't reach out, but let her explore; the ridge of bone at his shoulder, the lean muscles below, the bud of the flat nipple that tightened and hardened beneath her fingers, his arm, and his hand as she brought it to her own breast.

"Touch me." The words whispered through the shadows of the room.

Her skin was like warm satin, her breast filling his hand as he gently stroked the darker nipple. She could have pulled away. She didn't.

"Do you know what happens between a man and a woman?" he asked as he kissed her, brushed her bottom lip with his tongue then slipped inside, just inside.

The air rushed out of her, then she slowly breathed and opened for more. More...

She knew what was whispered in the dark of the room she shared with Ellie at the academy, her friend's vivid descriptions from her encounters with a particular young man, and from those whispers she imagined that warm veined flesh pressed against her.

Does it hurt she had asked then—naive, inexperienced, having only known the wandering hand of a beau who assumed too much, the experience leaving her with a strange ache inside afterward.

"At first," Ellie had admitted as they lay there in the dark.

"But you're ready and he's ready for you."

"How?" she had asked, grateful for the shadows in their room so that Ellie couldn't see the red at her cheeks.

"He makes you ready with his hands... and the way he kisses you."

She felt it now, the sudden warmth between her legs, the way her body tightened inside, waiting for...

"How do you know he's ready?" she had asked.

"It's there when you touch him. That's how you know and then..."

"And then...?"

She looked up at him, refusing to be afraid, refusing to hide from the storm that had slipped into the room.

She had no illusions about anything: who she thought she was, what her life might be. She had no family, no way of knowing who she was. She had nothing. She couldn't even be certain her name was her own. All she knew was what he made her feel safe—from the storm.

"Show me..." she whispered as stunning sensations swept through her at just that simple touch of his thumb stroking her. Curious and a little terrified at the same time, the whispers in the dark of that room she had shared with Ellie, were there. She wanted to know what passed between a man and a woman. She wanted to know, all of it. That dark gaze fastened on her.

He silently swore as he eased her down on the bed.

"If you want me to stop..." Could he if she asked it, demanded it?

She pressed her fingers against his lips. That dark gaze locked with hers.

DID she know how beautiful she was? That any man in his right mind would want to be with her, that just the sight of her with her hair spread across the bedcovers was enough to make a man come undone, and the expression in her eyes—innocence and that strength.

'I want you to show me'—the words were like a match set to lamp oil as he brushed the hair back from her cheek.

"I don't want to hurt you..."

Hurt her? He had protected her... saved her life. Whatever else was between them—the truth she was determined to find, his duty to hunt down the Daltons...

The answer was there in her hands at his shoulders as he moved lower and she closed her eyes, felt as he brushed his lips at the bend of her knee then at her thigh, then held her breath, her fingers clasped over his shoulders as he stroked lower.

Whatever Ellie had told her, whatever she had imagined

couldn't have prepared her for that first touch as he parted her, lightly stroked sensitive flesh, then slowly slipped past.

Her breath caught, he withdrew then slowly returned, gently stroking that sensitive flesh as he slipped past again. And again, then slowly withdrew.

She was restless, the heat at his mouth and his touch, and she ached for... something.

"Ranse...?"

He pressed his forehead against hers. "Do you want me to stop?"

He would... If she asked it.

She saw it in that dark gaze, something secret, something that waited there, waited for her. She didn't want him to stop.

"Show me..." she whispered, then went still at the tenderness of his mouth on hers, and his hand as it moved over her again, slowly over her belly, and that ache tightened as she instinctively moved her hips.

Then, yes! Yes, as he stroked that sensitive place that throbbed and ached, then slipped inside her once more, gently caressing, stretching her, then moving deeper still until she thought she couldn't bear it.

"Ranse!"

He heard it in her voice, that breathless whisper, the way her breath caught as her hands clutched at his shoulders, then felt it as her body tightened, the stunned look in her eyes, then the way she closed them, her head thrown back, her hips instinctively moving to take him deeper inside her.

"Are you sure?" he whispered against her lips, breathing her in, wanting more of her, like a starving man who could never get enough.

This, she thought, was what Ellie had spoken of—something dark, maybe even a little dangerous in the way it shattered all her previous notions about what passed between a man and a woman.

Breathless, her body still aching. "Yes."

He stepped away from the bed. The bed dipped under his weight when he returned, the feel of his long body against hers... his legs moving between her legs, his hip brushing her hip startling, the heat pulling her closer as he pulled her closer.

"There may be pain the first time..." he whispered, a hand closing around hers.

She nodded, her eyes widening as he wrapped her hand around his already engorged flesh. He needed for her to understand, giving her this last chance to stop.

Her other hand slipped behind his neck. "Kiss me... "

Her answer in those two words, the way her eyes closed... the way she tasted as his lips closed over her and then his tongue slipped inside, taking all of her—the sounds she made, the way her breathing changed, that dark taste, as he stroked her hand with his, then that moment when her hand tightened, moved down the length of him, her nails scraping at that flared tip.

Who was she now, he thought as fire burned at the base of his spine, the need to be inside her thickening him almost painfully?

Laine Dalton? The sister of ruthless outlaws wanted for murder? Or that educated young woman he'd first encountered? Both? Neither?

None of it mattered as his lips closed over her breast, tasting, teasing, tormenting himself as his teeth grazed her sensitive nipple until she moved restlessly under him and he pulled the taut flesh into his mouth.

Then, she felt those long fingers touching her, spreading her, slipping inside her. Dear God, how was it possible that she wanted that at the same time she thought she might shatter from the pleasure of it.

She was slick and warm, her fingers still wrapped around him as her breathing changed, deepened, then hitched.

"All of you," he whispered, almost a harsh sound as he grazed her nipple with his teeth. "Inside you."

He looked at her then, one last chance for her to tell him no.

Her eyes were wide and dark, the blue almost disappearing at the edges, her lips parted with every breath as she pulled him against her and pressed his engorged flesh against the slick folds of her body.

What did he see there? Fear? Regret? None of those, only the needy sound she made as he covered her hand with his, pressing past that opening, still watching her as he braced a hand against the headboard, then felt that faint shift as she moved her hips, her hand low on his back, pulling him closer.

She was unbelievably small and tight, and he cursed himself that he wanted to feel that more than anything, at the same time he forced himself to go slow, pressing inside her, withdrawing, then pressing inside again, easing her body around his, gently stretching her, withdrawing, then returning. And that moment as he pressed against that flesh barrier, her gaze locked with his, and he realized that she felt that resistance, the way her body refused him... her slender hands low at his back as she suddenly thrust her hips against his, taking all of him on a startled gasp.

"Easy," he whispered, his gaze finding hers as she slowly opened her eyes and the question there with the last of the pain, her fingers trembling slightly as she pressed them against his lips.

"It won't hurt again," he whispered against her fingers.

She slowly nodded, the tension easing from her body, resistance slipping away as he began to move inside her, slowly at first, withdrawing then returning as his fingers stroked that sensitive flesh, her body slick once more, easing him deeper inside, filling her, retreating, then filling her again.

"Move with me," he told her, lifting her hips, guiding her,

building the heat with every stroke. He wanted all of it, all of her. His fingers closed around her knee, lifting it at the same time he stroked deeper.

She thought she might break, then he took her further, filling her, retreating, then filling her again as he stroked the flesh where they joined, and she watched it all through the shadows—watched as he stroked his thumb there, watched as his thickened flesh disappeared inside her.

It was intimate and more, as she moved with him, moved her hips, feeling that tightness grow even as he filled her again and again. Her head went back as she moved her hips, taking more of him, and then she was falling, tumbling over some invisible cliff, sensations clawing to get out deep inside her as she shattered... as he shattered her.

He swallowed the cry she made, then pulled away. Not for her, he thought. This was bad enough... wrong, for all sorts of reasons.

This was what Ellie hadn't spoken of—the afterward, perhaps hadn't experienced as clothes were hastily pushed back into place before anyone discovered them. But she ached for more, even as her breathing slowed, the damp scent of their bodies thick in the air, as she lay there confused, filled with self doubt and that nagging voice that whispered deep inside.

He pulled the satin cover over her. Just the sight of her in the half-light that flickered in the room, then rumbled at the glass, and he wanted more and cursed himself.

Her lips were slightly swollen from kissing her and that look in her eyes... not fear, he knew that look, man or woman, but something different, something that reached out through the shadows, through the scent of her body, slick from loving her, the way her gaze widened slightly at the sight of his naked body and the way his flesh begged for her again.

"Are you all right?"

She nodded. Everything Ellie had told her was true, but

there was more. More than the discovery of her own body and pleasure that could be found there, then those last moments when he retreated and his curse in the darkness of the room.

"I didn't know.... " She didn't know what to say, what to do as humiliation and a dozen other emotions swept over her...

"I thought... then you left, and I... "

"Shhhh," he quieted her with a kiss at her forehead. "It's not you, it's not something you did. It's me, I shouldn't have let it go this far. It was wrong." I was wrong, he thought to himself.

"Go to sleep. The storm is over."

THE DEPUTY ARRIVED from town just after daybreak. Ranse saw him from the second-floor window. He looked over at the bed.

She was still asleep, a hand tucked under her cheek on the pillow, a frown at her mouth. Regret was sharp, he shouldn't have let it go so far. And now?

Too many questions with no answers as he leaned over her, inhaling the faint muskiness of her body that even now pulled at him as he gently stroked her hair back her from her cheek.

She moved but didn't waken, her lips softly parted, and he ached at the memory of the taste of her mouth, the almost feverish touch of her hands at the same time she was uncertain, that innocence, the look in her eyes as they came together.

Only in those last moments had he seen the surprise, the vulnerability, the silent question, then the way she had cried out against his shoulder.

He dressed, then retrieved his jacket and hat downstairs, along with biscuits from the kitchen, and headed for the stables.

Doubts, regret—both were there as he met the deputy and frowned at the message the sheriff had sent with him. There'd been another robbery, deep in the Territory. Several men had died.

Was it the Daltons again, he thought as he glanced up at that set of second floor glass doors.

"Damn!" He wadded up the note and tossed it to the ground.

Things had gotten complicated and even more dangerous, and she was right in the middle of it.

But not if he could prevent it, convince her to leave and let him do what he had to do.

HE WAS GONE.

What had she expected, Laine thought, as she tossed back the satin cover and left the bed.

She couldn't help the anger that came then. At him, at herself. She'd been a fool... the storm, old fears.

She was such a fool.

She went to the washstand, the sight of the dried blood on her thighs, a reminder of what had passed between them the night before. A mistake, another loss in a long list of losses of her life. And now he was gone.

The truth was that she hadn't expected anything, hadn't thought of the consequences. She had been so afraid... the storm, and then he was there.

And now?

He had warned her, tried to convince her that she shouldn't come to the Territory. But she had refused to listen.

The truth was that she had no choice. Everything had been turned upside down when he arrived in Philadelphia with his questions, that certainty that she was hiding something. And then?

There had been no other choice. She knew it then, and now. She had come there for a reason, the only reason that mattered, she thought with grim determination as she stood at the glass doors. And it wasn't there at the Oaks, or with Ranse McCandliss.

"MAKE certain those baskets are in the back of the buckboard," Hannah told Annie as Laine arrived downstairs.

She looked up with a nod. "It's late for starting out to town, with the storm and all. But we need supplies."

Laine felt the look she gave her.

"Looks like the storm kept you up, too," Hannah commented. "Heard Ranse moving around up there.

Laine knew that she looked tired, she had seen it in the mirror as she dressed. There was a question at the woman's voice and in the look she gave her. She chose to ignore it.

"Where is everyone?" she asked, the big house unusually quiet.

"Mr. Stanton rode out with the men to look for lost cattle. It happens when one of those storms hit. Ranse was already gone by then..."

"Didn't bother to eat, just saddled up and rode out like the devil was on his tail with that deputy from town."

Deputy?

Something had happened.

"I'd like to go with you into town... I have a letter I need to post, and maybe purchase some things."

There was that look again. Hannah nodded. "Fine by me if you're feeling up to it. There's plenty of room in the wagon."

She had seen little of the town of Guthrie when she first arrived, followed by that ride out to the ranch, and remembered little of it. She was surprised at how big it was, two streets intersecting the main street, lined with stores and shops, including the mercantile and grocer where Seth pulled the team of horses around to the back.

"I'll check on that new harness, Mr. Stanton ordered," he told Hannah as they entered the back of the store and walked to the front where Hannah gave her order to the storekeeper, Mr. Ames.

"I'll put this together for you," he told her.

He glanced past them to the front counter where jars of candy were displayed just out of reach of the boy who stood there, stretched up on his toes, eyes wide as he stared at the bright colored pieces of candy.

"Your mother know you're down here, Kit?"

"Yes, sir, she'll be over in a while. She's over at the ladies' shop."

"His ma, Lou, does sewing for Clarice over at the shop," Hannah explained. "Lou's a widow with the boy to care for. Her husband was a sheriff before he was killed. She makes do best she can without any other family around. Young Kit, there, works the small farm. They have pecan trees and I buy from her for my pies when they're in season. That, and the church ladies help out."

It was a reminder of the difference between life here and in Philadelphia. Here, it was harder, there weren't the modern conveniences, cable cars through town, electric streetlights, or police... but here, most people knew each other, including a young boy with his nose pressed against the glass at the candy counter.

"I like the lemon drops," she said as she joined him at the candy counter trying to remember when everything had once been as simple as a piece of candy—*once upon a time.*

"It's sweet and tart at the same time," she pointed out.

Kit's expression was serious, his dark eyes wide as his mouth twisted into a frown.

"The lemon drops are good," he replied with a serious expression, "But I like the licorice."

"I can see that you're going to need one of each."

Kit shook his head. "Not today... "

She looked over at the shopkeeper. He sadly shook his

head, the message obvious—that there was no money for candy treats. She reached inside the pocket of her skirt and retrieved a silver nickel.

"Is this enough for two pieces of candy?" she asked Mr. Ames.

"More than enough," he replied with a small smile on his face.

"Then we would like two pieces of candy; one lemon drop and one piece of licorice."

Kit stared at her, then Mr. Ames as he opened the first jar and held it out to the boy for him to take a lemon drop.

"Ma says we don't accept charity," he replied, eyes even larger as he stared at the jar and repeated what he'd obviously been told.

She caught the look Hannah gave her as she knelt beside the boy.

"It's not charity," she assured him, that dark gaze so like another's fixing on her, uncertainty there along with the frown.

"It's a gift."

She saw the indecision in his dark eyes—the struggle with what he'd been told by his mother against the possibility of having a piece of candy.

"I s'pose it's all right since yer the marshal's wife."

There it was again... small towns and the way something seemed to take on a life of its own, rumors, gossip.

"Not exactly... " When she would have explained, his attention was already fixed on another jar.

"Can I change my mind and take a different piece?" he asked.

In the end, she didn't try to explain. It was all far too complicated for a young boy to understand.

"Of course, you may."

"My ma likes the cherry candies, like my pa used to bring her."

It took her a moment, the boy's sincerity, his thought for his mother, so important that he would give up what he wanted.

"You may have whatever pieces you like."

He nodded. "I would like a cherry candy and a licorice candy," he told Mr. Ames.

When the transaction was completed, she had Mr. Ames keep the change.

"For future purchases," she told him with a nod toward Kit.

"Thank you, ma'am," Kit replied, the two pieces of candy in a brown paper bag, for later, so that he could share with his mother.

"My name is Laine... " she would have given him her last name, but stopped under the circumstances that would have been even more confusing and it was a name that people had learned to fear.

"Get on with you, boy," Hannah gently told him. Your ma will be wondering where you are."

He grinned. "Thank you again, Miz McCandliss."

Hannah, bless her, didn't make an issue of that little exchange with Kit or his innocent assumption of what was obviously all over town.

"Kinda reminds me of someone else," Hannah commented. "Those dark eyes, the proud way the boy carries himself. Ranse was like that, before he lost his pa, had a bit of the devil in him, and could sure talk a lady out of a piece of candy. That all ended when he took it upon himself to go into the outlet to bring his pa's body back. He was just fourteen then, not a man yet. That sort of thing, what he saw there and almost didn't make it back, has a way of makin' a boy grow up fast, shapes him, makes him into a man, the things he had to do, the decisions he's forced to make."

There was that thoughtful look again, and Laine wondered how much she knew, or guessed.

"I've got business down the street," Hannah told her. "The

greengrocer for some potatoes and such, and then I need to deliver an order over at the livery for Seth, if you want to come along."

"I need to post a letter and then send a telegram. And I thought I might see about some new clothes since mine were... "

"Post office is next to the telegraph office, both across from the hotel down the way. The ladies' shop is just across the way. Say hello for me. Mrs. Adams runs the shop and can get most of what you need."

She thanked her, then left the mercantile for the shop 'just across the way'. There she encountered a young woman who was just leaving with a thick wrapped bundle in her arms. She had those same sad dark eyes and she knew this had to be Kit's mother. Life was simple and hard, but it included a cherry candy once Kit returned to find her.

The ladies' shop was an establishment that provided elegant evening gowns as well as other garments that a woman might want or need, including a walking skirt on display, shirt-waists that could be made to size, ladies' hats, gloves, and jackets.

It was an eye-opening experience since most of her clothes had been provided by the trust fund set up for her by her guardian.

That was then, this was now. With limited funds and the uncertainty of how long she would be there, she placed an order for another walking skirt since hers was somewhat the worse for wear with the wine stain from her travel out there, along with a new shirtwaist, and additional undergarments.

The owner of the shop informed her that the dry cleaners down the way—with their new way of cleaning clothes—might be able to remove the last of the stain. She smiled at yet another modern innovation that had just arrived in the frontier town—dry cleaning.

Adjoining the post office was the telegrapher's office immediately next door. An elderly gentleman completed his transaction and stepped away. Dressed in a long- sleeved, starched, white shirt worn under a dark-green, wool vest, the postal clerk was obviously suffering from the heat that had collected in the office over the long hours of the morning.

Only the swirling blades of the fan overhead seemed to give any relief from the stifling heat that had built through the morning. Dark shades had been drawn down over the windows that faced onto the street to give ease from the glare of afternoon sun. Though the office was much cooler than the street beyond, it was still overly warm inside. The postal clerk finally looked up.

"Philadelphia? That's a good ways away. It will go out by rail on the morning train tomorrow."

She gave him the necessary coin for postage and turned to leave.

"You are finally up and about, after your unfortunate 'accident'."

There was no mistaking the obvious hesitation in that one word, as Elisabeth Summers stood in the doorway and greeted her with unmistakable coolness.

"Good afternoon."

"Everyone has been most concerned about your recovery," Elizabeth continued. "After all, your arrival in Guthrie was quite... memorable."

Laine supposed one might call being shot an accident. As for polite conversations...

"Excuse me," she politely told Elizabeth. "I have several errands to run."

"Of course, I understand. We'll be seeing more of each other in the very near future. I've invited Ranse and Addison to our annual picnic. And since I hear that you've been staying at the Oaks, you're welcome to attend also, if you feel up to it."

The afterthought of an invitation was unmistakable. She

had encountered similar attitudes in Philadelphia from those who thought her lack of family was both curious and amusing, and a weapon for wagging tongues from time to time, particularly when it came to the question about a particular beau and prospects for marriage. It seemed that was one thing that was the same in Guthrie.

She could imagine what Ellie would have said, something blunt and colorful.

It was too tempting. "Oh dear," she exclaimed. "It seems that you've stepped in something. I hope you haven't soiled your gown, too."

It was undoubtedly petty and small-minded, but she couldn't help a small smile of satisfaction as Elizabeth had suddenly gone speechless with whatever her next remark might have been. She looked down and lifted the hem of her gown to inspect the damage to her skirt as well as her boot.

10

Waves of heat rose from the street and shimmered in the afternoon air as Laine left the telegraph office.

She passed several people on the boardwalk, asked directions from an elderly gentleman, then crossed the street to the local newspaper office.

She still had time to make some inquiries at the newspaper office before meeting Hannah back at the mercantile where she'd placed her order for the week. She'd been thinking about how to go about this to find what she needed. She hesitated at the door, then pushed it open.

She had come there to learn the truth. Her search had to begin somewhere.

"Can I help you?"

A bespectacled, older man never bothered to glance up from beneath the visor of the green shade over his eyes where he worked at a desk behind the counter. He continued reading the printed sheet from time to time to mark through an item that didn't meet with his approval or to circle another that perhaps needed changing.

At the rear of the office behind another counter loomed the

massive presses. A young man was bent over one of the presses, setting the letters into the blocked rows for printing, while another brought the next page to the be-speckled editor for proofreading.

Her friend, Ellie, would have pulled this off without missing a step. She was determined to do the same thing. One thing she'd learned from her friend, among other things, was that a good bluff was hard to beat. The other piece of advice—don't get caught.

"I'm doing a story on outlaws," she explained. "And I'd like any information that you have on them, stories that might have been published, that sort of thing."

"You might be here a while," the editor, Edward Melrose, by the lettering at the window told her.

"There's plenty of articles."

"I'm specifically interested in information about the Dalton Gang," she explained. "I understand they used to live nearby."

He nodded. "We keep copies of all editions of our paper." He rubbed his chin thoughtfully. "Things have been pretty quiet since the family left, but I can get you what we have."

"Did you know them?"

"Just about everyone around here for any amount of time knew the family."

"Do you know where they went?"

"Adeline and the girls moved up near Stillwater. That was almost a year ago. There were always people coming around, trying to find the boys. Some of them not the sort you'd want to meet up with. And now the Pinkertons that came in a few days ago. But the Sheriff or Marshal McCandliss might be able to tell you more."

Might be able to. But hadn't. Why? And now he had left with a deputy and ridden into the outlet. After the Daltons?

"I'm interested in that, as well as any other information

about the family. I understand the family used to have a place near Kingfisher."

"It came over the telegraph late last night. We're setting it up for the afternoon edition now and you'll be able to read about it then."

"I appreciate it, and any of your back issues would be very helpful."

"What newspaper did you say that you work for?" he asked as he called for one of his employees.

"The Philadelphia Herald." It was the first thing that came to mind. Mrs. Ralston had it delivered to her house when she was alive.

"If you have a few minutes I'll have Adam get you some of the back issues."

She thanked him.

"You're asking about the Daltons?"

She turned to the slender, blonde-haired young woman who had come into the office just after her, and had obviously overheard her conversation with the editor.

"That's right." Keep it simple. Ellie's rule number one, anything complicated was very likely to trip her up, get muddied with the details. And it was possible the young woman had overheard her conversation with the editor of the newspaper.

"Most people in these parts know all about the Daltons," the young woman replied.

"They have quite a reputation," Laine added. "It's for a story I'm writing. Do you know the Dalton family?"

"Everyone in these parts knows about them."

The young woman's answer was vague. She shrugged. "I heard about the robbery in the Territory."

That had only been a few days earlier, Laine thought. Word certainly traveled fast.

"Are you a reporter?" the young woman asked.

There was something different in her voice now, something careful.

"I'm working on a story. I'm from Philadelphia."

The young woman hesitated, then eventually introduced herself, although she seemed hesitant.

"Ginny Morton," she replied, but didn't offer her hand.

"So, you're interested in the Daltons," she said, that first interest now had an edge. "You need to be careful."

"Careful?" It sounded like a warning.

"You can't always believe what you read in the newspapers. They make stuff up, make it sound more important than it is. It sells more newspapers."

"I can imagine how difficult it must be for the family."

"I don't think you can."

The sudden sharpness in Ginny's voice surprised her. It seemed somehow... personal.

She wanted to ask her more but in private.

"I think these will get you started," the editor told her as he returned from the back office with several past issues of the newspaper folded over his arm.

"I am very grateful... What do I owe you?" she asked as the door behind her snapped shut. Ginny Morton was gone.

"We usually provide back issues free," the editor explained. "But since you have several... "

"I understand," she replied with growing impatience. "How much for these copies?"

After all that, he shook his head. "You don't owe me anything. Consider it a courtesy for a fellow— journalist. You might add a mention of the paper as a source for your article."

She gave him a quick smile as she gathered the issues of the paper, again with a quick glance out the window of the office.

"Here," he told her, reaching for the bundle of papers. "Let me tie those for you or they'll be all over the street.

"That's not necessary..." she started to explain, only to have him waive it off as if it was no bother.

The bundle was neatly rolled and tied with a thick string. He handed it to her.

"Remember, mention the paper in your article."

"Yes, of course," she replied as she tucked the bundle under her arm and ran from the office.

She was too late. Ginny Morton was gone. She returned to the newspaper office.

Mr. Melrose glanced up.

"Is there something else?"

"There was a young woman here a few minutes ago. Can you tell me where she lives?" Laine turned back to the editor.

He shook his head. "I don't recall... "

"I was just talking to her when you went to get the copies of the newspaper for me. You must have seen her," she replied with mounting confusion. "She seemed to know a great deal about the Daltons... " She gave him a description of Ginny.

"That description could fit any one of several young ladies here in Guthrie. I'm sorry, I don't recall. Is there's nothing else I can help you with? I need to get back to my work."

"No, thank you." She didn't bother to hide her disappointment. "You've been very helpful."

He had been helpful as far as providing back issues of the paper were concerned, but the rest of it...?

She glanced down both sides of the street before turning back toward the mercantile store.

Her thoughts still back at the newspaper office and that odd encounter, she failed to see the uneven board at the planked walkway. The toe of her boot caught on the uneven board and she stumbled.

"Whoa!" A familiar voice as she caught herself with the help of a hand at her arm.

"Be careful. You don't want to re-injure that shoulder." Tom Travis' smile broadened as she looked up.

"And I thought the heat was bad today," he commented. "Did you leave any wounded behind?"

A friendly voice in spite of the reminder about her shoulder.

"Would it have anything to do with Elizabeth Summers?" he asked. "I saw her a few minutes ago. She extended an invitation for Saturday. She mentioned that she had also invited you. That must have been some conversation."

She saw the sympathy in his expression as he tucked her arm through his.

"It's an annual tradition, and an opportunity the past couple of years for her father to try to promote his campaign for Ranse to go to Washington and push for statehood."

She heard the amusement at his voice. "Addison has mentioned that."

"And good luck," he replied. "It would make sense. There's no one better qualified, but Ranse has no ambition for politics, much to Summers' great disappointment. That doesn't mean he won't try to convince him."

"What is his ambition?" she asked.

"For now, it's the Daltons. And in a way it's personal. He was once real close with Frank Dalton... But that ended when the boys made other choices. Now they're on opposite sides of things."

"He left the ranch early this morning." She thought of that note that Seth had found.

"I saw Hannah earlier, she told me."

"It's dangerous, isn't it?" She shouldn't care what Ranse McCandliss did. It was his job.

"Dangerous enough."

"He won't stop until..." She was about to say, until the Daltons were either in prison, or dead.

"No, he won't. It's who he is."

Who he was... and that put the two of them on opposite sides. It had from the beginning, and she needed to remember that in spite of what had happened the night before.

"Hannah mentioned something about checking the bandage on your shoulder. I don't think that is really necessary. Two more days and you can remove the bandages permanently. But the only excitement I want you to consider for the next few days is that picnic and dance.

"By the way," he continued. "I understand Judge Parker will also be attending Daniel Summers' little get-together. He's a friend of Addison's. He's earned quite a reputation for himself in the Territory. He and Ranse have worked closely over the last three years."

"Judge Parker?"

Ranse had mentioned him. The 'hanging judge', he was called, and he had sworn to see the Dalton gang tried and hung for their crimes.

"Are you all right?" Tom asked. "Let's step inside," he indicated the shop they stood in front of. "It's cooler in here. It's not good for a doctor to have a patient faint on him."

She would have reminded him that she did not faint. But he was already pulling her with him into the shop.

"What flavor do you like?"

Judge Parker would be at the picnic...! Would Ranse meet with him when he returned? About what? About her?

"Emily owns this shop next door to the boardinghouse," Tom explained. "That's her daughter Laurie behind the counter. Seth is sweet on her. If he can't be found at the ranch, then he's here," he continued.

She forced a small smile as she tried to wrap her head around what it meant that Judge Parker would be in Guthrie, and at the picnic.

"You choose," she told him. "Any flavor is fine."

"I can personally vouch for all of them." He gave their order to Laurie.

"How are you getting along out at the Oaks?" he asked as they sat together over dishes of ice cream. "I imagine that Hannah can be a handful, she likes to be in charge. But the truth is Addison would be hard put to replace her."

"She's been very kind, and she's incredible how she manages it all." She was thoughtful.

"But I need to see about moving into town for the time being."

"That won't go over well, if I know Hannah."

She caught that slight hesitation that he would have said more but chose not too—that it might not go over well with Ranse?

"How did she come to be at the Oaks?" she asked.

"It was all a long time ago, after Addison's wife died and then his son... He expanded the ranch out, acquired more land. I think it was to have something that kept him away from the house as much as possible after all that.

"The ranch took most of his time and he hired her on as cook at the house. She stayed on after Ranse went to live with there. Then, Addison sent him off to school back east the same as his own son, but you know about that. When he came back Addison had built the gristmill down by the river, and just a couple of years ago set up a generator plant for the town." He gestured to the overhead fan and electric lights in the shop.

"Now the mill serves a dual purpose—grinding grain that's produced around here and providing electricity to the town. The workers at the mill freeze whole blocks of ice during the winter and keep them solid down in that underground cooler through the summer months," he took on the role of historian and storyteller.

"At Ranse's suggestion, Addison hired some of the local schoolboys to deliver block ice. Emily is a regular customer," he motioned to the girl behind the counter. "I'll tell you another secret. When the heat is bad, like today, people set a big block of ice in a wash basin and hook up one of those electric fans to blow across it. It cools a room down quick."

The knot of frustration she'd felt since leaving the newspaper office began to unwind. Tom Travis had that effect on her, as opposed to someone else she could name.

"Hannah has that in the kitchen out at the ranch." She had seen it just the day before the storm came in.

"She stores food in a cooler."

"Modern conveniences," Tom said as he finished his bowl of ice cream. He was thoughtful.

"You've never said much about your family."

"I don't remember anything about my real family. I went to live with Mrs. Ralston when I was very young."

"Then Ranse must have been acquainted with Mrs. Ralston. He said that's how you met," Tom continued, nothing in his voice to indicate that he thought any differently.

She hesitated. "We met through... mutual acquaintances in Philadelphia," Laine replied.

"What has Ranse told you about the Daltons?" she casually asked.

Tom sat back at his chair. "He doesn't talk about his work. It's confidential, for only the sheriff and now the Pinkertons since they've been brought in to help with bringing them in. The pressure is on him from Governor Seay to bring an end to this.

"It's gotten political, the Governor can't hope for reappointment if he fails to stop the Daltons and these attacks. That was made pretty clear when we were all in Washington.

"Ranse has more authority than any other lawman in the Territory," he continued. "Most have no jurisdiction beyond their own county or township. He can go anywhere necessary to find the Daltons, but that authority carries a heavy responsibility."

"You've lived here for a long time," she commented. He certainly seemed to know a lot about the town and its people, including Ranse.

"My grandparents came out here in the early days. My grandfather was a doctor, the first physician here when Guthrie was nothing more than a stage stop with a store, a saloon, and a boardinghouse that had some... young ladies who worked there."

She laughed. A boardinghouse with young women who worked there?

"Enterprising, were they?"

"Well, there was a lot of... demand from the cowboys who came through. My grandfather had an interesting clientele. And then my father after him."

"And he sent you to medical school as well," she concluded. "To go into the family business."

He nodded. "The town has grown up quite a bit since then. It's respectable now. More or less, except for a few holdouts."

"Such as the Daltons," she added. "Ranse mentioned that the family lived near Guthrie at one time." She wondered what he might be able to tell her.

"The family moved around quite a bit over the years, mostly due to the old man. He never could keep a job for long and kept moving them around when work played out, or when he decided to move on.

"I heard that if it wasn't for Adeline Dalton's perseverance and the small farm they had, the family wouldn't have survived. Many people think it was because they were so poor that the boys took to robbing trains. I believe that Adeline and the girls moved back to Kingfisher about three years ago."

Kingfisher.

"How far away is that?" Keeping in mind his friendship with Ranse, she tried to hide anything more than casual interest.

"A good day's ride west of here with an early start. There's a stage run that goes in that direction."

A full day's ride.

"Are you all right?" Tom asked with obvious concern.

She looked up and nodded. "Do you know a young woman by the name of Ginny Morton?"

"Your first day in town, and you already met someone?"

"I ran into her at the newspaper office." She didn't elaborate. The less said, the better.

"Ginny Morton? Can't say that I do. Were you looking for the latest edition of the Guthrie Herald? Something to read out at the ranch?

"We have a small but impressive library across from the Sheriff's office. The Ladies Auxiliary of Guthrie raised the money for it. It would have better reading material than the latest crime and political news."

He walked her back to the mercantile where she was to meet Hannah.

"I'll want a dance on Saturday," he told her, a reminder of Elizabeth's invitation. She had hoped to make some excuse to escape the annual picnic. That seemed to have disappeared.

"Of course," she replied and thanked him for the ice cream and the company. At least she had one friend in Guthrie.

"Tom's a good man," Hannah commented on the ride back to the ranch.

"Yes, he is."

"He and Ranse have been friends for a long time."

She knew that. Was there some other reason for telling her?

"It would be a shame for something to come between them."

A warning? But there was nothing more than a friendly expression on Hannah's face.

"I doubt that would ever happen," she replied. And it

certainly had nothing to do with her, in spite of what had happened the night before.

It was nothing more than the store, those old memories out of the past, and her own foolishness.

As far as what had happened... it didn't mean anything to either one of them. That was abundantly clear when Ranse left without a word, without...

What? What had she expected? Nothing. And it would continue to be 'nothing' as soon as she was able to leave the ranch.

She should have an answer to the telegram she'd sent to Philadelphia in a couple of days. A loan was all it was, even though she knew what Ellie's response would probably be— that she didn't need to pay back the money she asked to be wired to the bank in Guthrie; that she should come home and forget all about everything that had happened; that Ellie's father would help her...

But that was just the point of all of this and something she'd tried hard to make Ellie understand before she left. Her friend had a family that had always been there for her, a family that cared for her even if they were a little blind to some of her more colorful tendencies, and a family that would always be there for her.

Ellie knew who her grandparents were, and their grandparents before that. Her friend had a history whereas she had... nothing beyond a note that had been pinned to her dress as a small child, an orphan taken in by an extremely kind and generous woman.

She told herself that it should have been enough, and it might have been if she had never met Ranse McCandliss. Everything had changed. He had changed everything and as soon as Ellie wired her the money she needed, she would be gone.

Just a few more days, she told herself. She now had information about the Dalton family. Surely that would lead to more information. She might possibly be able to find out more about Ginny Morton. In the meantime, she had the roll of newspapers to go through.

Just a few more days, hopefully before Ranse returned and the Saturday picnic that she'd received an invitation, too. Then, she wouldn't be forced to endure Elizabeth Summer's sly comments and innuendos.

Just a few more days...

11

————

She spent the next two days going through the half dozen newspapers Mr. Melrose at the newspaper office had provided. Having read several stories about the *'Wild West'* in popular dime novels, she was familiar with the vivid descriptions of some of the more colorful and notorious articles.

In some articles the events were described as *'incredible'* and almost *'heroic'*, with one describing how a child was saved by one of the members of the gang from a stampede in the middle of the small town where they'd robbed the bank.

But most of the articles described the *"horrific events that had robbed the bank and the next town of safety and tranquility"* as the gang *"descended"'* on the dispatch office and robbed it of the railroad payroll with the clerk badly wounded.

The most recent article was almost two months old and none provided any information about the Dalton Gang's whereabouts other than they were last seen riding deep into the Territory and beyond the reach of authorities and representatives of the railroad who were trying to find them.

She thought of the Pinkerton agents who had been aboard

the train from Washington. They had continued on to Tulsa according to what she'd later learned. And from there?

She needed to go into Guthrie to see if there was a response from Ellie at the Western Union office.

She made the excuse of picking up items that she'd purchased and accompanied Seth into town to pick up harnesses that were being mended at the leather goods next to the livery stable.

A telegram from Ellie was waiting for her.

"Didn't know where to deliver this," the agent told her. "Glad you stopped by, miss."

According to the telegram, Ellie's father had made arrangements for funds to be sent to the bank in Guthrie in her name, in spite of the fact that she might be related to the Dalton gang. But it would take a couple days for the transaction to go through. As far as a loan was concerned, he refused to consider it for his *other* daughter, as he had often called her.

"Will there be a response, miss?"

"Yes."

She wrote out the message for Ellie, letting her know that she had received the message. She thought of adding something more, but decided against it and simply said that she would stay in touch. She certainly wasn't going to mention the fact that she'd been injured in a hold-up attempt on the train.

After leaving the Western Union office, she went to the bank, but the funds from Ellie's father hadn't yet arrived. And it was Friday, which meant the next day that they might possibly arrive wouldn't be until Monday according to the clerk.

Two more days.

She made additional inquiries about Ginny Morton, but that proved to be almost as impossible as trying to find the Daltons. Everywhere she inquired, including the ladies' shop where she picked up purchases she'd made, turned up nothing. It was as if the young woman had simply disappeared.

Tom Travis had told her that the old Dalton farm in King-fisher was a day's ride to the west. It seemed more and more that was where she needed to go if she was to find out anything about the family.

She returned to the livery stable to meet Seth for the return ride to the ranch. Several pieces of harness, including a saddle that had been repaired, were already in the back of the buckboard wagon.

"Said he needed to make a stop down the street," the leather-maker told her with a good-natured grin. "That boy sure makes a lot of trips into town."

Down the street, could only mean one thing—the ice cream shop.

She tucked the invoice into her reticule and was about to cross the street when the man at the shop pointed down the street.

"Looks like the deputy just got back."

Laine glanced down the street where a dust cloud churned up beneath the hooves of horses as riders came up the street from the far edge of town. Four horses, three riders, and one of them was Ranse McCandliss.

Her first reaction was an undeniable feeling of relief that she quickly pushed back. She told herself that it didn't matter whether or not he'd safely returned.

That was immediately followed by the leather maker's comment, "Looks like they got somebody with 'em."

A third rider sat astride one of the horses, slouch hat pulled low over his face, hands bound behind his back. The fourth horse carried another man laid across the saddle.

"One of 'em is dead."

Her stomach lurched. Who were the two men? Was it possible Ranse had found the Daltons?

A crowd had already gathered, following them from the edge of town to the sheriff's office where Ranse and the deputy reined in their horses. Seth was among the crowd as the sheriff came out of the office as they dismounted.

The deputy pulled the bound man from the back of his horse as Ranse rounded the other horse with the fourth man tied across.

Laine stepped out of the shop as other townspeople gathered. It was as if the circus had come to town, she thought, or some country fair as other people streamed out of shops and the hotel.

Seth was among them, threading his way through the bystanders to reach Ranse as a man in a black pipe hat and long coat appeared, and she realized the man must be the undertaker.

She stepped back as Ranse looked up through the crowd, Seth beside him, and that dark gaze shaded by the brim of his hat fastened on her. He nodded to Seth, then led the horse with the man's body through the crowd, along with the man in the long coat.

"Some excitement today," the saddlemaker commented. "Wonder who they brought in?"

From what Addison had said just that morning, he wasn't expected to return so soon. These trips into the outlet could take several days even weeks. In spite of Addison's hospitality and assurance that she could stay as long as she wanted, she had decided to be gone after the picnic at the Summers' ranch, no later than Monday when the funds from Ellie's father arrived.

Now he'd returned.

What was done was done, as far as she was concerned. That night was a mistake, and not one she intended to repeat. The plain and simple truth was that he had a life here, presumably with Elizabeth Summers. She had no idea where her search would take her or what she would find at the end of it. And afterward?

She had no idea where that would take her. Possibly back to Philadelphia. Ellie and her family were there. She might continue her studies as she'd planned, perhaps teach afterward, or...? But at the moment, the last thing she wanted was an encounter with Ranse McCandliss.

"Is there a boardinghouse where I might be able to find a room?" she asked the saddlemaker.

"Bessie Pollard has a place with rooms to let if she's not full up. It's over on Second Street." He angled his head in the direction, opposite the crowd that had gathered.

She had less than four dollars left of the money she'd arrived with after the purchases she'd made, and no idea what a room might cost per night. It was best that she didn't return to the ranch now that he had returned. But first she needed to know who he had brought back to Guthrie.

Was it the Daltons? Or someone else? Would her search end here, one man dead and another arrested?

She had to know; it was the reason she'd come there.

Among the bystanders, she caught sight of Seth, head and shoulders taller than most in the crowd that had gathered. She made her way toward him, no small effort with the curious bystanders who had gathered.

He steadied her with a hand at her arm, as those around them jostled and pushed for a better look.

"Be careful, miss," he cautioned. "You don't want to re-injure yerself."

That was the farthest thing from her mind.

"Who were those men who were brought in?"

"I heard someone say that the man they have inside is Jim Bitters, the other."

"What do you know about him?"

"Rumor has it that he once rode with Bob and Grat Dalton. They say that Marshal McCandliss caught up with them in the outlet where the Daltons used to hole up. Don't know about the other fella that the undertaker took away."

Jim Bitters. It wasn't a name she was familiar with. Was there a possibility that she might be able to speak with him?

The crowd continued to gather and she caught comments of those around them; mostly curious, but there were also other comments that surprised her, that sympathized with the two that had been brought in.

"Can't say as how Jim deserves this, after what that posse did to his wife and son."

"I knew Mary, a real sweet young woman... She didn't deserve that."

"Heard the dead fella is Texas Jack from over Tucson way, a cold-blooded killer. Man, woman, child... didn't matter, and better off dead by my way of thinkin'."

"I best get you back to the livery," Seth was saying as he escorted her from the crowd. "This is no place for you."

No place? A world so far from the one she knew. But was it? That long train ride almost twenty years before, and that note pinned to her dress...?

"You back to the ranch... I have some business I need to take care of."

"Mr. Stanton wouldn't like me going off and leaving you."

"I won't be returning to the ranch. I'll be staying in town... "

"Hannah didn't say anything about that... And yer things are there."

What there was of them, she thought. Most of what she'd brought with her, other than her recent purchases and the one gown, she was either wearing other than her jacket and a few personal things.

"Once I've made arrangements, I'll send word to Mr. Stanton and ask to have my things delivered into town. I appreciate your help... "

"Seth... "

That deep voice with that edge of authority had them both looking up.

"Yes, sir," Seth replied as Ranse McCandliss slowly walked toward them. "I was just fixin' to get back to the ranch with the harness and saddle that Mr. Curry needed repaired."

Laine looked away, refusing to meet that dark gaze that fastened on her.

"He's right," Ranse said then, "this is no place for you."

She did look at him, then several emotions, not the least which was surprise along with anger, and something else that she pushed back.

"I don't recall needing your permission where I go, Marshal McCandliss." She turned to leave with the intention of finding the Pollard boardinghouse.

"You need to go, Seth. Mr. Curry will be needing that saddle," Ranse told him. She didn't stay to hear Seth's response, but kept walking in the direction the saddlemaker had said she would find the boardinghouse. She got as far as the corner of Second Street, the boardinghouse in sight.

"We need to talk."

He saw the stiffness in her back, the way she squared her shoulders, then slowly turned around.

"There is nothing to discuss, Marshal McCandliss, unless you intend to arrest me."

There was a great deal to discuss and all of it had to do with that last night at the ranch. It had worked at him that long ride into the outlet, when they caught up with Bitters and Texas Jack, and the long ride back—who she was or might be, the reason she was there, what should never have happened but had.

She plunged ahead, humiliation adding to the anger. "I haven't committed any crime, and I don't owe you anything."

"No, you don't. It's what I owe you."

She would only have been more surprised if he had arrested her.

"I owe you an apology. I had no right to... take advantage of the situation. You were frightened and vulnerable, and I had promised to protect you... "

And the fact that she had obviously never been with a man before, that she was naive, vulnerable... But looking at her now... the anger that was there, that she had every right to, she seemed anything but frightened or vulnerable.

An apology? The last thing she wanted or expected. But it was there along with something else in his voice, in the deep lines at his eyes, and the exhaustion from where he'd been and had to do.

Damn him. She didn't want to care about Ranse McCandliss, and God knows she didn't owe him anything.

"I don't want your apology. I don't need your protection. And I'll find what I came for without your help."

"This?" he gestured to the boardinghouse they stood in front of.

"It's better that I don't return to the ranch."

There was more to it than what had happened between them. She had given it a great deal of thought. If it turned out that she was part of the Dalton family, she thought too much of Addison, respected him and owed him too much for the past weeks she'd been there, to cause a scandal not to mention the questions it would raise. Such was the notoriety of the Dalton Gang.

"I don't agree."

"It doesn't matter whether or not you agree."

"What about Addison?"

"I'm thinking about him."

"Are you? He's taken a liking to you. You've given him something that he hasn't had in a long time."

"It's because I'm thinking about him that I've made this decision. I don't want him hurt if it turns out that the Daltons are my family."

"You're not a good liar."

"I beg your pardon."

"I've known Addison a long time. He isn't afraid of anything, but that's not the only reason."

"I don't owe you another reason."

"You're right, you don't. But you owe him."

Guilt slipped to the surface. "It's better if I take a room here."

"Maybe better but probably not likely."

"Excuse me?"

In spite of the bone-wearying exhaustion of the past days not to mention the outcome, with the Daltons slipping away once more, he smiled at her reply. There were times, she was the prim and proper well educated young woman he'd first encountered in Philadelphia. Then there had been that last time before he left...

"Bessie is usually full up with regulars, and with certain guests arriving in town, my guess is that the hotel and any rooms she has left will be taken."

"Guests?"

"A gentleman by the name of Roosevelt is supposed to come in on tonight's train, and a few others."

She wondered if that included Judge Parker.

"Then I need to make certain I can get a room before he arrives." She turned to the gate in front of the boardinghouse, but a sign in the front window answered the question—*NO ROOMS AVAILABLE*.

"I'll find some other place to stay." She said as she turned around and would have pushed past him.

"What do you want me to tell Addison?"

That stopped her. Damn him! He knew that it would.

"Seth has already left with the buckboard."

"Maybe the livery has a horse I can ride."

"Not that he won't charge you an arm and a leg," Ranse replied. "And that shoulder might not be strong enough yet. I'm going back this afternoon. You can ride with me."

"No... " she shook her head.

"You don't know how to ride?"

She bristled. "I know how to ride."

"I need time to wash some of the trail dust off," he told her. "And then I'll be ready to leave. I'll turn in my report later."

She nodded as another thought came. Would there be something in the report that might tell her something? Returning to the ranch might give her the opportunity to find out what he'd learned about Bill Doolin and the Daltons.

It had been a while since she'd ridden a horse and then it had been sidesaddle on a docile horse selected for her by Ellie's father. In spite of the long ride back to Guthrie from the outlet, Ranse's horse was anything but exhausted or docile. And it was more than a little discomforting to be seated in front of him in the saddle on that long ride back to the ranch.

"Do you want to stop to rest?" he asked when they had been on the road for some time.

"You don't need to worry about me," she answered stiffly, trying to move away from the contact of him at her back, long arms wrapped around her, those hands at the reins in front of her, the purchases she'd made that day tied behind the saddle.

Her previous ride to the ranch had been when she first arrived after that terrifying train trip and the attack, hardly in any condition to be aware of the countryside. Her only other exposure to the Territory was at the ranch—the wide open space of it, pastures still green rolling away to distant hills, and the scent of lupine.

Now, from the back of a horse as they left town and that dirt road and rode mostly in silence, the flat countryside bordered by gently rolling hills as they left the wagon road and followed the course of a river.

"It's called the Cimarron," he eventually said as he guided the horse along the edge of the river and through a stand of cottonwood trees that sat atop the rust-red sandstone riverbank.

"It runs all the way to the Arkansas river. In winter it can rise over the edge of that red escarpment and flood the surrounding prairie."

"And the cattle?" she asked, curious in spite of the fact that she swore they had nothing to talk about.

"The ranch is on higher ground. Addison has the men bring most of the cattle in before that happens, and there is grass they can forage."

"Most of the cattle?"

"The ones they can find."

"And the ones they can't find?"

"Some of them make it through. Others end up caught in the river. Then there are the others that are picked off."

A different part of the country, different language, and different people. Like the man she rode with, who kept his arm around her, his hand clasped over the pommel to prevent her slipping or falling.

"Picked off?"

"Cattle rustlers. There's been a lot of trouble from them, stealing cattle, changing the brands, selling them off to those who deal in such things. It can be a big loss for Addison and the ranch."

'Those who deal in such things'. Cattle rustlers.

"Have the Daltons' ever stolen cattle?"

He eventually answered. "Not that they've ever been caught. They usually prefer banks and payroll offices: easier profit.

And people got killed.

She heard the change in his voice, the silence that followed as he guided the horse over a fallen tree, then down an embankment, one arm going around her to steady her as the horse carefully picked its way up through rocks then under an overhang of that rust-red sandstone escarpment that rimmed the river.

"Is Bill Doolin part of the Dalton gang?" Would he tell her, or would he refuse, she thought. But she had to ask.

"He's ridden with them, then goes off on his own."

He and a man called Texas Jack, according to Seth. And Texas Jack was dead, which had to mean there was a confrontation or an attack. Like the attack on the train?

"Does he know where the Daltons are?"

She had no business knowing any of it, but the truth was Doolin had been caught red-handed doing what he did best—picking off the stage that left two good men dead.

There was that silence again. Then, "Not that he was willing to tell us." Even though Texas Jack had reportedly been seen with the Daltons only weeks earlier in the outlet.

"Do you know a woman by the name of Ginny Morton?"

She felt his sudden shift in the saddle behind her.

What did she know? What had she found out, he thought. And not a clue how dangerous it could be for her.

"There was a family by the name of Morton that lived in the area," he answered carefully. Not a lie, but neither was it the answer she was after.

"They've been gone a long time."

If there was more, it was obvious that he wasn't going to tell her.

He caught the change in her expression, the way her brows came together with the frown on her face at the only answer he could give.

The easy gait of his horse covered another mile as silence

expanded, except for the sound of the horse's hooves and the occasional call of a bird as it swept over the river.

"Are you all right?" he asked, as she continued to hold herself rigid in the saddle in front of him.

"My shoulder is much better. Tom says the bandages can be removed in a couple more days."

"That's not what I meant."

She closed her eyes. She knew what he meant and was grateful that he couldn't see the embarrassment she still felt.

"I'm fine, there's no need to bother yourself on my account."

'Fine'—that one simple word that came too easily, that didn't require anything more, end of the conversation. Except that it wasn't the end of it.

He felt it in the stiffness of her back, the way she pulled further away, the anger there in her voice, and it cut at him. It cut deep and left a raw feeling like a wound that had been opened.

He told himself that she was an unfortunate part of this. That the only thing that mattered was finding the Daltons. Then, why did that night and what had happened feel as if he'd been opened up and his insides cut out?

The ranch came into sight just over the rise, the sprawling house with those balconies, the stone path that led to the stables and pens below, with that shimmering heat that brought the last scent of lupine as it dried and drifted on the wind.

"You need to tell Addison you plan on leaving," he told her as they rode into the stable yard, and Addison was there with Seth as they unloaded the buckboard.

"But I won't let you hurt him; he's already had a lifetime of that."

A warning? she thought, as he stepped down from the back of the horse, and then reached for her, gently easing her to the ground.

Addison nodded a greeting in that way that men greeted each other, but his smile was for her—caring, welcoming, with faint lines of concern.

"You had us worried when Hannah told me that you'd ridden off this morning with Seth, and then this young yahoo came back alone. Sure glad to see you, young lady." His arm gently went around her shoulders.

"I want to show you something," he walked her around to the back of the buckboard.

"I had this repaired at the saddle shop in town."

She recognized the saddle she had seen earlier.

"It belonged to my wife. You're about the same size, and obviously you can ride. I thought you might get some use out of it."

Her gaze met Ranse's. Such a fine gift and obviously one that meant a great deal to Addison.

"I don't know what to say... I can't..." She tried to find something to say.

"Say that you'll use it and I'll have Curry pick out a good, broke horse for you once that shoulder is strong enough to handle the reins. It means a lot to give it to you."

Give to her? If Ranse McCandliss hadn't just returned, she would have thought he had something to do with this. And that warning, 'I won't let you hurt him... '

"Was there something you wanted to tell him?" Ranse reminded her, that dark gaze fastened on her.

Damn, she thought. And damn Ranse McCandliss.

"Thank you," she told Addison.

"Well, it was just sitting there in the tack room, and I couldn't see it being wasted when there's someone who could make good use of it."

She nodded. "It's just that... " She wanted to tell him that she was leaving, but couldn't. And Ranse knew it.

"What's that?" Addison asked.

"It's very kind of you," she finally replied.

"Not at all, young lady. As I said it's a pleasure to see someone getting use out of it. If you feel up to it, we'll all ride over to Summer's ranch tomorrow for this get-together of theirs.

No one had ever given her something that obviously meant so much. True, she had everything she needed growing up, generously provided by her guardian; everything except a connection to family.

The saddle obviously held great meaning for Addison, something that connected him to his wife that he wanted her to have. Thanking him seemed so very inadequate. He couldn't possibly know what it meant to someone who never knew who her family was.

And that was the problem. How could she possibly tell him now that she was leaving without seeming ungrateful for the kindness he had shown her the past two weeks, welcoming her into his home, and now this?

The truth was that she couldn't, not yet. Not until there was something out there that she could explain, and hope that he would understand.

In the meantime, there was the annual picnic at Daniel Summers' ranch, and Elizabeth Summers would be there.

She might have been able to use the excuse that she was still recovering from the wound, but riding back from town with Ranse had pretty much eliminated that when she told him that her shoulder was much better and that Tom Travis told her that she could remove the bandages in a couple of days.

Just a few more days, she told herself as she turned and walked up the path to the house. As soon as she had the money that had been sent, she would find a way to explain that she needed to leave.

In spite of what Ranse had told her that the Morton family hadn't lived in Guthrie for a long time, she was determined to find Ginny Morton.

There was something about the woman, about the vague answers she had provided to her questions, as if she was hiding something, and had then disappeared.

She needed to go to Kingfisher where the Dalton family once had a farm.

Would she find answers there? There was only one way to find out.

HANNAH HAD STARTED EARLY in the kitchens the next day, baking pies for the picnic. Annie informed her that they were all to go over after noon. The men would be riding over and Hannah and Annie would follow with the wagon.

Laine planned to ride over with the women, but Seth had informed her early that morning that Addison had him grooming a horse selected for her to ride with the saddle he'd given her, if she felt up to it.

She didn't care to spend more time with Ranse McCandliss, but if she chose to accompany Hannah and Annie begging off with the excuse of her shoulder, then she would be expected to stay longer until she was stronger. She chose to ride over with the men, wearing a split skirt shirtwaist that she'd purchased in town.

"You look just like that woman in the Wild West show I once saw a poster for in town," Annie complimented her. "She's a sharpshooter in the show. Can you imagine that?"

She had pulled her hair back and wore it tied at the back of her neck. She liked Annie.

"I don't intend to shoot anyone," she assured her. "I'm just going to put in an appearance and then return."

"Oh, these things go on into the night. "

"It's just a picnic..."

"That's during the day, then there's the sit-down supper at night. I hear that Mr. Summers is plannin' on having music and a dance floor set up special on accounta Mr. Roosevelt's gonna be there. Do you want me to pack that pretty red gown Mr. Addison gave you? I heard they'll be leavin' soon."

She hadn't counted on an all-day affair. Her plan had been to return to the Oaks as early as possible after putting in an appearance.

"It doesn't matter," she replied.

If possible, she intended to leave long before supper and return to the Oaks. She only agreed to go out of courtesy to Addison. He had been more than kind to her.

"What about Mr. McCandliss?" she asked.

She had discovered in the short time that she'd been there that Annie knew just about everything that went on at the Oaks. Hannah was far more close-mouthed about it, but Annie had no such hesitation.

"Oh, he left for town early this mornin'. Something about the report he needed to write up after he brought that man in yesterday. I heard him tell Mr. Stanton he wasn't sure when he would be back."

That suited her just fine. It eliminated any more contact between them than absolutely necessary. All she had to do was get through the afternoon and then she would be gone.

JIM BITTERS LEANED against the back wall of the jail cell, that penetrating glare fixed on Ranse McCandliss.

Bad luck, he thought, gettin' caught by him. Anyone else and he mighta gotten away, but not McCandliss. He was persistent and stubborn. He'd heard that he'd once ridden a horse deep into the outlet, trailing another one behind. When one gave out, he'd simply cut it loose and saddled up the second horse, and kept goin.'

Stubborn, determined, and had a reputation for always gettin' his man. Now it was the Daltons. And the hell of it was, he'd once ridden with Frank Dalton, the older of the brothers.

There were all sorts of stories; some of 'em came from Grat Dalton. That sort of story usually came with a good joke about how the man he was after messed up, underestimated the man who was after 'im. Then the boastin' started along with whiskey passed around. But not when it came to McCandliss.

Relentless was another word they used.

"The man just don't stop!"

It was Bob Dalton, who told those stories more than once, staring into the fire. When others they rode with started in with the boastin' and braggin', more than once he'd seen him get up with a hard expression.

"Ye'er a damn fool. You don't ever want him comin' after you. There's only one way it will end."

"You scared of 'im?"

"I know the man. The reward don't matter. It never did. It's about what's right and what's wrong. That's all."

Now, Jim Bitters sat there, listening to the conversation in the office beyond the cells. The questions would come next, he thought, as he heard the scrape of the chair on the wood floor, then the turn of the key in the door that separated the two parts of the jail.

Relentless, the word came again, something he'd learned on that ride in the outlet, certain more than once that he and Texas Jack had lost him and that deputy.

Wrong. Now Texas Jack was dead, and that door was being pushed open.

The man had an uneasy feelin' start in the pit of his stomach. He knew what he wanted—the Daltons. He knew what would happen if he gave them up. They'd come after him... sooner or later. Especially Grat Dalton. Crazy they said, and he'd seen signs of it more than once. He just needed to keep his mouth shut, he thought, even as those words came back.

"The man just don't stop..."

12

L aine glanced at the clock that sat atop the mantel in the guest room at the Summers' ranch where she had gone to change for supper.

She had tried to leave after the picnic, having managed to avoid Elizabeth Summers most of the afternoon. The woman's one comment when escape had been impossible had been, referring to the split skirt, shirt, and boots.

"A riding costume, how charming. Will you be doing riding tricks for our entertainment later?"

But Addison refused to hear of her leaving, and as the day grew longer and evening set in, it was obvious by the amount of drinking that had taken place that it might be dangerous to set off with Seth after dark.

"There will be music and several young people from town, including that young man's sweetheart. And I want you to meet Mr. Roosevelt."

That the girl would be there pretty much decided the matter. And she did want to meet Mr. Roosevelt. Addison had introduced her as Laine Ralston, using her adopted name.

She found Mr. Roosevelt to be boisterous, charming, and

friendly, and they quickly discovered that they knew several people in common in New York through Ellie's father.

"I understand there was a bit of a to-do on your travel out here. Bad business these train robbers. I hear that you were injured. You look to be the picture of health now. No lingering effects?"

She laughed as she was finally able to get a word in. *"No lingering effects, I assure you. I'm sorry that your rail car was damaged."*

"Not anything that can't be fixed. I'm confident the Pinkertons and Marshal McCandliss have things well in hand. You know, you remind me very much of my daughter, Alice. She's only six years old, but I see that same look in her eyes that you have—spirit. That's what it is. She would make an excellent markswoman. Do you shoot, Miss Ralston?"

He was off on a long conversation about the hunting he had done in the Montana Territory.

"I keep trying to get Stanton to join me, but he is always too busy."

And she had been persuaded, rather forcefully, to stay.

"What brings you to the Territory?" he had asked.

"I'm hoping to connect with distant family," she had told him, and not far off the truth.

"What do you know about Mr. Stanton's family?" she now asked Annie as she finished helping her dress for the supper that was being given in Mr. Roosevelt's honor.

"He doesn't talk about them much. It all happened a long time ago, before I came to the Oaks. But Hannah was there then. She's told me some of it. I know that Mrs. Stanton died only a few years after the big house was built," Annie replied.

"Were there children?"

"There was a boy, born just after the house was built—John Stanton," Annie replied.

"He was killed several years back, both he and his wife. There's a picture of them in the library at the Oaks—dreadful how it all happened. But you probably know that," Annie assumed. "This gown belonged to her, but she never got the chance to wear it.

She smoothed her hands down the watered silk skirt. The color was a deep rich wine color and she wondered about the young woman it had been purchased for.

"According to Hannah, young Mr. Stanton and his wife were in New York for a few years, their first child was born there.

"They decided to return to the Oaks. There was even talk at the time that she was expecting a second child and wanted to have it born there. They were killed in an accident. From what I hear, Mr. Stanton changed a lot after that, but he's sure been different since you arrived."

"Did Mr. Stanton have any other children?"

Annie shook her head. "His wife died in childbirth with a second child. The baby only lived for a few days."

A hard land, she thought. And it took hard people to survive in it. Like the Daltons, and Ranse McCandliss.

"How did Mr. McCandliss come to live at the Oaks?" she asked.

"Mr. Curry brought him back from Fort Supply after going to pick up some horses Mr. Stanton bought. His folks were dead, he was around fifteen years old then and a real hellion according to Hannah. He went into the outlet all by himself and brought his father's body back after he was killed.

"I guess there was a need in both of them. Mr. Stanton was alone and here was this wild boy needing a home. There was a rough patch when he took off with one of the Dalton boys. Something bad happened with that but Hannah never said what it was. Only that Mr. McCandliss was changed after that.

"Mr. Stanton got him to come back, told him there was just two ways to go and gave him a choice—prison or schoolin' back East. He chose to go to school and then law school. He sure turned out to be a fine man. Mr. Stanton sets great store by him." Annie stopped long enough to give Laine a last, critical inspection.

"You look just fine," she exclaimed.

Seven o'clock in the evening. She had only to endure the next few hours.

As she descended the long, curving staircase, the glass walls of the outdoor pavilion where guests gathered caught the of sunlight from the last light of the day, creating a kaleidoscope of colors that spilled across the gleaming wood floor.

The pavilion was octagonal with steps leading off in different directions for walks in the gardens that rimmed the pavilion. A cupola overhead was supported by columns with glass paneled doors that might have been more at home in New York or out on Long Island. They stood open to the breeze from the river while on a dais at one side was a small orchestra.

"I thought maybe you had decided to return to the Oaks, dressed in your riding skirt."

It could be none other than Elizabeth Summers as she slowly turned around, a term she was rapidly learning the meaning of—ambush.

"And you have changed, an improvement. Although your gown doesn't appear to be the work of our local seamstresses."

"New York, I believe. It was a gift," Laine replied, since it seemed very likely that the gown had come from there, considering who it once belonged too.

She didn't wait for a response, with no appetite for more questions that were sure to come. "Excuse me," she politely added as she glanced across the pavilion and saw Addison in conversation with Mr. Roosevelt. She wanted to thank him. Let Elizabeth Summers think what she wanted to think.

She spotted Addison in conversation with another gentleman. He introduced him as she approached.

"You look lovely, my dear." He took hold of her hand and kissed her on the cheek.

"You do me a great honor wearing the dress."

She smiled. "Thank you."

"And no more bandages?" he pointed out.

"They didn't go with the gown."

He threw back his head and laughed

"If I were twenty years younger, I swear I would be tempted to scandalize these good folks and steal you away for myself." Addison smiled at her, making it impossible for her not to feel his light spirit.

"Well, perhaps thirty years younger," he corrected himself. "I forget just how young you are, and how old I am. But I swear it makes me feel young just to have you around."

"Are you flirting with me, Mr. Stanton?" she asked enjoying the conversation. He had that effect on her, as opposed to Ranse McCandliss.

"Just pleased to see that you're recovering nicely. I was beginning to be a little concerned. There's nothing bothering you is there? You're feeling all right?" he asked.

"Nothing that good company wouldn't cure."

He glanced in the direction where she had entered the pavilion, and the woman who stood there in conversation with another guest.

"I sense a varmint in a purple dress. Mostly harmless but let me know if she bothers you."

Varmints came in all shapes and sizes she was discovering.

"I've been told that what I need to watch out for are rattlesnakes," she replied.

Addison seemed to suddenly have difficulty with his drink, seized by a fit of coughing mixed with laughter.

"Particularly purple ones," she added.

"There's a cure for that," he managed to say as the orchestra began another piece, a waltz this time. He set his drink aside.

"Excuse us, Robert. I want to dance with this young lady." He turned to her.

"May I have the pleasure?"

She placed her hand in his and he led her out onto the dance floor. "I'm going to apologize in advance. It's been a long time since I accompanied a beautiful young woman."

She smiled. "Just follow my lead."

As she suspected, he had greatly exaggerated his lack of skill, even after all these years as he claimed.

"I needed to make an excuse in advance," he told her when she called him out for being deceptive about his ability.

"Mrs. Stanton was from Boston. She was very good at these things. I either had to acquire a few skills in order to win her or forget about her."

"And you chose to acquire those skills."

He smiled at the memory. "I still managed to step on her toes a few times, which she never let me forget."

In spite of the sadness, it was a good memory.

"You're a lot like her. Not so much the way you look. She was fair with green eyes, a strong woman to set out with a man like me." Something changed in his voice.

"I see that same strength in you."

She would miss him when she left, that gruff affection, the way a smile crinkled the corners of his eyes, his direct manner, and honesty. As he guided her around the dance floor, she wished that life had been gentler for him, without that loss so young but also sensed that it was part of the man he was now.

It was impossible not to know when Ranse finally arrived. If Addison hadn't noticed as the dance concluded, then Elizabeth's reaction made the announcement as she swept across the floor toward the three men, including Tom Travis, who had now joined the guests.

"It's about time he got here," Addison commented. "And Judge Parker."

She had known that he was supposed to be there, the

'hanging judge' as he was known. Still, she felt more than a little uneasy.

The man's reputation wasn't unwarranted. She had read about it in the newspapers back home. His determination to *'clean-up the outlaw element'* was well known. His determination to have the Daltons and others like them *'put out of business'*, as one newspaper had quoted, and made him quite famous.

"Is something wrong?" Addison asked as she held back when he would have escorted her over to greet them.

"It's just that... "

He followed the direction of her gaze that included the two men and Elizabeth Summers.

"Not a rattlesnake, just a pesky porcupine dressed in purple."

She couldn't help but laugh. *Porcupine* seemed very appropriate.

"Damn the torpedoes, full speed ahead."

"Torpedoes?"

"A quote I read once. Seems appropriate, don't you think."

She had to admit that it fit the situation. "You don't approve of Elizabeth Summers?"

"It's not for me to either approve or disapprove. Ranse is his own man." He patted her hand where it lay over his arm.

"He makes his own decisions, has since he was fifteen. I trust that and so can you."

If there was something else behind his words, she told herself that it didn't matter.

Ranse saw them as Addison walked with her to join them. One of the men at the ranch told him that she'd ridden over earlier that day.

"She rode over with Mr. Stanton. She has good hands; shoulder didn't seem to bother her none."

She wore a gown in a deep shade of red that clung to her,

the bandages gone with only dark pink skin in the shape of a star at her shoulder and her dark hair pulled back.

"It's the most amusing story," Elizabeth Summers was saying. "And then that dreadful attack of the train. We might have all been killed. Oh, and I'm certain you'll want to meet Addison's guest."

She pulled back as Elizabeth made introductions to those around them, that cool blue gaze narrowing as it met hers.

"Such an interesting story... Most amusing."

Laine suddenly found it difficult to breathe. Rattlesnake, indeed. The venom was there. The woman all but hissed, and she dreaded what came next.

"You just won't believe it," Elizabeth continued.

Elizabeth Summers had somehow discovered the truth about why she was there and the very real possibility of who her family might be. She knew what came next. Addison's hand covered hers, but she pulled away.

Ranse saw the color drain from her face as everyone nearby heard the conversation. Tom nodded as they exchanged a look.

"Come along, Elizabeth," Tom told her, taking her by the arm. "You look as if you need some refreshment. I know that I need a drink." He forcefully took her arm and pulled her away before she could say more.

Laine felt as if she was suffocating. It was only a matter of time until Elizabeth managed to tell everyone who she was and the reason she was there. She needed to leave, to get as far away from these people as possible if she was to find the truth.

"Please, excuse me," she told Addison as she turned and crossed the pavilion toward those double doors that led to the main house, ignoring the looks that followed her.

When Addison would have gone after her, Ranse stopped him. He shook his head, then went after her.

She ran down the flagstone path that led to the house. She was wrong to come there. If it hadn't meant so much to Addison, and the dress he had given her... She had only wanted to please him. She should have known better, should have refused, made any excuse...

He caught up with her at the steps into the house. "Laine..."

He pulled her into the shadows that surrounded the house.

"I need to leave," she told him trying to push him away.

Her eyes were dark and tears streaked her cheeks. But it wasn't fear he saw there. It was anger as she balled her fists and would have struck him. He pulled her against him, holding her with one arm, his other hand at her hair.

"I know," he whispered.

He had felt that same anger a long time ago; at the stares of people, at questions that he couldn't answer after that long ride deep into the Territory to find his father's body, and the hole deep inside that could never be filled up after that.

The questions were still there and would probably never have answers. The stares had gradually disappeared. But the hole was still there. Addison had tried to fill it, with kindness and strength, and he'd learned to live with the emptiness that was all he'd found on that long ride.

He brushed the tears from her cheek.

"I can't stay, I won't stay."

He nodded. "I'll take you back to the ranch."

She changed her clothes, the gown that Addison had given her left for Annie to take back to the ranch. Ranse was waiting for her at the stables.

"What about Addison?"

"Tom will let him know."

He'd saddled her horse and held him as she climbed into the saddle. Then he mounted his own horse.

A three-quarter moon lit up the night sky and the trail they followed, their horses settling into an easy gait with the warm night air and the distant yipping sound that broke the silence.

"Coyotes," he told her. "They've caught something."

Sure enough, there was silence that followed.

They rode on through that silence, the lights from the ranch coming into view in the distance.

The answers she needed weren't there at the ranch. She had to leave and they both knew it.

He unsaddled the horses and turned them into the paddock, then walked with her up to the house. Only a few lights shown through the downstairs, left on by one of the men who'd stayed behind. They let themselves in.

He went to the library, for lack of a better name for it. It was also Addison's office and a place he'd discovered that first day when he'd arrived after trying to steal from Curry just so he could buy some food and survive.

Whatever conversation passed between the two men, the next thing he knew Curry had hauled him up to the big house and into that room. He'd been angry, defiant, and scared, with no idea what Addison Stanton, one of the most powerful ranchers in those parts, intended to do to him.

"What's your name?" He had asked him, the memory coming back as if it was yesterday as he poured a drink at the side table.

"What's it to you?"

For about two seconds he thought about lying just to get the hell outta there. Curry had cuffed him in the shoulder, the memory sharp and clear.

"Show some respect, if you don't want to find yerself in jail."

He had no reason to respect Addison Stanton by his way of thinking at the time. But the man hadn't yelled or threatened. He'd simply asked the reason he tried to steal. He had puffed himself up to his five-and-a-half-foot height at the time and glared back at him.

"I was hungry!"

"Where's your family?"

"Don't have any!"

It was then Curry had spoken up and added that he was the

boy who'd gone into the outlet after that cavalry troop from Fort Supply was ambushed and butchered by a band of Comancheros that had been terrorizing outlying ranches and farms.

He was certain then that Addison would simply pack him up and take him into town. He didn't.

"*Hungry*," Addison had repeated what he told him. "*I suppose that's a better reason than most.*"

At the time, that had confused him. That didn't last long.

"*You can obviously ride.*"

In spite of himself, with growing curiosity, he had answered, "*Yes, sir.*"

"*Know anything about cattle?*"

All he knew was that the man had a helluva lot of them.

"*We're shorthanded around here,*" Addison had gone on to say. "*If you stay, you'll get all the food you can eat, and some new clothes... along with a decent pair of boots. You'll need them and you'll be expected to work for it, and there won't be any lying or stealing. If you're caught, you're gone, same as for any of the men.*"

If you stay—those words had given him the opportunity to make the decision for himself.

He carried a lot of anger and pain around with him back then, part of it being fifteen years old, the rest of it suddenly finding himself an orphan with no family, no way of surviving except what he'd been caught at.

At the time it didn't seem like a choice at all, just a way to survive. It had changed, slowly and he didn't steal or lie. He earned it the way his father had taught him, and Addison became like a father.

What did she have? A name linked to one of the most notorious outlaw gangs in the Territory, dozens of questions and no answers, an unknown past, and old secrets. And he remembered that fifteen-year-old gangly kid, not quite a man, had confronted those same questions and doubts.

Who am I? What will happen now? He downed his second drink and poured another.

She sat in one of the chairs across from the desk, her arms wrapped around her as if she was cold in spite of the warm evening.

"Drink this." He handed her a tumbler and wrapped her hands around it.

She took a swallow, inhaled sharply as it burned down her throat, then took another.

"Easy on that, it's strong. You're not used to it."

She didn't want to be careful, she wanted to forget, for just a little while.

Was he afraid that she might get drunk? She wouldn't have minded. Not that she had any experience with that, but Ellie once told her that after drinking too much champagne at one of her parent's boring supper parties, she'd been fairly intoxicated.

"There's nothing to worry about," she had explained. "Not my marks at the academy, not who my mother wants me to meet as a prospective husband, nothing. Everything just sort of goes away for a while... "

"Judge Parker will find out who I am, won't he," she said. There was no keeping it a secret now. She took another drink, wishing that everything would just go away.

"What will happen then?"

He knew that she meant Judge Parker, and she was right. Probably sooner after that conversation out at Summer's ranch. The judge was a smart man. He would have picked up on the fact that they had waylaid Elizabeth and what she would have told him.

He knew there was no avoiding that. It was only a matter of time, possibly already.

"There will be questions, won't there?" she asked. "The same questions you asked that I couldn't answer. And he won't stop."

He knew Judge Parker. The truth was that he wouldn't be satisfied with those answers. He'd vowed to see the Dalton Gang hang for their crimes, and he would use whatever was necessary to do that, including using her to get to them no matter what the truth was.

It was what everyone, including him, felt was necessary in order to clean up the crime and put outlaws away, and the damnable truth of it was that they were caught on opposite sides of it.

"No, he won't stop," he replied.

The whole truth, no half truths, no lies, no telling her how foolish she was being about all of this. Painful as it was, he was the only person she trusted to be completely honest with her.

There was only one thing she could do and they both knew it, Ranse thought. She had to leave, go back to Philadelphia. Mrs. Ralston's attorney was there and he could help her.

If she remained, there was every chance that Parker would have the sheriff take her into town for questioning. He had the power to keep her there as long as he wanted even if she didn't know anything. From there, he could only guess and there was nothing either he or Addison could do to help her.

She sat back in the chair, a thought slipping just out of reach.

Her hand shook slightly, and he saw it in the expression on her face as she took another swallow.

The whiskey was strong, it burned into her stomach. That glow that Ellie told her about was there, wrapping around everything as she emptied the tumbler. It spread through her arms and legs.

Tomorrow, she thought as her chin lowered and she nodded off, slipping into that warm glow.

Ranse set his empty glass aside then walked over to the chair where she sat, her head angled slightly to her shoulder, eyes closed, lips slightly parted. He took the empty glass from her hand and set it on the desk. Those eyes fluttered open and she mumbled something vague in protest and the thought came back to him—she had grit.

She'd needed it to get this far and reminded him of himself all those years ago; angry, determined, fighting against things he couldn't change. She protested as he slipped an arm behind her and another under her legs.

"You've had enough to drink," he told her as he lifted her in his arms.

The fight had gone out of her and she curled against him, her head tucked under his chin as he carried her from the library and up the stairs.

13

————

She wakened, her eyes slowly adjusting to the shadows in the room.

It was morning, slivers of light slipping around the edges of the drapes at the glass doors. She sat up, pushing back the bedcovers and winced at the faint headache that reminded her of the evening before: leaving the Summers ranch with Ranse after that encounter with Judge Parker, arriving back at the Oaks, and that last conversation with him...

Her gaze went to the chair that sat before those glass doors as another memory returned. Had Ranse been sitting there through the night?

The split skirt and shirtwaist that she'd worn on that ride back to the ranch lay over the foot of the bed, her boots on the floor, as another memory returned. He had undressed her!

She vaguely recalled him carrying her upstairs and placing her on the bed. Then? He had unlaced her boots and removed them, then unbuttoned the skirt.

She had been too tired—the whiskey—to protest when he then unbuttoned the shirtwaist, and...?

She was still wearing her camisole and bloomers.

Then, she remembered him pulling the cover up over her. She had protested, insisting that she wasn't tired, there was something she needed to do, something she needed to remember now as another memory returned and she touched her fingers to her lips.

He had kissed her. *"Go to sleep."*

When she closed her eyes now, she could almost feel the touch of his lips against hers, the taste of him—that combination of whiskey and something she'd glimpsed that night when...

She had wanted that again, wanted the touch of his hands, the safety that she felt with all the chaos, the fear from the storm that night that became something more... She glanced over at that chair again before those doors.

"Go to sleep. I'll be right here."

Watching over her as he'd promised?

But he couldn't protect her from Judge Parker. And he knew it. She had heard it in his voice as they talked in the library. He wanted her to leave, to go back to Philadelphia. But she couldn't.

The house was quiet as she dressed. Ranse's room across the hall was empty as was Addison's large room at the end of the hallway. Downstairs was equally quiet as she let herself out and walked down the path to the stables.

The horse Addison had picked out for her was there in the paddock, the saddle he'd given her over the top rail where Ranse had put it the night before. She stepped into the stables, drawn by the faint smell of smoke.

A small fire burned out the far end of the stables, a coffee pot hung over with a cast iron pot set on the coals. Curry looked up from where he sat at the edge of that campfire.

"I couldn't find anyone up at the house," she said.

Curry nodded as he poked at the fire. "Everyone usually camps out over at the Summers place after these get-togethers.

Mr. Addison came back early and rode out with Ranse, had some business to attend to with the herd." He frowned.

"I've got biscuits and coffee." He gestured to the pot at the fire. He squinted at her through the smoke of the campfire.

"You eat yet?"

She shook her head. "I need to go into town." She left it at that.

He nodded with that same quiet expression, a lot like Ranse's, that made her think that he understood a great deal more.

"I cook up a batch for the boys when Hannah is out. You're welcome to help yourself. It could be a while before she gets back."

"I'm not hungry." With everyone gone, she wanted to leave as soon as possible.

"Plannin' on riding in alone? You might wait until Mr. McCandliss gets back."

She shook her head. "It's not far, I know the way. There are some things I need to do."

And someone she wanted to find. There was that look again.

"All right." He pushed to his feet. "I'll saddle the gelding for you."

She thanked him when he led the gelding around to the front of the stables, then held him steady while she pulled herself into the saddle. He handed her the reins.

"Take it slow and easy now, miss. You wouldn't want to hurt that shoulder."

She thanked him again and turned the gelding toward the wagon road that led from the ranch.

In Philadelphia most businesses would have been closed on Sunday, but not here. Church services were over, people on the boardwalk or in the restaurant across from the livery stables.

Music tinkled from a piano in a nearby saloon, the doors

open as the day warmed. Wagons and carts filled the street, a reminder that with farms and ranches, every day was a workday.

She left the gelding at the livery, then walked to the newspaper office.

The editor smiled as she entered the office.

"Looking for more information about the Daltons?"

"There was another young woman the last time I was here. She told me that her name was Ginny Morton. Do you know who she is?"

He claimed that he hadn't seen her, now she saw something different in his expression. What did he know?

"You're the one staying out at the Stanton Ranch."

She was reminded again that there was little that remained a secret in small towns. She was relying on that now.

"Do you know Ginny Morton?"

He called into the back of the shop. An older man came out, wiping his hands.

"Hey, Gus, do you know anything about a Morton family that lived around here."

"There was a Hal Morton, had a place out past the river. Got himself killed in a raid by renegades. His wife tried to hold onto the place, but it was too dangerous back then. I heard somewhere that she and the two children left and were someplace up in Ohio. But I could be wrong about that."

"How old were the children?" she asked. "Was there a girl by the name of Ginny?"

"Two girls as I recall, don't remember any names. They'd both be about your age now though. There was an older boy. He use to run with the Daltons, but he got himself killed not long after the father. There was some talk that he'd thrown in with the younger boys."

"Do you remember anything else? It's important."

He shook his head. "It's been a long time, over fifteen years, and all the trouble with the Daltons. They were better off going back to family in Ohio. A lot of folks left back then."

Left and then came back? Why? The next question was, how much did Ranse know?

Gus was on his way over to the restaurant for a bite to eat. He'd been there since four o'clock in the morning setting up the press.

"Miss Jane over at the restaurant has been around a long time. She might know something about the Morton family."

She waited as he removed his gloves and apron, then grabbed what passed for a hat and walked with her down the street to the restaurant.

It was past midday. Families that had stopped in for Sunday breakfast after church were long gone, returning to their homes or driving back to the outlying farms and ranches.

"Well, if it ain't the handsomest man in town," a gray-haired woman called out from behind the counter. "And who's that with you, Gus?"

Gus waved off her comment. "This is a friend of mine," he said by way of introduction even though she had just met him.

"You still got something for a meal back there? And maybe a piece of pie." He swept off his hat as he pulled out a chair for her at a nearby table.

"I've got a couple pieces of deep-dish apple pie left."

It was a reminder that she hadn't eaten that morning.

"Bring 'em on," he said good naturedly.

The meal arrived first followed by what passed for apple pie. Instead of slices, it was two small pies in baking dishes.

Gus patted Miss Jane on the hand. "This young lady is... " He looked at her then, obviously realizing that he had no idea who she was.

Laine introduced herself as she placed a napkin in her lap, giving her first name. Better that way, she thought, to avoid questions that she couldn't answer.

"She was asking about the Mortons used to have that place out beyond the Cimarron." Gus tucked a corner of his napkin into the neck of his shirt and grabbed a fork.

"I was tellin' her that you might remember them since you've been here longer than God." He chuckled at that and received a smack on the back of his head.

"Kate Morton," she remembered, pulling a chair from an empty table and joining them.

"Real sad, losin' her husband that way, and the boy got himself on the wrong side of the law. It seemed he was just trying to take care of the family after his pa was killed, but made some bad choices. After the boy got on the wrong side, Kate and the girls left. They couldn't manage that place by themselves and it was just too dangerous, a woman out there alone with young girls. "

Gus was well into a cut of beef and potatoes. He gestured with his fork. "What was the names?"

Jane thought about it for a minute. "Lou was the older girl. The younger one was Ginny. They'd both be grown women now."

"Gus said they went to Ohio?"

"That's what I heard. They was real close with the Daltons," Jane added. "But Lord knows that Adeline Dalton had her own troubles with the three youngest boys taking off like they did, leaving her with two young girls."

"I heard that they had a farm in Kingfisher," Laine commented.

Customers had entered the restaurant, cowboys by the look of them. Jane told them to take whatever table they wanted. They brushed past and took a nearby table.

"They had that place for a while," Jane added. "The old man took off, then the boys. There was no way Adeline could run it by herself. Then, all the trouble that followed and all sorts comin' around; some of them with the law, and others," she shrugged. "Let's just say those were bad times. Some of it spilled over into town and some people got killed.

"Adeline finally picked up stakes and left too," she continued. "Last I heard, she wasn't well. But that was some time ago. She might have passed on by now."

It was disappointing, but she wasn't going to give up.

She had learned valuable information. Ginny Morton had lived near Guthrie as a child and her family had known the Daltons. It was an even smaller town then. Unless there was another young woman named Ginny Morton, it seemed that she had returned.

The question was, why? And why had she then disappeared since no one recalled seeing her?

She thanked Jane for the information and the pie. It was wonderful. When she tried to pay her, the woman's comment stopped her.

"Yer that young woman that was badly hurt during that attempted train robbery a couple weeks back. Been stayin' out at the Stanton place."

Small towns, Laine thought, where it seemed everyone knew everyone's business.

"Looks like you recovered well enough. Addison takin' good care of you? Don't worry about the pie." She pushed away from the table.

"I gotta see what those boys want and then get back to the kitchen. Won't be long and more folks will be comin' in for supper." Jane gave her a smile. "You take care of yerself. Two bits will cover the meal and pie, Gus."

He laid a quarter on the table. "I need to get back and check on the press for the morning edition."

She thanked Gus for the information and the introduction to Jane and watched as he ambled down the boardwalk to the newspaper office. She had information but she needed more.

Where had Ginny Morton gone? Was she staying in town?

She inquired at the hotel, then the boardinghouse. The answer was the same. No one by that name or description was staying at either place.

Disappointed, frustrated, with no idea what to do next, she passed the mercantile on her way back to the livery stables. Like most of the businesses in town, the mercantile was open, a woman and boy coming out the front with wrapped bundles. But she stared past them through the store to the back entrance where large doors were open, daylight showing through that showed a young woman with the owner of the store. Ginny Morton?

She crossed the street, ran up onto the boardwalk and into the store.

"Can I help you, miss?" the young clerk asked from atop the ladder where he was stocking shelves, as she ran through the store.

The owner was just closing those double doors at the back and looked up in surprise.

"The woman who was just here?" Laine asked.

He nodded. "Just loaded up her wagon..."

She pushed past him and called out as she ran out the back of the store.

Ginny Morton turned in the seat at the buckboard.

Laine stared at the kegs, a crate of canned goods, and other bundles wrapped in brown paper, and thought of Hannah's kitchen at the ranch stocked with canned goods, jars, and bins full of potatoes.

"I need to talk to you," she told Ginny as the woman reined in the team of horses. "Please, it's important."

Ginny tried to brush her off. "I need to go."

"Where?" Laine asked.

Ginny looked at her with a combination of confusion and uneasiness.

"Please," she said again. "I need to talk to you about the

Dalton family."

That caught her attention. "I know that your family knew theirs. I was told that you moved away, but now you're here. Please. I need to ask you some questions."

Ginny shook her head. "I can't."

She had begged and it obviously wasn't going to work.

"Where are you staying? Your old farm? Some place else?"

That brought a startled look.

"I gotta go."

Desperate to stop her, the only chance she might have to learn something about the Daltons, she called out as Ginny gathered up the reins and would have left.

"My name is Laine Dalton."

Ginny turned and stared at her. "That's not a wise thing to be tellin' people."

"I didn't choose it."

"You with someone in town?"

Laine shook her head. "I came in alone. My horse is at the livery."

Ginny finally nodded. "There's a stand of cottonwood trees out past the edge of town. I'll meet you there."

She was taking a chance she realized, as she ran back to the livery stable. There was every possibility that Ginny would simply keep going and disappear as she had before, and she might never find her again. She desperately hoped that she was wrong.

She found the stand of trees that Ginny had told her about. She was there, along with a man she didn't recognize. He sat astride a horse, sheltered in the trees. Ginny gave her a cautious look.

"I'm takin' a chance on you and what you said. It's dangerous enough for me to go into town."

She understood and appreciated it.

"A lot of people make claims," she continued. "They want

the attention though God knows why. What did you mean back there?"

Laine glanced to the man who sat astride a horse some distance apart. Who was he? One of the Daltons? Or a friend of Ginny's? He hadn't accompanied her into town. Obviously he didn't want to draw attention to himself, and he looked the sort that might have drawn attention in the stained pants and shirt, the hat that was pulled low, and the gun he carried.

"My name *is* Laine Dalton," she repeated. "I'm looking for my family."

She took out that stained note that had been pinned to her collar years before and handed it to her.

"A. Dalton," Ginny read the name at the bottom.

Laine nodded. "I'm trying to find Adeline Dalton."

She caught the faint movement of the rider, the way he shifted in the saddle as Ginny stared down at the note and then looked up at her.

"You're not looking for information for a story?"

"I'm trying to find information for myself. As a child I was sent to Philadelphia with that note pinned to my collar. I've been told that your family knew the Daltons. Do you know where Adeline Dalton is?"

Ginny looked up and then over at the man who kept apart.

"I might know."

"If I could just speak with her, ask her a few questions about that note, why I was sent away..."

Ginny shook her head. "I can't promise you anything." She looked back down at the smudged note with worn edges. "That's a long time ago... "

"Please."

The man who waited apart in the tree cover had grown impatient.

"Ginny... "

She shook her head at him, then asked, "Where can I get word to you?"

It had been difficult enough to track her down and she was obviously being cautious. She had to be careful here, or Ginny might simply leave and she would never see her again.

"I could meet you back here," she replied. "Tell me when."

Laine saw the hesitation. She wouldn't have been surprised if Ginny simply refused to help her.

Ginny looked down at the note again. "Can I keep this?"

Now it was her turn to hesitate. It was her only link to the past, that and the crystal that had been in her pocket when she arrived in Philadelphia; a sparkly object that she refused to part with according to her guardian.

She nodded. "When can we meet again?" Her thoughts churned.

Would Ginny send a telegram? Or was it possible that she wanted to talk to someone else about it first? And then, what?

It's all she had to go on.

"Meet me back here, tomorrow afternoon."

There was no good-bye. Ginny didn't wait for an answer, she simply picked up those reins and drove off.

The man who'd waited in the shadows didn't immediately follow, but held back for some reason, watching her. Waiting to make sure she didn't follow?

He continued to wait and watch her as the buckboard disappeared around a bend in the road.

Uneasy, Laine turned the gelding around toward town. When she looked back, he too was gone.

Was she a fool to trust someone she'd just met? Would Ginny meet her the following day? Or was it just a ploy to get rid of her?

It made sense with that wagonload of food, she must be staying somewhere nearby. Her family's old farm? Or with the man she'd seen?

Tomorrow was a long ways away.

"THINGS GOT interesting after you left yesterday evening." Addison angled his horse around a group of cattle that had wandered from the herd during the night.

A half dozen of the men had returned with him that morning, then set out to move the herd, pushing them to better grazing. Ranse had gone with them.

The wild grass down by the river was better grazing with the early summer grass already grazed off where the herd had been earlier. It was the same every year, following where there was forage, then bring them in closer for the winter.

"Elizabeth had her wind up; she made certain just about everyone got an earful about Laine."

Ranse could imagine that earful had included what happened in Washington DC, and Laine's deception about being his *wife*.

"Seems she also found out that Laine's last name isn't Ralston." They exchanged a look. Daniel Summers might have had something to do with that," Addison continued. "He knows a lot of people, and we both know that he's got plans for you."

Ranse nodded. "I make my own way."

"I know," Addison replied. "Be careful. Like I said, he knows a lot of powerful people and he'd like to see you married to his daughter."

Powerful people who wanted to control whoever was governor once the Territory achieved statehood.

"That could be important for the future," Addison added.

Ranse shook his head. "Daniel Summers doesn't have anything I want."

They rode on a ways, going after the occasional stray that

darted away from the main body of the herd, cutting them back in.

"I like that young lady," Addison said, staring out over the herd. "She's got fire in her; doesn't much matter what her name is."

Grit, Ranse thought; stubborn, strong, and she had grit. He couldn't think of many others who had gone through what she had, far from anyone she knew, coming out to a place she knew nothing about, going through the attack on the train coming out, being shot. Grit and courage.

A whistle from one of the other men finally caught their attention. The man gestured to a rider approaching south of them from the direction of the ranch. Ranse recognized that paint horse as Curry rode hard toward them. He reined in as he reached them.

"Glad I caught up with you. One of the sheriff's men rode in. There's been some trouble over at Mr. Summers' place."

"What kind of trouble?" Addison asked.

"Seems with all the folks out there yesterday, people comin' and goin', there was some things stolen."

"What sort of things?" Ranse asked.

"Jewelry, some of it pretty valuable, and some cash," Curry replied. "The sheriff wants to talk to Miss Laine."

"What reason would the sheriff have to want to speak with her?" Ranse demanded.

"Seems Miss Summers told him that she came upon Miss Laine in her room last night. She also told him that she has been hiding who she really is."

Ranse and Addison exchanged another look.

"Where is the sheriff now?" Ranse asked.

"Still out at the Summers' place. I didn't tell the deputy that Miss Laine wasn't at the Oaks."

"Where is she?" Ranse demanded.

"She had me saddle up the gelding you gave her to ride, Mr. Stanton. She rode off not long after you left."

Ranse cursed. "Which direction?"

"Looked like she was headed for town and didn't come back by the time I left to come tell you." There was more.

"The sheriff wants to talk to her. Seems Miss Summers wants to press charges."

Powerful people, playing their games. "The men and I can handle the herd," Addison told him.

Ranse nodded as he turned his horse toward town. He needed to get to her before the sheriff or one of his deputies.

14

"She did it!" Elizabeth Summers accused in front of everyone. "And her name is Dalton, something she tried to hide from everyone! I want her arrested!" She was furious, the skirts of her gown fairly crackling as she paced back and forth across the large room at the Oaks.

"That's a lie," Laine replied, looking at the expressions of those that had gathered there—the sheriff, Daniel Summers, his daughter, Ranse, and Addison.

What did she see in Addison's expression? Doubt? Disappointment?

She had no idea why it hurt so much. She'd only been there a couple of weeks, but it was there, after his generosity and kindness. And all she could do was deny the accusations.

Judge Parker sat in one of Addison's large chairs, watching her much like a cat ready to pounce on a mouse. He had vowed to see all the Daltons hang or put in prison. Her stomach tightened.

And Ranse. What was he thinking?

He had caught up with her on the road into town as she returned to the ranch. She had argued with herself that she should tell him about meeting Ginny Morton. At the same time, she wondered if he knew Ginny was nearby all along.

She didn't want to risk her meeting the next day with Ginny, and had simply explained that she had gone to check on the funds she was expecting at the Western Union office. Looking at him now she saw that same closed expression of Marshal Ranse McCandliss.

What would he say? Would he tell the judge that he'd gone to Philadelphia searching for someone who might very well be part of the Dalton family, hoping to learn something about the brothers?

She had seen that same expression on his face in Philadelphia and again in Washington, a look that said it was all business—his official duty. She didn't expect him to understand now anymore than he had then, and what had happened between them... done, over, best forgotten.

The only thing that mattered was that she meet Ginny Morton the next day. It was the only way to find answers to questions she'd had her whole life. Who was she? What had happened to her family? Why was she sent to Philadelphia?

That she should have been grateful that she hadn't ended like so many orphans she heard about that were sent back on those 'orphan trains', who often ended up in workhouses, or on the streets.

Yes, she'd been fortunate in that regard. Her guardian, Althea Ralston, had provided a home and education for her and a handful of others. Philanthropist the city fathers had called her with her efforts to help those less fortunate.

She was deeply grateful, but it didn't fill the hole deep inside that should have been filled with connections to family, no matter what the truth was. Good or bad, at least she would know who she was. Althea Ralston understood and never begrudged the endless questions she had asked as a small child.

"Where's my mother? Who is my father? Where are they?"

The simplest answer that a child might understand, was that they were *'gone'*. As she grew older, she assumed that meant that they were dead. Then, with the help of friends— Ellie and her family, she needed to look toward the future. What would she do after she left the academy.

Teach? Become a governess to one of the families that Mrs. Ralston knew? Marry and have a family of her own?

But always there was that question—who was she, that ruled out marriage into one of the mainline families. They were not inclined to welcome an orphan with no proper family connection, or 'heaven forbid', someone who might not be up to their standards.

She had learned not to care what they thought, and more and more had considered leaving Philadelphia to find a position someplace elsewhere where the label—orphan, didn't follow her.

She had to admit that the Oklahoma Territory wasn't exactly what she had planned, but after that fateful meeting in the headmistress' office she had no other choice. She had to take a chance that she might finally learn something about her family, no matter what that was. Now she was faced with the possibility that her name—Dalton, might be more than a little dangerous.

"I had nothing to do with the stolen jewelry," she repeated, needing them to believe her.

They had no sooner returned to the ranch that afternoon than the sheriff had arrived, along with Judge Parker, and it seemed that she'd already been condemned. Elizabeth and her father had followed, along with the accusations and no way to defend herself other than with the truth.

"I had nothing to do with this! You have to believe me!"

"You were in the house," Elizabeth accused her. "You were in my room!"

"There were several people there, coming and going all day," Laine replied. "I changed clothes in your room, but I didn't take anything."

"Blood tells," Elizabeth fired back. "She was there last night! I saw her."

"You didn't see anything."

Several pairs of eyes fastened on Ranse McCandliss.

"You couldn't have seen anything, because she was with me all night."

Elizabeth whirled around, her expression pinched with a frown. She crossed the room to where he was standing and laid her hands on the front of his shirt.

"What are you saying, darling? You know that's not true... For God's sake, Ranse! Tell them the truth. She's a thief, she should be arrested."

He took hold of her wrists and gently set her from him.

"I just did."

"You're just saying that... you're trying to protect her. I don't understand why..." Elizabeth protested.

"We left early. She was with me all night here at the ranch."

Laine felt Addison's gaze on her. "Both their horses were in their stalls this morning when we rode out."

"It seems we have different stories here," the sheriff finally commented. He looked over at Ranse. "It is just your word against Miss Summers'. She could easily have come back here later. We have only your word that it was early in the evening and that she was with you all night."

"That's right," Ranse told him. "You have my word."

Judge Parker frowned. "Do you want to press charges, Daniel?" he asked Summers.

"Of course, we're going to press charges," Elizabeth whirled round, shaking with anger.

"You've got nothing to hold her on," Ranse replied. His voice was quiet, sure of himself at the same time he knew that he was walking a thin line. Things were different here where law and order was dealt with a heavy hand.

It had to be, in a place where the outlaws and thieves often outnumbered the farmers or citizens in town, along with those meant to keep that law and order. Too often the local sheriff had a questionable background.

Several names came to mind, along with them Wyatt and Virgil Earp over in Tombstone. They ran the local gambling hall that dealt in bootleg whiskey, table games, and women at the same time they wore badges. A long time ago, he might have taken that same path with Frank Dalton, but life had dealt him a different hand that had started with the death card—the loss of his father and that trip into the outlet.

Then a different card—the ace of diamonds, if someone was trying to find some meaning in all of it. That ace of diamonds was Addison Stanton, who saw somethin in him that nobody else saw. When he might have walked away from that out of sheer bullheadedness, Addison had been there with a choice—jail or and education that might provide a future. He'd made a choice then that had included law school where with that same bull headedness and determination, he'd succeeded. He made another choice now that put him up against the judge.

He threw down that gambling hand. He knew the law.

"You've got no witnesses that actually saw her take anything. You've got my word that she was with me. You've got nothing legal to hold her on."

Hesitant, uncertain, the sheriff looked over at the judge.

"Think what you're doing," Daniel Summers told Ranse. "You're throwing away your chances, throwing your career away, for this... throwing your career away? For someone who is a criminal?" He made a gesture in Laine's direction.

"Think what you're doing, what you're saying!"

"I just did."

Summers turned to Judge Parker. "Her name is Dalton! What are you going to do about it?"

"That's enough!" Addison told him. "We've known each other a long time, but this is my house. Ranse has told you what happened. I believe him. That's all that needs to be said!"

She watched as Judge Parker slowly stood. Ranse had explained everything on that ride back to the ranch. The judge had the power, if he chose, to have her detained if he chose until the matter of the stolen jewelry was solved, which might never happen. It was the nature of thieves to disappear after they'd stolen to keep themselves out of jail. Now, he had taken a stand against both the sheriff and the judge.

"I want a written statement from you," Judge Parker finally said, that gaze that had no doubt stared down the worst criminals boring into Ranse.

"And you'll take full responsibility for her while the sheriff investigates this further."

"Now, wait just a minute..." Daniel Summers started to protest.

Judge Parker held up a hand. He looked over at Addison. "You'll take responsibility for keeping her here?"

Addison and Ranse exchanged a look. Addison nodded. The judge looked over at her.

"You're to be confined to the ranch until this is straightened out. Is that understood?"

Confined to the ranch? That single word had her coming out of her chair. How was that different from being arrested... for something she hadn't done. She looked over at Ranse.

He had spoken on her behalf, sounding very much like a lawyer in a situation that had spun out of control with Elizabeth's lies. But what would happen now when she had just discovered someone who might be able to help her find answers to those questions that had haunted her entire life? What would happen if she failed to meet Ginny tomorrow?

Afterward, with no other choice but to agree, Elizabeth had paused, telling Ranse that they needed to talk, that he couldn't just throw away everything between them. Her father had simply shaken his head.

"A shame. You had such a bright future."

As for the judge, he had parted with a final comment, accepting Addison's offer of the ranch carriage to return to town.

"I'll give you that argument. But when a witness is found, are you prepared to defend her in court? To throw away your legal career?"

It was a warning that Judge Parker had accepted Ranse's original argument, but wasn't convinced that she was innocent.

She needed air, even the smothering heat of the afternoon, as she left the house and went to the stables after they had all left. It was only after she was there that she wondered if the stables were included in her 'confinement', or if she had just broken the judge's instructions.

The gelding had been turned out into the paddock beside the stables, along with Ranse's horse. He walked over, neck outstretched, catching her scent. She rubbed his neck, inhaling that scent that she'd discovered—a mixture of sweat, hay, and heat at that coat that gleamed under the afternoon sun.

Ranse's horse had wandered over and joined them, one on either side of her, competing for attention and strokes at their muzzles the way Mr. Curry had showed her. The ears of both horses suddenly perked up. She heard it then, the faint crunch under boots as someone approached.

"One step and you could get crushed between them."

Ranse McCandliss, she thought. Protector as he had once promised? Or her jailer now?

She didn't turn around, but continued to stroke those velvet muzzles, first one then the other even as she struggled with what had taken place up at the house, almost like a trial. She

had been on trial, Elizabeth's accusations ringing in her ears—
that she was a Dalton and that was all that was needed. Painted
with the same brush, convicted before there was even a trial?

Was she a Dalton?

There was only one way to find out, and that had just been
taken from her.

Confined to the ranch. When he would have said something, she shook her head. She should be grateful that he had
spoken on her behalf.

"I'm sorry," he told her, watching her. "I'm sorry that I had to
tell them that you were with me last night." He knew what that
might mean for someone like her, with her upbringing, for any
young woman.

It wasn't what she expected and caught her off guard.

"What will happen now?" she asked, smoothing the gelding's forelock, gently stroking around an eye that closed with
obvious pleasure.

"The sheriff will question all the guests."

Looking for a witness, she thought. Determined to find one,
and with Daniel Summers' influence, would they find one
willing to lie that they had seen her take the jewelry in
exchange for... what? Political favor? The same political favor
that Daniel Summers and his daughter had hoped to influence
Ranse McCandliss? And then?

This, she thought, was what the Dalton family had faced—
suspicion, accusations, even possible imprisonment because
what the older boys had done.

It was no wonder Ginny Morton had been reluctant to
speak with her and had constantly watched over her shoulder.

She hadn't told him of meeting with Ginny. Now it seemed
that she had no choice, if she was to be able to keep that
meeting away from the ranch, and against Judge Parker's
orders. She couldn't let the chance slip away, the only chance
she might ever have.

"I found Ginny Morton when I was in town." She waited. He didn't immediately reply and she thought he might not have heard. She turned and looked at him, that dark gaze meeting hers, a frown at his mouth.

"She was picking up supplies at the mercantile."

That dark gaze narrowed on her. "Where is she staying?"

"I don't know, but she agreed to help me meet with Adeline Dalton." She left the corral then.

"I'm going to meet her again tomorrow afternoon outside of town." She wasn't asking for permission.

"And risk getting yourself arrested?"

"Did you know that she was here all along?"

He heard the emotion in her voice, the anger that flashed in those blue eyes. He shook his head.

"No. I didn't know. Did she tell you where she's staying?" If Ginny had agreed to help her, then that had to mean that Adeline was there too. Unless it was an excuse to get rid of Laine.

Ginny had learned to be careful in the past. She had to protect herself and Adeline and the girls. She had been the one to move them out of Guthrie almost five years ago. Supposedly Adeline and the girls had gone to live with her sister. After that he lost track of Ginny and had no way of knowing where she'd gone.

Why would she come back with Adeline and the girls now?

"You can't break the judge's orders and go out there tomorrow. I know Judge Parker. The only reason he agreed to the confinement was because of his friendship with Addison, and ... "

She cut him off. "And he expects you to enforce it."

He nodded. "If he hears that you've broken the order, he'll have you arrested and there's nothing I can do to help you."

Her entire life had been upended because of a name. With

the anger, came the frustration at all the unanswered questions that came with it.

"I'm going to meet her tomorrow," she repeated, shaking with anger. "It may be the only chance I'll ever have to know the truth about who I am. You owe me that much!"

Ranse swore. He saw it in the expression on her face, and angry tears in her eyes. Stubborn, determined. Grit. She knew the risk and she was willing to take it. And she was right, he did owe her this, to allow her to go there to find out what she could.

If he had never gone to Philadelphia following that trail of money deposited into that bank account, the Dalton name on the bank records, she wouldn't be here. She would probably never know the truth, but she wouldn't be risking arrest. She wouldn't have been caught in the middle of a train robbery and shot. He swore again.

"I won't let you go alone."

He intended to go with her? That could ruin everything.

"If Ginny sees you... " she started to protest.

"No," he cut off her objection. "I'm going with you. It's the only way."

He didn't tell her how dangerous it could be, that the risk of Judge Parker finding out could be the least of the risk. The Ginny Morton he remembered was smarter than to let anyone get to close if she was alone. She'd had to be, keeping the Dalton family secrets. If she was here, there was a reason, and likely there was someone with her.

"What will you tell Addison?" she asked.

"Do you care?" he snapped, letting the anger loose. She was being a fool, but he already knew there was no talking her out of it, short of tying her up.

"You know that I do."

"Then you might think what this would mean for him, the trouble it could put him in."

He was being deliberately cruel. She *was* thinking of Addison. Once she found out what she could, she had no intention of returning to the Oaks and bringing more problems down on him. If she wasn't there, then no one not even Judge Parker would be able to hold him responsible. Just how she would do that, she wasn't certain. But she would do it.

I am thinking about him. She didn't say it as she pushed past him and returned to the house.

She had no appetite at supper and excused herself, ignoring Addison's look of concern. Ranse hadn't joined them, but had ridden out in the direction of town, and she worried about that all evening.

It was near midnight when he returned according to the clock on the mantel in her room, the sound of his boots muffled on the carpet in the hallway. Not that he had wakened her. She wasn't able to sleep, dozing, then waking, pacing the shadows in the room.

It was the heat, she told herself, clinging to her skin, that scent from the hillside filling the room, the hours seeming to drag by. She had no idea when she finally slept, only that her head ached and clouds were outlined by gray as the sun slowly appeared.

Hannah had returned to the ranch the day before along with the rest of the ranch hands, and Annie. She had breakfast set on the sideboard in the dining room. The candles had been lit in the chandelier overhead against the dark gloom of the day and she was just raising it over the table.

She still had no appetite, pouring herself a cup of coffee.

"Mr. Stanton rode out earlier," she said by way of conversation. "He was headed over to the Summers place."

"Ranse came down earlier and he's out with Mr. Curry, working one of those young colts he wants to get under saddle.

Both out of the house, Laine thought. It was just as well. She had no idea what she would have said to either one of them.

"You keep frowning like that, your face is likely to freeze in place," Hannah told her.

She looked up from her coffee. "It's just a headache," she made the excuse.

"It happens sometimes when we get weather comin' in." She angled her head toward the glass doors.

"There's a storm sittin' out there, probably hit sometime tonight. Let me know if I can get you something to eat. I'll be in the kitchen." She gave her a long look.

How much did she know about what had happened the day before? That look said a great deal, and as she'd already discovered there was little that went on at the Oaks that the woman didn't know, either by gossip, talk among the men, or from Addison.

"Things have a way of working themselves out," she said now. "You need to trust the people who care about you."

After she had gone, Laine went to those glass doors. The clouds were dark where they hung in the sky in the distance, a warm wind sweeping across that distant hillside, the lupine that remained a purple wave beneath a purple sky. At the stables, she saw Ranse at the paddock, the colt on a long line as he sent it first one direction then the other.

She helped Hannah with the midday meal in the kitchen, needing to keep busy until the time came to leave to meet Ginny. She felt as if she was all thumbs until Hannah gave her instructions to set the table for Addison and any of the men who might come in. That, at least, she could do.

When she glanced toward the stables again, the colt was in the paddock but Ranse was nowhere around. And a thought occurred to her that he might have changed his mind or the possibility that he had no intention of allowing her to leave in spite of what he'd told her.

The men started to come in through the service porch to

the smaller dining room off the kitchen. Ranse wasn't with them.

Trust the people who cared about her...?

Had he lied to her? Did he have no intention of allowing her to leave the ranch?

She ran upstairs, to get the hat Hannah had given her, the gloves Mr. Curry had given her when she took one of the horses out for a ride—*"You'll have blisters soon enough if you don't wear these,"* and the small carpetbag.

With most of the men in the house, she would have to saddle the gelding herself. She returned downstairs, glanced toward the kitchen where the men had gathered, then slipped out the door and ran down the foot path to the stables.

Ginny had said to meet her at the same time and place that day. It was the only chance she might have to find the answers about her past, and she was determined to keep that meeting even if it meant that she might get caught.

"You sure this is the way you want to play this?" Curry asked. "You're putting a lot on the line. You don't know what you'll find out there."

Ranse nodded as he led the gelding out of the stall. "I'm sure."

"You're the boss."

They both looked up as Laine ran into the stables then suddenly stopped.

"I thought ... "

He knew what she would have said, that she thought he'd decided against taking her to meet Ginny Morton. And she was determined to leave along if necessary. He saw it in the gloves in her hand and the small bag she carried over one shoulder.

Ranse walked past her, leading the gelding. His own horse was already saddled and tied at the rail at the far end of the stables where it was less likely they might be seen leaving. She exchanged a look with Mr. Curry.

He tipped his hat with the usual greeting, but that crisp blue gaze that seemed to see everything didn't quite meet hers as he walked past and seized a set of reins from the hook outside one of the other stalls.

She followed Ranse out the opposite end of the stables. She knew he was taking an enormous risk allowing her to leave the ranch. He was disobeying direct instructions from Judge Parker. With the reputation the man had, what were the consequences Ranse might be facing if it was discovered that he'd not only allowed her to leave, but had helped her leave?

She realized she had misjudged him as she reached the end of the stables where he made the final check of the saddle rigging.

"I thought... "

He cut her off. "Best get going."

He knew what she thought, he saw it in her expression when she entered the stables; that he had decided against letting her go to meet Ginny. If Ginny would even be there.

He knew the Daltons, and he knew Ginny Morton even though it had been at least five years since he'd heard anything about her or the family. Now, to learn that she was back? Who was with her? Had Adeline returned after all the years, the heartache, the danger?

The family had been driven out of Guthrie because of the boys and what they'd done over the years, leaving Adeline and the girls to work the farm. And then they too were gone, up north he'd heard, to live with Adeline's sister.

What had brought her back, if she was here at all? And what about the young woman who was determined to have this meeting? What would she find?

She was chasing after something that was almost twenty years old—the past, looking for answers. He knew as well as anyone that there often were no answers, just more questions. He'd lived it, a long time ago.

He hadn't found any answers out there, only his father's body and more questions about the man he had barely known, being uprooted and following him to one post after the other, his mother's death when his father was gone, left to strangers, making his own way. Then that last post to the Territory, trying to keep settlers, farmers, towns safe.

There was no safe place. Only a handful of men had returned that last time. His father wasn't among them. The stories he heard whispered among the soldiers after their reports were made, and that long ride alone, for what.

He didn't know at the time, only that he had to go. *"Let it go, boy,"* the chaplain at the post had gently said at the time after attempting to prevent him leaving. But he had to go.

Maybe that was his way of letting go, he thought now. He had to go, even if it meant that he might not come back. Just as she had to go now. He saw it in the look at her face, she would have gone without him.

He gave her a leg up into the saddle. That look was still there, along with something else.

"Thank you," Laine told him. He didn't respond. The disapproval was there, but he said nothing.

He handed her the reins then went to his own horse. Once astride, he removed the badge he usually wore, tucked it into his vest pocket, then rode past her.

The clouds she'd seen earlier were bunched in the sky, ominous, waiting, almost like a warning, and Laine shivered in spite of the heat as they rode in silence, almost as ominous as the sky.

They left the ranch, followed the road, then cut away from it and from town, eventually circling back, avoiding anyone who would be on that road and might see them.

What would she find? Would Ginny even be there?

15

Ranse saw the horses first, partially hidden in the stand of cottonwood trees. There were two riders, that familiar instinctive warning that had saved him more than once tightening at the back of his neck.

Ginny Morton was there, and the man beside her, a familiar face in spite of the heavy growth of beard and the hat that was worn low—Bill Newcomb.

He pulled up a short distance apart, reins in his left hand, his right hand free as Laine pulled up beside him.

There was recognition in the expression at Ginny's face, then from Newcomb and a tight-lipped nod, his rifle carried across the front of his saddle. Cautious, and every reason to be for a wanted man.

"Ranse... didn't expect you," Ginny said.

"It's been a while," he replied, then nodded to man beside her. "Newcomb."

"You were supposed to come alone," Ginny reminded her, her voice tight.

Laine saw her opportunity slipping away. But before she

could find something to say, Ranse provided the only reason there was.

"It's too dangerous," he replied with a glance over at Newcomb. "With the Dalton name, you should know that better than anyone, Ginny."

"Are you planning on arresting us?" Ginny's voice was cautious.

Ranse shook his head. There was a lot of history with the family, but not Newcomb. He was a small time criminal, who'd ridden with the Daltons brothers from time to time, like a parasite feeding at the fringe of the brothers' crimes, one of the hangers-on. But arresting him today served no purpose.

"I'm not here in an official capacity. I only came along for the ride."

"Well, that's good, McCandliss. Real good, or else I might have been tempted to kill you," Newcomb replied, his hand still resting on that rifle.

"Not today," Ranse replied.

The silence was as thick as the clouds that gathered overhead as Ginny finally nodded.

"I want your guns, McCandliss," Newcomb demanded. "Hand 'em over."

Laine glanced over at him. Would he give the man his guns?

They were a part of him, she'd never seen him without them, except at the Oaks or the Summers' ranch, set aside along with the other men's weapons on that long table at the barn. It was a reminder of this place, a frontier that was still wild and dangerous, as dangerous as the man who demanded that he surrender his guns.

"And you'll stay right here, McCandliss," Newcomb added. "Right where I can keep an eye on you."

The air seemed to crackle between them like the storm that hovered overhead.

"She doesn't go in alone," Ranse replied. "And as I recall that you have a habit of shooting unarmed men in the back."

Laine glanced over at Newcomb. What would he do? Would her hopes to meet with Adeline end here? It was Ginny who ended the confrontation.

"I want your word, Ranse, that you won't make a move against anyone. Or you can turn around and leave. You too," she looked over at Laine.

He didn't like it, but he agreed. He sure as hell didn't trust Newcomb, but he trusted Ginny. He looked over at Laine. She had said it—he owed her this much.

"You have my word."

Laine saw the look that passed between them. Whatever his history was with the Dalton family, it was enough.

Ginny nodded. She didn't ask for his guns as Newcomb had. She swung her horse around.

"Follow me."

They rode through the stand of trees, then through a field thick with lupine and other tall grass. They turned east, away from the town.

She had no idea where they were going as they passed a run-down farm, followed an almost invisible wagon path through thick grass, then reached the river and crossed through water that swirled around the horses' bellies, then north, where those storm clouds crowded over flat, empty countryside.

They might have ridden right past the rundown farmhouse, much like two others they'd passed, except for the buckboard wagon at the back, and horses in a side corral, with broken wooden crosses in a side yard. It looked abandoned, the front porch sagging.

"I'll go in first," Ginny announced.

Laine followed, easing her horse down the slope to the yard below. As they approached closer, she saw that flowers lay at the base of the crosses.

She stepped down from the gelding as Ranse and Newcomb followed. Another young woman stepped beside the front door as Ginny climbed the steps. Nothing was said as Ginny then entered the house and the young woman stood to the side, holding the door open.

Laine hesitated. This is where the past weeks had brought her.

What would she find inside? Answers after all these years? She felt Ranse's hand at her arm, oddly reassuring since he had first refused to let her come there. She stepped inside the small front room of the rundown farmhouse

The room was steeped in shadows, the only light coming through badly stained windows. But she was able to see a young woman who had opened the door for them, Ginny as she took off her hat and laid it on a table, and another young woman who stood beside a rocking chair that sat before the windows. The only sound was the faint creak of the chair as it slowly rocked back and forth.

The two younger women stood together, staring at her, their expressions both curious and cautious. They both wore faded gingham dresses of a style Laine had seen in town, with scuffed boots, the toes just visible at the edge of their skirts. They resembled one another and might have been near her age or slightly younger.

"Annie and Eva," Ginny said by way of introduction. "This is Laine, the woman I told you about."

They nodded, then glanced past her.

"Uncle Ranse?"

"Hello, girls," he replied. "It's been a long time. You're all grown up."

Confused, they looked over at Ginny.

"It's all right," she assured them, then crossed the small room and laid a hand at the shoulder of the woman who sat in that chair, still rocking, rocking, back and forth.

"This is Adeline," Ginny made the introduction.

There was no response, no turning of the head from the woman who sat there, only that steady rocking back and forth.

Laine removed her gloves and slowly crossed the room. This is where the past had brought her, a moment she had thought she would never have. She reached out, not even certain what to say now that the moment was here.

"My name is Laine," she finally decided, looking for any sign that name meant anything to the woman who sat there, thin, almost shrunken into herself, her face careworn, hands thick with veins.

"I've come a long way to meet you," she added.

Whatever she could have expected or hoped for, there was nothing, no response, not even a flicker that Adeline Dalton had even heard her.

"It happened two months ago," Ginny explained. "The doctor over in Stillwater said it was a stroke. She was in bed for a while, then seemed to get better. She wanted to come back here where her babies are."

Laine realized what that meant—the wooden crosses she saw in the side yard, babies that hadn't lived. And that other larger cross? Her husband?

"Three weeks ago, was the worst of it, another stroke," Ginny continued. "Afterward, she couldn't speak, didn't seem to recognize anyone. Just sat, staring, like you see her now. It's all I could do to get her to take some food.

"The girls and I brought her back here like she wanted, hopin' it might make a difference, might bring her around, a familiar place and all."

What did she see in that faraway gaze? Laine thought. Memories that only Adeline could see, those small graves where her babies were buried, these walls where she had tried to raise a family, the hardship that her older boys had brought down on the family?

"You sent a note pinned to my dress," she told her. "Your name was on the note, a long time ago. Do you remember?" Laine looked for a sign, some reaction, but there was nothing. She felt Ranse's hand at her shoulder.

"You tried," he gently told her. "That's all you could do."

It was as if time had stood still, as if all the years in between had never happened, and he hadn't taken a different path at the faint flicker of recognition at Adeline Dalton's eyes and for a moment that faraway look changed.

She tried to mouth something. It was only a whisper, but Laine heard it as Adeline whispered his name.

"I'm here," he told her, bending over and taking her hand.

The reaction from the girls was as surprised as her own as Laine stared at Adeline Dalton.

Her speech was slurred. There were only a few words, but for just that moment, she was there trying to lift her other hand. Ranse took it in his hand.

"It's been a long time," he told her. "This is Laine. She's come to see you."

Again, there was that faint reaction as Adeline tried to lift her hand. Then it was gone.

"That's the most I've seen out of her since that last stroke," Ginny said.

But what did it mean, Laine thought? Adeline had reacted to Ranse's voice. She had whispered his name. The rest of it? There was no way to know if it meant anything.

She tried once more, telling Adeline everything she knew, including the name of the woman she had traveled with to Philadelphia as a child. But there was nothing, no reaction at all. Eventually those sad eyes closed and she seemed to doze.

"Come on," Ranse said gently. "We need to go."

"Hold it, right there," Newcomb told them, his revolver pointed at Ranse. "You didn't think you were gonna just walk in here, pretty as you please, and then leave?"

When Ginny tried to protest, he told her to be quiet.

"Now that you been here, how do I know you won't bring the sheriff and deputies down on us? Not to mention them damned Pinkertons."

"You have my word."

"Yer word? Just like what happened to Frank? He gave his word. You think I don't know about that? Take it off," he gestured to the revolver in the holster in Ranse's belt.

"That was a long time ago, before your time. You weren't there. Frank shouldn't have gone for his gun."

"That's not what Bob said."

"Like I said, that was a long time ago, and Bob wouldn't know because he wasn't there either."

"Not good enough. Take it off and drop it to the floor."

Laine stared at Ranse. What would he do?

"All right, but put the gun down. You don't want to hurt the girls." He slowly unbuckled his belt and let it slide to the floor.

Laine thought of the attack on the train. Everything had happened in a matter of seconds. No one had been killed, but this was different.

She didn't know anything about Newcomb except what she'd seen that day, but it was enough to make her realize how dangerous he was. How did Ginny know him? Was he part of the Dalton Gang? What would happen now?

"You," he pointed his gun at her. "Come over here. You're gonna be my guarantee that he don't follow me."

She exchanged a look with Ranse, then glanced at the girls. She slowly crossed the room toward Newcomb. He grabbed her by the arm and she winced as pain shot through her shoulder. Newcomb waved the barrel of the revolver at Ranse.

"Get over there with them," he motioned toward the two girls.

"Don't be a fool... " Ginny started to tell him. He swung the revolver toward her.

"You get over there too."

He still had a hold of Laine's arm as he slowly backed toward the door, taking her with him.

Laine felt the barrel of the revolver pressed against the back of her head, the threat very real. When Ranse would have taken a step toward them, Newcomb pressed the tip of the barrel harder against her head.

She closed her eyes. The wound at her shoulder had been painful, something she'd never experienced before. Would this be the same? Would she even feel it if he pulled the trigger? Or would it simply be all over?

"Please don't hurt anyone." Was that her voice? Where did that come from? As she thought of those broken wooden crosses in that side yard and the feeble woman in that chair.

She opened her eyes to keep herself from stumbling as she was pulled backwards, and her gaze met Ranse's. He was the same, the angles at his face the same, the shadow of the beard, his mouth tight, that dark gaze the same—as on the train when he had found her and told her to hold on.

Did he say it again or did she only imagine it as Newcomb dragged her out the door of the farmhouse?

"Get on your horse," he ordered.

Shaking, her shoulder throbbing, she managed to pull herself into the saddle. Newcomb was already astride his horse. He leaned over and seized her reins.

"If you follow, I'll kill her!" he told Ranse.

Ranse grabbed his holster as they rode off. He could have taken the shot, but with her horse trailing behind Newcomb's he took the chance that he might hit her. He swore as he ran to his horse. Ginny had followed him from the house.

"Where would he go? Tell me."

She was clearly torn what to tell him.

"Coffeyville... " she finally whispered through her tears. "He's supposed to join the boys in Coffeyville."

Kansas. What the hell were they doing in Kansas?

"What's in Coffeyville?"

Again, she was torn what to tell him. She finally broke down.

"A job. That's all I know. "Ranse...?"

It was there in Ginny's eyes as she ran toward his horse, the pain, the agony of living with secrets, the secrets of a wife who had watched the man she loved ride out too many times, not knowing if he would come back—Bob Dalton. And now the choice she was forced to make so that someone else wouldn't die.

"I'm sorry, Ginny." He swung his horse about, regret sharp.

It was his fault this had happened. Against his better judgment, he'd allowed Laine to keep the meeting with Ginny. And for nothing, nothing that Adeline could remember. But if he hadn't?

'You owe me this.'

He had been willing to give her that much, the chance to find out what that note meant, who had sent her to Philadelphia all those years before.

But not this.

He had the rifle and revolver, but nothing more, definitely not what it would take to ride north into the outlet where Newcomb was headed, but he couldn't spare the time to go back for more men.

It wasn't lost on him that it was a ride he'd made before, into territory that had no law, only outlaws, renegades, and death.

How tough was she? If Newcomb didn't simply put a bullet in her head, could she survive the ride?

Grit. She was going to need it to stay alive.

"Let me go," Laine urged Newcomb when they stopped to water the horses as the sun appeared briefly below the clouds then disappeared.

"You're far enough away now." But how far, she wondered? "Just let me go."

They had been riding for hours and she had no idea where they were, only that they'd been riding steadily north.

Newcomb shook his head as he drank from a canteen, then threw it at her. Those cold eyes watched her.

"Not clean enough for you?" he sneered.

As much as she was loathe to drink where he'd taken a drink, she took a long swallow, and forced herself to think.

What was north? The outlet, she'd heard Ranse talk about? It seemed most likely. And then? Where was he taking her? What would happen when they got there? Then another thought—that he might not intend to take her anywhere. That she might die out there.

It would have been so easy to give into the fear. Too easy, she thought, and as she'd already seen, he seemed to feed off it, even enjoyed it. Her cheek throbbed where he'd struck her when she tried to force her horse away from him.

He'd caught her, dragged her from the saddle, struck her, and then tied her wrists together and then to the saddle horn. Trapped, caught, and how many miles more when she was certain she couldn't stay in the saddle any longer, and now a brief stop and rancid, stale water.

"Get back up there," he snarled, holding the reins of her horse.

He swung up on his horse and they continued on until well after dark and the rain started.

They were both soon soaked and forced to stop, the rain blinding them as the wind came up. He pulled her from the saddle and shoved her toward a rock outcropping.

She was exhausted, bruised and every muscle ached, but

the storm that had held off and had now stopped them for the night was warm, driving against the rocks in waves. Mercifully there was no lightning, only the wind and rain.

She crawled as far back under the outcropping as possible, wrapped her arms around her knees, and thought about a fifteen-year-old boy who had ridden into the outlet alone, and had then returned a man.

What had he seen? What had changed him? A boy, not quite a man. Was he out there now?

She shifted against the hardness of the rock at her back and stared into the darkness across the small clearing of rocks where they'd made camp for the night. Newcomb was wary they were being followed and refused to risk a campfire. She heard the subtle scraping of the metal spoon against the flat metal plate. Her stomach grumbled at the sound. Newcomb hadn't bothered offering any of the cold beans or peaches he produced from a knapsack rolled inside his bedroll.

A faint flickering of light split the darkness as Newcomb struck a match and lit a cigarette. It was just as quickly extinguished. Laine turned her head away from the choking, bitter smoke, far different from the slender cigarettes Ranse always smoked.

She couldn't see him, but she could smell the rancid, foul stench of Newcomb as he approached. He threw a blanket at her.

With rock at her back, there was no place to retreat further. She felt the damp dirt beneath her hands as she tried to crawl away from that voice. Her left hand brushed across a rock.

Before the thought could register, Laine's head snapped back, pain stinging her cheek. She fell back, her hand closing over the small rock. She struck Newcomb. He grunted painfully, falling back into the shadows.

He screamed with pain, "You broke my nose!"

Laine lunged in the direction of the horses. Before she had

taken a half dozen steps, a powerful kick knocked her feet out from under her, sending her sprawling into the mud where Newcomb sat only moments before.

She fought the pawing hands that seemed everywhere at once on her body, dragging her across the clearing back to the rocks. She choked as a filthy hand closed with bruising strength around her throat.

If she fainted now, she knew exactly what her fate would be. She had seen it in Newcomb's face through the long hours of the afternoon. She twisted hard to her left, bringing her knee up sharply to gain some leverage against his body.

She'd be damned if he'd take her alive. If she was dead, it would hardly matter what he did to her.

She gasped at the sudden rush of cool, sweet air that filled her lungs. Her dry, bruised throat ached, but she was able to breathe again. She opened her eyes, struggling to understand. She stared at Newcomb, close, too close. He seemed as badly shaken for the ordeal. His labored breathing came in deep rasping gasps.

"Damn you!" he swore. "Try that again, and I'll put a bullet in your head."

She struggled and would have lunged across the encampment again, only to be jerked back down into the dirt at Newcomb's feet as she felt a rope around her neck.

"Now, we'll see Miss High-and-Mighty. You move just one inch off that spot and I'll jerk this rope. You understand?" he told her.

"I don't give a damn what kind of marks that rope leaves on you. I'll still get my price," he growled at her.

Price? What was he talking about?

"It don't matter much to me who you are," he continued. "But I can't afford to have the marshal following me. I got to get rid of you, and I know someone who can do that and at a nice profit to me.

"Do you hear me?" he jerked on the rope. "I don't stand to gain nothin' from havin' you dead, and I don't much like the idea of mountin' a corpse. So you listen real careful. Don't you try nothin' and I just might let you live."

Her cheek ached from the blow, and she felt the rope bite into skin at her neck. She was tired, hungry, and scared.

"If you come near me again, I swear I'll kill you," she whispered, her throat raw. "Somehow, some way I'll kill you. Do you understand?" she spat back at him.

He eased his hold on the rope.

"Don't go gettin' yourself all riled up. You're right about one thing—you're worth more to me alive than dead. Just don't try my patience none. I might do something I'd regret later, but by then it would be too late. Let's just say this rope is for your own protection." He pulled a filthy bandanna from around his neck.

He wrapped it across her mouth, forcing the loathsome fabric between her lips, then tied it off at the back of her neck. In one, final gesture of authority, he twisted his filthy, stained fingers into her hair, jerking her head back, so that she was forced to look up at him.

"You'll be good and quiet now even though there ain't no one to hear you." He gave her a hard shove down onto the ground.

"You just remember that. And in case you start forgettin' I'll just give a little extra pull on this rope to remind you." With a final warning, he settled himself a short distance away.

Laine fought back the tears that would have been too easy. Dear God, what was to become of her? Who were these people he was taking her to?

She slumped against the rock. That slight movement cost her dearly, as Newcomb jerked viciously on the rope—a reminder that he was only a few feet away.

In the dark she let the tears come.

16

A nother cold camp, and no trace of either Newcomb or
Laine.

Ranse kicked at the remnants of the fire with the toe of his
boot. Newcomb was a crafty bastard. He'd been after him the
past two years, but he always managed to disappear.

Newcomb had ridden with Bob and Grat Dalton for the last
three years, and from what Ranse knew, even they didn't trust
him as far as they could throw him.

There had been some rumor that Newcomb had tried to
organize a takeover of the Dalton Gang. The plan had failed
when everyone but Bill Doolin had sided with the brothers. Of
course, it was all rumor, and stories about the Daltons were
constant.

For the last three days, he had done little more than search
for hoof prints through the rocks of the rugged hills, combing
the landscape for some sign Newcomb had passed that way
through scrub oak and thorny tumble weeds.

Now, he squinted into the midday sun from beneath the
sweep of his wide-brimmed hat, tiny wrinkles at the corners of
his eyes.

North... Their course was steadily north, when he could find it. But he hadn't seen tracks since early yesterday morning.

Instinctively he had continued to follow the course of the Cimarron River, with only vague impressions left in the sandy soil along the riverbank, that might easily have been made by wild animals. Again, as he had continuously the last days, he pushed back the fear that knotted his gut. Would Newcomb kill her?

The outlet was wide open territory. There was no law here, except what each man made for himself. That was exactly the reason renegade Indians fleeing the reservations came there. It also provided a haven for every other type of renegade unable to live in civilized society.

It was hoped that the land rush three years earlier that brought settlers, farmers, families, would also bring law and order to the Territory. Land had been claimed and farms had sprung up as families moved in and settlements were established. But there was still danger and risk. Those same settlers found themselves having to constantly defend and protection their land claims.

It wasn't uncommon for a farm or settlement to be raided, people killed, anything of value stolen, children left orphans or dead alongside their parents. But that happened farther and farther between as the Army established outposts throughout the outlet. Still, there were others, holding on to that way of life —Newcomb, the Daltons, and others like them.

Ranse checked his revolver once more, then re-holstered it. The Winchester was in the scabbard beneath his knife, fully loaded. He felt the firm pressure of the long, smooth blade, against the calf of his leg down the inside of his boot.

He knew this land, and he was careful. Along time ago he had ridden some of these trails, knew where the water was, and the places where a man could be ambushed. He knew it all, seared into the memory of a fifteen-year-old kid. In the years since, the job had taken him to various places in the outlet. But this was different. This was personal.

He'd spared neither his horse nor himself and felt as if he carried a good portion of trail dirt on his face and neck. He had accepted the offer of water and food at a farm the day before, the man and his wife relieved to see the badge he carried. No, they hadn't seen anyone that resembled Newcomb riding a dapple gray, with a woman.

Ranse had described her, hoping against hope that she was alive and not left someplace for the animals to finish what Newcomb had done.

He didn't stay long enough to rest or shave the growth of dark beard that covered his face and made him look as dangerous as the man he was after. He paid the farmer for the food his wife wrapped in a burlap sack for him, then pushed on.

Now he scanned the horizon. There were a million places a man like Newcomb could hide in the outlet. But there was something he was missing, something he and every other lawman had been missing all along, all those many months they'd pursued the Daltons and the bloody trail they'd left behind.

If you wanted to catch a thief, you had to think like a thief. If Newcomb wanted to kill Laine, he would have done it already. There was some other reason for taking her so far into the outlet. Ranse shrugged off the idea of Newcomb turning her over to the Indians. That was too easy. He knew from experience that Newcomb was a coward, and he was greedy. He wouldn't go near the Indians, except if there was a profit to be made.

Save her for himself? He rejected that. There would hardly have been a need to take her into the outlet for that. There was something else the outlet offered Newcomb. And he knew where he was headed when he found the tracks of two horses just before sunset the fourth day. His horse snorted as he sent him down the riverbank and they crossed the North Canadian River.

LAINE COLLAPSED in the only shade to be found, under a scrawny tree. Her lips were cracked and bleeding from lack of water. Her entire body ached from long hours in the saddle, and a welt burned her neck from the rope Newcomb had tied around it to prevent her escaping.

She flinched as beads of sweat rolled across tender, raw skin, and silently cursed Newcomb. When he turned his back to take the canteen from his saddle, she continued to work at the leather thong that bound her wrists. She was careful to watch for any sign that he saw what she was doing. Any movement usually resulted in the rope being tightened.

Laine had found herself considering that death might be favorable to the hell she was forced to endure. She stopped working the rope at her wrists as he turned. He thrust a canteen at her.

"Drink, but not too much or you'll be sick. That's all I need, is a sick woman. And try to do something with yourself before we get to the settlement, make yerself presentable. But don't think you can get away. I'm not about to let go of this rope. You make one move I don't like, and you know what it will get you."

As if she needed reminding, Newcomb jerked on the rope, causing her to choke on the first swallow of water she had taken since morning.

She glared at him.

"Still Miss High-and-Mighty ain't you? I guess it must be somethin' in that fancy schoolin' back East. Well, your fancy ways don't mean nothin' out here at the auction." Newcomb growled in her face.

There it was again. What was he talking about, an auction?

She fought the nausea that threatened to bring dry heaves. There was nothing else that would have come up if she had been sick.

She had refused to eat any of the food Newcomb offered her. If she could slow his progress, she might buy herself more time to escape whatever he had planned. Now the thought that they approached a town of some kind offered her new hope.

She weaved in the saddle. Newcomb yanked brutally on the rope, the coarse rope biting into raw flesh. A slow leer split his grizzled face as he found momentary enjoyment in the pain it caused.

Instinctively, she raised her bound hands to ease that tightening about her neck. She thought it unlikely that she would ever be able to draw a full breath again, so bruised was her throat. They had stopped and for the first time in hours, Laine felt cooling shade.

She opened her eyes slowly, wondering why they had stopped so early in the day. She had learned to gauge the hours they travelled by the dull, throbbing ache in her back and muscles. Her gaze widened at the sight of the ramshackle building in front of her. A poorly made sign tilted crazily over the extension of porch where several rotted boards had given way. They'd reached a place called Cherokee Springs.

The doors suddenly flew open and a man came flying through the air and landed in the dirt in front of the horses.

"You hear what I say?" Someone bellowed out the door behind the prostrate man.

In the next moment, the gaping doorway was filled with the largest and most outrageous woman Laine had ever seen. At least she was fairly certain it was a woman. She was certainly dressed the part, or overdressed might have been a better description. Her costume rivaled a circus tent in size and garish color.

"You try to cheat me again, and I'll blow your head off.

There's two things in this world I can't stand—bad whiskey, and men who cheat at cards. I don't mind cheatin' in bed. That's how I make my livin' in this hell hole, but I'll be damned if I'll tolerate cheatin' at cards. Now get your worthless hide outta here."

It was impossible to deny the danger of the threat, with the sun glinting off the steel barrel of the revolver the woman held. She continued to stare threateningly at the departing shadow of the hapless patron for a long moment as he pushed to his feet and then staggered away. Suddenly aware of the two riders who sat watching the exchange, the woman's gaze narrowed as she squinted into the afternoon sun.

"That you, Newcomb?" she grunted.

She slowly stepped down the last step of the wooden porch and gazed into the hard gaze underneath the brim of Newcomb's hat.

"Damned if it ain't. It's been near a year since you and the boys last rode through. Come on down here you and let me have a good look at you."

There was obvious caution in the large woman's tone as she exchanged crude banter with Newcomb. Where she had handily given no hesitation to booting a man, a full eight inches taller and much heavier than Newcomb out of the saloon, she was now extra watchful.

Laine watched her from beneath the floppy hat she'd worn the last several days. Despite her size and the gun she still clenched in her hand, this hardened woman kept a careful distance between herself and Newcomb.

"I thought you might have sold out, Rose, and headed for San Francisco by now," Newcomb grunted. "You should have a good amount of gold stashed away with the prices you charge for whiskey."

"That might be," she replied, "if you and the boys didn't swing through here, bustin' things up. After that last time, it cost me a pretty penny fixin' things up again. One thing led to another, and I decided to make some improvements.

"I got tired of walkin' down them stairs in the middle of the night when the urge hit me, never knowin' what kind of varmint was waitin' in that outhouse," she continued. "I added a privy upstairs. Besides," the woman reached up to smooth a tangled mass of hair, back from an ample cheek with a fake beauty mark that shifted and swam in the middle of a deep wrinkle.

"I just wasn't too certain San Francisco was ready for me. I hear they've got a couple of fine houses up there though. That half-breed keeps tryin' to get me to throw in with him and sell this place.

"Says he can get us in a real deal at one of the places where he supplies the women. Says they need a woman to ride herd on the girls." She patted a pudgy hand on the well-padded swell where her hip might have been. The keen, dark gaze narrowed as she stared at Laine a full, long moment.

"What's that you got there?" Rose pointed with a grimy finger.

"That's some business I got with the half-breed. When you seen him last?" Newcomb shifted the revolver at his hip, his other toying with the end of the rope.

"He's layin' in upstairs with Lucy. You remember her. She was here the last time you, Bob and Grat rode through. Anyway, I don't have her washin' dishes no more. I got better uses for her now. And she's taken to upstairs work real fine and it makes me money that way.

"But the breed won't be in no condition to see anybody for a few more hours," Rose went on to explain. "He put away two pints of whiskey last night, and started wavin' that knife of his around, talkin' how he was goin' to cut everyone up, including Lucy.

"Well, that little gal was worth every bit of the twenty dollars that I paid for her. She got him upstairs and started sweet talkin' him. The next thing I know it's all quiet upstairs. I didn't know what I was goin' to find, but Lucy came down a little while ago, with only a few bruises and the half-breed was out cold.

"If you got business with him, you're gonna have to wait. And if that's the business you got... " Rose waved a hand at Laine. "You better get her cleaned up some, or she won't bring you more than fifty dollars. He's gotten real picky since he's been takin' women to San Francisco. Says they have to be real fine lookers to get top dollar."

San Francisco?

Dear God, Laine thought, where had Newcomb brought her? Fifty dollars?

Rose reached out to lift the edge of Laine's skirt for a better view of the merchandise. In spite of her weakness, Laine kicked out at that ham-like hand that lifted the hem of her skirt for closer inspection.

Rose stepped back with surprising quickness in spite of her girth and ample weight.

"Oooeee, this one's got a temper. That'll please the half-breed He likes 'em spirited, that might even make up for the way she looks. But I'll tell you what, Newcomb. I'll make you a real deal. Twenty dollars in gold, and I'll make a real looker out of her. A little soap and water will work wonders."

She reached up, her big hands reaching up, poking Laine in the ribs, passing over the swell of a breast as if she inspected a piece of livestock at auction.

"You touch me again and I'll kill you!" Laine whispered. Rose drew back as if she had been stung, a wide grin revealing several missing teeth.

"Twenty dollars, Newcomb, in advance, or you get nothin' from me. We'll see then just how much you can get for her," Rose countered.

"All right," Newcomb grumbled, as he yanked on the rope, dragging Laine down from the saddle. "You got a deal. But she'd better look good, or I'll come back and take that twenty dollars out of yer hide."

Rose gave him a teasing look, her humor restored at the prospect of the extra money.

"I've been waitin' a long time for you to come back and do just that, Newcomb. I may even give Lucy the night off tonight, just to make sure you get your money's worth. I've had plenty of varmints in my career, but I ain't never had me a lowlife snake like yerself. Might prove real interestin'."

Rose reached out, boldly caressing Newcomb's groin. When he pushed her hand away, her laughter filled the hot, stifling air. She continued to laugh all the way inside the saloon.

Newcomb jerked Laine along behind him. The saloon reeked of sweat and stale whiskey. The air was still and stifling, but it was a relief from the heat of the sun.

She ignored the stares that fastened on her, as Newcomb jerked on the rope, leading her upstairs, Rose leading the way.

At that moment nothing else mattered but the promise of relief from the dirt and heat of the last days even as a nagging thought remained, something Rose said about a half-breed, and money. She stumbled on the last step, and Newcomb pulled viciously on the rope.

"You go on jerking that rope like that, marking her up, and you won't get a plugged nickel for her. She don't look like she could stir up much of a fight. Give me that rope." Rose stopped in front of a door at the top of the stairs. Without knocking, she thrust the door open.

Sprawled on the bed in the center of the room was a blonde-haired, young girl, almost naked except for the sheet she clasped to her thin body. Beside her lay a dark-skinned man, with long, unkempt, black hair. He was turned away from the door, a long, jagged scar running from his shoulder to his waist.

"Get some clothes on Lucy and come along. I'm gonna need your help. The Injun won't miss you. Looks like he's gonna be out for at least another three to four hours."

At the crisply barked command, Lucy scampered out from under the sheet and darted about the room looking for her clothes. Rose left the door ajar, and pulled Laine across the narrow hallway towards another door.

"This here is my room, and that is the new privy I had built last year. Comes in real handy." She shoved Laine inside the room.

"Go on! Get outta here," Rose told Newcomb. "It's gonna take some time to get all dirt off her. I'd think you'd take better care of somethin' you want a good price for.

"Tell Charley I said to get you somethin' to eat," she called after him.

Seeing that Newcomb was still uncertain about leaving Laine in her care, she waved those great ham-like arms in the air.

"I got that special whiskey you like. A shipment came in last month. Have a bottle, on me. It will help calm your nerves, and it'll give me time to get her washed. In her condition, she ain't goin' nowhere," Rose spoke convincingly. Newcomb grunted reluctantly as he turned to leave, pressing past Lucy in the narrow hallway.

"You start fetchin' buckets of warm water up here," Rose told the girl. "We got us a real chore ahead of us." Rose sighed heavily as she lifted a matted and snarled tangle of Laine's hair.

An hour earlier Laine would have denied that the bath alone, could work such wonders as she leaned against the windowsill, feeling the cooling night air lifting her still damp hair from her shoulder as she seriously considered the long drop to the ground from the window.

"I wouldn't try it if I were you," the girl, Lucy, told her as if she had read her mind.

"Rose wouldn't have left the room if she thought you'd have any luck climbin' out that window. That's a thirty-foot drop to the ground, and what's below sure as hell ain't worth any price droppin' into. You're better off with Newcomb than to try that," the girl spoke softly. As if giving proof to her words a foul, horrible stench lifted on the night wind and filled the room.

"That's the new privy you're smellin'. Rose didn't have no idea where to drain it all off. In hot weather, it pretty much dries up, but once in a while the whole thing runs over and causes a dreadful stink. Rose had a bath this mornin', first time in a week. So, it's a bit ripe, with everythin' else, if you know what I mean.

"She knew the half-breed was comin' in and she likes to be sweet smellin' for him," she continued. "She says it's better for business. Men get enough of smellin' themselves. At any rate, that privy can't much handle more than two baths in the same week, much less the same day. But orders is orders, and Rose wanted you cleaned up real good. By mornin' the smell will be gone when the morning breeze changes direction. Hey! You're not lookin' too good. You'd better have a swallow of this."

Lucy thrust a stained glass of amber liquid under Laine's nose. The scent of the whiskey alone had a sobering effect on Laine's reeling senses. She took a tentative sip, and realized Lucy was right. The deceptive liquid stole like molten heat through her weakened limbs, easing some of the pain in her back.

Across from her, Lucy tossed down a second tumbler-full, not even flinching as the heady brew went down.

"Thank you," a whisper was all that Laine could summon from her bruised throat.

Lucy shrugged. "It helps me forget who I am and where I am, at least for a little while," the girl added. "But real soon, I'm gettin' outta here, and I won't need any more to forget."

Laine smiled weakly. She admired the girl's spirit.

"What did Rose mean about the Indian?"

Lucy met her gaze evenly. "He buys women. Then he takes them to places like Phoenix and San Francisco, and gets a real good price for them in the whorehouses there. Says, it's his revenge against the settlers."

Lucy poured herself another drink. Laine shook her head when she offered her more.

"He's a renegade half-breed," she explained. "He comes here a couple of times of year, cause he knows Rose will arrange to have women for him, some of 'em settlers and farmers from the outlet. He pays her in gold and whiskey. She must have a small fortune buried somewhere in this hellhole of a place."

"How did you get here?" Laine mouthed the words as her voice failed completely.

"My pa sold me and my two older sisters to Rose. The Indian took Clair and Amy to Phoenix last year. I ain't heard from them since. Rose started me out washin' dishes and cleanin' the place cause I hadn't got my woman's figure yet. But earlier this year, I got *promoted*." Her laugh was a harsh sound.

"I've been workin' upstairs ever since. Helluva promotion." There was that harsh laugh again. "Rose usually makes the men pay her first before they come upstairs with me, but once in a while I do real good and a customer will pay me extra. I've been savin' my money, and I'm gettin' outta this place. I got someone special I met up with last year. A young fella came through with his folks.

"They was goin' towards Enid to do some farmin'. Said he had his own piece of land there. Wanted me to go with him, but Rose found out about it and tied me up in the privy. I was just doin' dishes then, but he was a real nice fella, with kind eyes and a soft way of speakin'.

"I'm goin' to Enid, and if he'll still have me, I'm gonna become a farmer's wife. He don't ever have to know about any of this." Lucy made a gesture with her hand.

"Help me get out of here and I'll see that you reach your young man in Enid," Laine told her.

For the first time in days, she had real hope of getting away.

"I know people in Guthrie, and I could pay you. Please, you've got to help me. We could leave here together. We would need another horse, some food and water. We could do it."

"I don't know. I always figured to go alone. It's easier for one person to slip outta here, but both of us?" She shook her head. "Rose watches everyone like a hawk."

"Please, wouldn't you like to go to your young man with some nice clothes and maybe a carriage with a fine horse?" She pleaded with mounting desperation.

The girl refused to meet her gaze. "We gotta get you dressed, or else Rose will be up here wonderin' what's keepin' us. She wants you downstairs to meet the Indian. The auction's goin' to start right away. It usually goes on for hours, with lots of whiskey and haggling goin' back and forth. That's how Rose makes her money, plus a percentage of what the Indian makes on his end."

Laine grabbed Lucy's too-thin wrists in desperation. "What auction?" she whispered frantically.

Lucy struggled to free herself. "The auction. That's why Newcomb brought you here, to auction you off to the highest bidder or sell you off to the Indian. We got enough people comin' through, that he's gonna have to come up with more than usual. There'll be a lot of drinking and bidding." Lucy squirmed and tried to twist free.

"Let go, you're hurtin' me. For a refined lady like Newcomb said, you sure got yourself a real mean grip. And don't go gettin' yourself all riled up. I didn't say I wouldn't help you." The girl finally jerked her wrist free.

"You will?"

"I suppose now is as good as any time, but I gotta personal score to settle with Rose first. It won't do her reputation no good when word gets around that she can't even hold onto two scrawny women. And that's for sure what we are." Lucy rubbed her wrist.

Laine threw her arms around the girl and squeezed her tight. Both jerked around at the knock at door.

"Almost ready!" Lucy yelled through the door. She turned to Laine. "We gotta put on a real good show downstairs, and don't go gettin' all riled up no matter what goes on down there. If we're gonna escape, we gotta get everyone real drunk. That Injun can't even find a horse, much less sit on one, when he's got a good amount of whiskey in 'im." Lucy headed towards the door as Laine tucked her shirtwaist into the waist of her skirt.

"You any good with a gun?" Lucy looked back over her shoulder.

"I can be if I have to," Laine told her.

Lucy nodded. "I know where Rose keeps her shotgun. We just may have to shoot our way out." Lucy took another look at her. "On second thought, leave that to me. I saw Newcomb's face. He said you hit him with a rock."

Laine nodded. "It's all I could get my hands on at the time."

Lucy grinned with growing excitement. "Between the two of us and a good amount of whiskey, we might just pull this off."

THE LONE RIDER slipped silently through the night.

In the distance, lights and music filled the cool, night air.

Cherokee Springs, the darkest hell-hole in the outlet. A place where anything could be bought for a price—gold, guns, and women. The tip of a cigarette glowed for an instant, reflected in that dark gaze as Ranse slowly exhaled.

If he was wrong, if Newcomb hadn't come here, Laine might well be lost forever. And in that case, she was better off dead.

Deep inside, his gut twisted at the thought and with a deep need to see Newcomb dead. He reached for the rifle and laid it across his lap as he eased his horse down the slope toward those distant lights.

Laine followed Lucy down the stairs to the first floor of the saloon. A sudden quiet filled the saloon as she reached the last step.

Rose tossed down a full glass of whiskey. "Well, look here, Newcomb. Told you water and a bit of soap would do some good. Don't seem like the same gal, does it? I guess, old Rose sure earned every bit of that gold piece."

A broad smile split her face, revealing gaps between rotted teeth, and Laine decided that Rose's wrath was better than her humor.

Lucy reached behind her and gave her hand a reassuring squeeze. Two strangers entered the saloon, slapping trail dust from their clothes. They approached the bar, calling for the bartender to pour a couple of whiskies.

The bartender nodded, taking his time as he delivered a newly opened bottle to the table occupied by Newcomb and the Indian.

Lucy pulled Laine across the room and seated her in the corner. An old man at the piano received a swat on the top of his balding head from Rose as she made her rounds of the customers. He quickly resumed playing, that tinkling sound filling the saloon.

Laine refused a bowl of greasy stew that Lucy had brought her, deciding instead on the slice of thick bread.

"You'd better eat somethin'," Lucy whispered. "If we're gettin' outta here, there ain't no tellin' when we'll be able to eat next."

Laine eyed the unidentifiable chunks that floated in the grayish broth. Her stomach lurched. She shook her head as she considered herself much safer with the bread. But she smiled at Lucy. She didn't want her to think that she was ungrateful.

"This will be fine. I haven't had this much in the last three days. I don't think I could handle the stew," she told her.

She downed the bread in small bites, feeling the queasiness in her stomach ease. When the small loaf had been consumed, she felt strength slowly returning to her arms and legs. She watched the card game between Newcomb and the Indian, wondering if she had suddenly become the bet, considering what Lucy had shared with her.

According to the girl, Newcomb wasn't foolish enough to take a chance on losing her in a poker game. He wanted cash. That would come later, she thought. Laine's attention focused on Lucy, as the girl exchanged words with Rose.

Rose gave her a suspicious look. Had Lucy betrayed her after all? Her uneasiness faded as the girl returned.

"Rose wanted you to sing for the boys. It's all part of the little show she likes to put on. Sort of teases everybody, before the auction later on. I told her you couldn't even talk, much less sing, cause of that rope Newcomb had about yer throat. So I get to provide the entertainment for the evening.

"You just keep your mouth shut and your eyes open," Lucy continued. "If Newcomb or the Indian make any move in your direction, tell them you want a drink. Try and get as much whiskey down them as possible. Rose'll cooperate. There's nothin' she likes better than sellin' bootleg whiskey. Just remember what I told you, keep 'em drinkin'."

Lucy smiled at her and then crossed the saloon. She leaned over the piano player and whispered something to him, then turned back to face the room as the music began.

Notes with a haunting sweetness kept the customers attention. Conversations ceased as all eyes turned towards Lucy. She had never heard such an achingly, beautiful voice, perhaps all the more haunting for the melancholy sadness that filled the notes. The song ended and Lucy quickly began another lighter tune with colorful lyrics that had the men laughing and clapping with enthusiasm, their attention fastened on the pale-haired girl.

Newcomb licked his lips in silent appreciation of the slender, yellow-haired girl who sang so sweetly. The warm glow of the whiskey brought a familiar ache that hadn't been satisfied on the long ride out here.

Focused on the girl, he was only vaguely aware of the tall man who entered the saloon. He was dressed the same as the other two drifters who had come in earlier and looked as if he lived in the saddle.

Newcomb grumbled as the Indian poked at him with the tip of that menacing blade, a subtle reminder to continue their game. The half-breed was hardly interested in that little gal, he'd been enjoying for two days now.

"Two pair, queen high. Now see if you can beat that." Newcomb slammed his cards down, his eyes gleaming with satisfaction beneath the thick brush of his brows.

The Indian silently glared at him from behind the sweep of unkempt hair that was crudely tied back with a piece of leather. When Newcomb reached forward to claim the gold pieces and paper money that lay in the center of the table, the Indian grabbed the knife and with lightning quick swiftness drove the tip down into the wood of the table.

"You cheated!"

When Newcomb made a second grab for the money, the Indian lunged across the table, retrieving the blade. One hand grasped Newcomb by the collar of his shirt, the other held the blade against his throat. Across the saloon, Lucy went to stand at the end of the bar. Her gaze met Laine's.

Rose approached their table from the bar. "I don't allow no

cheatin'. If the Indian says you were cheatin' I gotta believe him. After all I do a lotta business with him. Put the money back on the table."

The entire saloon had gone silent. Would Newcomb refuse, Laine wondered? What would happen then? Would the Indian kill him?

"Put that thing away," Rose eventually told the Indian. "Let's get the auction started." Her suggestion met with hoots of enthusiasm from the men.

The Indian grunted as he released Newcomb who fell back in his chair. When the Indian reached to claim the pot of money, his only reaction was a warning look at Newcomb.

"Let's get this over with. I wanta get out of here," Newcomb snarled. He rose from his chair and crossed the saloon. He grabbed Laine by the wrist and yanked her out from behind the table where she'd been sitting.

Lucy caught the barely noticeable movement at far table. The stranger who had just come in laid a rifle on top of the table. By the looks of it, that wasn't unusual in a place like this. What was unusual was the second drink he refused, with a shake of his head, when the barkeep attempted to refill his glass.

Most of the men came to the saloon to get roaring drunk. This man had come for some other reason. There was a lean intensity about him that spoke of quiet strength and cool determination, as he watched with the ease of a cat that quietly contemplates its next meal. He leaned back, one hand resting on stock of the rifle, his features hidden beneath the brim of his hat. But it was there in angle of his body and the way he watched everyone.

He wasn't the usual drifter or renegade, easily satisfied with a few drinks and a quick toss upstairs.

What had brought a man like this to Cherokee Springs?

Lucy followed the direction he stared across the room.

Oh, boy, Lucy thought. So that was it. He'd come for Newcomb's prize lady. And there was goin' to be a gunfight for certain. She glanced about the saloon.

There was nothing to indicate that anyone else suspected anything. Charley was pouring whiskey and old Trapper continued pounding away at the piano. The Indian's attention was fastened on the dark-haired gal as Newcomb dragged her across the room.

Lucy glanced back at the stranger and saw the tightening of his fingers around the stock of the rifle. This man was willing to die for that girl. And a man willing to die for want of something was the most dangerous kind.

"All right, this is what I promised you. The finest little piece west of the Missouri," Newcomb boasted. "I got one price, five hundred dollars, in gold."

"One hundred," the Indian grunted, looking Laine over thoughtfully, his black eyes gleaming. He shoved one hundred dollars of the money he had won off Newcomb across the table.

"She's worth five times that amount and you know it, "Newcomb protested. "You'll get ten times that amount when you take her to San Francisco. Five hundred, nothin' less."

The Indian grunted, running a finger along the curve of Laine's arm. She pulled back instinctively. Newcomb pinched her.

"She'd got a lot of spirit. That's worth extra." And again, he named his price of five hundred dollars.

Ranse's his hand tightened over the rifle. He couldn't risk Laine getting hurt and forced his gaze away from her and watched the Indian. He reached inside the pocket of his vest as the two men argued back and forth. He lit a cigarette and slowly blew out a stream of smoke.

"Three hundred dollars."

If he had wanted to get everyone's attention, he couldn't

have picked a better way as all eyes turned towards the corner of the saloon.

Laine's head came up. She stared into the shadows at the stranger who sat at that table and slowly came to his feet. A cigarette glowed between the fingers of his left hand. His right hand rested casually on the rifle.

It took all her self control to not cry out. Dear God, how had he found her?

"Three hundred?" Newcomb rubbed his hands together. "Ok, Injun. Seems like we got us a real auction now. What's your bid gonna be?"

The Indian moved slowly as he rose from the chair. His dark eyes glinted as a smile slipped across his face and Laine felt that dark gaze on her.

"Five hundred dollars."

Lucy stared wide-eyed at the exchange. She couldn't believe what she was watching. No one had ever dared challenge the Indian for what he wanted. She glanced at the faces of the other men in the saloon as they backed uneasily away from their tables. The air was heavy and still like the calm before a storm.

Ranse took another draw on the cigarette. He glanced at Laine, warning her to silence.

"Seven hundred dollars." He upped the bid, never taking his eyes off the Indian.

Newcomb may be crazy, he thought, but he was also stupid, and unpredictable.

His pistol lay on the table where he had placed it at the beginning of the auction. Only he knew that Newcomb carried a small pistol in the inside pocket of his jacket.

The Indian's eyes narrowed. "Eight hundred dollars."

"All right, mister." Newcomb turned to Ranse. "Surely, you ain't gonna let this pretty gal slip through your fingers. She's real fine. Got skin like satin, and all nice and round in the right places, too."

"One thousand dollars," Ranse offered.

"Sold," Newcomb announced.

The Indian's expression hardened. He had outbid him, and Ranse saw the sudden change in the Indian's stance.

At the far end of the bar, Lucy slipped behind the bar. Directly in front of her, was the sawed-off shotgun Rose always kept behind the bar.

Ranse watched as the Indian glanced about the saloon. He'd wanted Laine. Now, he'd lost her. But he'd lost something more, he'd lost respect. He saw it in his eyes, something he'd seen a long time ago when he'd gone into the outlet and knew what would happen next.

"All right, mister, pay up. The woman is yours." Newcomb moved closer to Laine.

Then, as Ranse slowly circled the saloon and stepped into the flickering lamplight overhead, Newcomb exclaimed, "You! I should have killed you back at the farm!"

In one movement Ranse shifted the rifle to his left hand. Just as quickly, his right hand moved down, cocking the revolver, as chaos erupted in the saloon.

Laine took the only chance she was likely to have, and grabbed Newcomb's pistol from atop the table, as customers dove for cover while others struggled to draw their own weapons.

Rose shouted at Lucy, as the girl stood in her path. "Give me that shotgun!" She grabbed for Lucy.

"Leave her alone!" Laine shouted at Rose.

"Well, if it ain't Miss High-and-Mighty," Rose sneered. "I'm willin' to bet you ain't got what it takes to fire that gun at ole Rose."

She heaved her ponderous weight across the width of the bar and seized Lucy by the front of her gown.

Laine took aim and pulled on the trigger. A loud roar filled the air as the revolver went off. Rose turned and stared at her. Her mouth gaped open as she stared dumbfounded at her.

"You shot me!" Rose choked with surprise then anger, blood coming away at her hand where she pressed it against her rounded belly. The woman lunged toward her.

Laine yelled at Lucy and they ran across the saloon, and ducked behind the piano as bullets filled the air, splintering the wood of the piano. Lucy screamed as she was grabbed and pulled to the floor. Laine's gaze locked with Old Trapper who had been seated at the piano only moments before.

"The place is on fire," he shouted and pointed at the overhead fixture that had come loose with a stray bullet and dripped lamp oil onto one of the tables.

"It's gonna go up like a tinder box. I'm gettin' outta here, you outta do the same." Then he was gone, disappearing through a cloud of billowing smoke.

The Indian lunged, catching Newcomb off guard, hurtling the man's body towards Ranse. Gunfire filled the air. Newcomb grunted with the force of the blow, as he crashed to the floor.

Side-stepping Newcomb's body a moment too slow, Ranse felt the slash of the knife as the Indian rolled to the side and sprang to his feet. Blood was warm at his side.

The Indian waved that deadly blade back and forth at him. Ranse smashed the butt of the rifle against the Indian's jaw. He staggered back, the knife hitting the floor. He upended a table and crouched behind it.

Smoke filled the saloon as another lantern shattered on the floor. The flames scattered, catching the contents of shattered whiskey bottles and erupting into an inferno that quickly spread.

Through the smoke Laine saw a figure crawling through the doorway. Bittercreek Newcomb! And he was getting away.

A deafening roar filled the air as the shotgun erupted with a burst of smoke. The blast took out the bottom half of one of the doors. Bittercreek Newcomb suddenly pushed to his feet, then lunged headlong out the doors.

Ranse caught a glimpse of Laine. He reached the side of the saloon where the piano stood.

"Get out of here, now!" he told her, sending her toward the door.

The sudden change in the expression on her face had him turning around. The Indian stood only a half dozen feet away, a gun pointed at them.

A loud roar exploded amid the smoke and flames. Ranse spun around as the body of the Indian dropped to the floor.

He seized the revolver from Laine's trembling hands, then pulled her with him out the gaping doors as fire roared through the saloon behind them.

He pulled Laine with him and pushed her down behind several oak barrels as a stray shot came from inside the saloon. A man tumbled through the doorway of the saloon, his clothes aflame. He rolled in the dirt in front of the saloon in an attempt to douse the fire.

Rose emerged from the saloon, her ponderous size, taking the burning doors off their hinges as she charged out of the saloon. Stray tendrils of black matted hair smoldered. She immediately doused her entire girth in the water trough in front of the saloon. From every window, opening, and doorway, the hapless patrons of the saloon spilled out into the night air.

"Where's Lucy? Did you see her get out?" Laine struggled out of Ranse's grasp.

Those she reached all shook their heads, as they coughed and tried to wipe the soot and cinders from their eyes. Behind them the flames from the saloon consumed everything in its path, driving them back towards the far side of the settlement. Ranse pulled Laine back with him, holding her against him, turning her away from the horror of the flames, the nightmare of death.

"She tried to save me," Laine cried against his shoulder. "We were going to leave together." Behind them, Rose emerged from the trough, looking more like a drowned cow.

"Served her right, the little bitch." Rose winced, her hand pressing against the waist of her gown.

"And you...! You're to blame for this!" she screamed as she descended on Laine.

17

"Hold it right there, Rose." Lucy emerged from the billowing smoke that poured out of the building.

In only a few moments the ramshackle building that had been Rose's legacy to entrepreneurial success was completely engulfed, lighting up the night sky.

Standing flat-footed in the middle of the street, her ponderous breasts heaving from the effort to save herself, Rose glared at her.

Laine stared at the girl. "How did you get out?" she asked as she ran toward her.

"You might want to stay back," Lucy warned and held up a hand as Laine approached. "I don't think you want to be comin' any closer. The way I smell would rival Rose before Saturday night bath."

"Are you hurt?"

Lucy shook her head. "Here I was cursin' that damned inside privy. There was water in that sump at the ground floor. I can't say much for the way I smell, but that stinkin' hole sure as hell broke my fall." She grinned back at her.

"You jumped from the second floor?" Laine stared at her aghast.

"I had to go back for somethin' and there wasn't nothin' else to do. Those stairs was on fire when I tried to get back down. When it came to choosin' between bein' burnt to death and gettin my feet wet..." She shrugged.

"I suppose this will get me use to livin' on a farm. If Clint could only see me now." Then she asked, "Did that son-of-a-bitch Newcomb get away too?" she asked.

"No," Ranse replied with a look toward the saloon that was engulfed in flames, a slumped body motionless on the board-walk in front.

"Oh, well good riddance, the man was a pig." Lucy shifted the shotgun into the crook of her arm. The dimples in her cheeks deepened with the flush on her face as she got a look at Ranse.

"If I'd known the *cavalry* was comin,' I wouldn't have bothered bein' worried. I tried to go back for that money on the table, but the fire was fearsome."

They all turned as curses filled the air.

"You good-for-nothing little whore, after all I done for you..."

Lucy raised the shotgun and aimed it at her. "There's one more round in this shotgun," Lucy told her. "I figure all you got out of me the last two years, more than makes up for one meal a day, nothing but a hard floor to sleep on, and that damned chain you kept on me."

She lifted the shotgun and took aim. "Like I said, you got all you're getting outta me."

"I got an investment in you. You owe me." Rose reached to shove the barrel away.

"That debt is cancelled," Lucy told her.

Rose took another step toward her and Lucy punched her. Rose dropped like a rock.

"Is she dead?" Laine asked, staring as Lucy bent over the

woman who greatly resembled a beached whale she'd once seen.

"Nah! Just out cold. I've been wantin' to do that for two years, only I figured it would probably break every bone in my hand." She shook her hand. "It was worth it."

"We need to leave," Ranse reminded them, as he swung up into the saddle.

He handed Laine the reins to the gelding. As her fingers brushed his, she felt the wet stickiness of blood. Her startled gaze met his.

"You're hurt... "

"We need to get as far away from here as we can. You and Lucy will have to ride double." He turned his horse north.

How much blood had he lost? How serious was it?

Now was not the time, she knew that by the look at his face. But how far could they get with him injured and only two horses?

She pulled herself into the saddle then held out her hand to Lucy. The girl swung up behind her, then wrapped her arms around Laine's waist.

"I'll keep a look out," Lucy said as she laid the shotgun across her lap and they rode out.

THEY RODE for hours in silence, until the glow of the fire at the saloon disappeared in the distance behind them, and it became too dangerous to continue over uneven ground with just the light of a half moon.

"Where are we?" she asked as Lucy slipped to the ground beside the horse.

"A few miles from Cherokee Springs," Ranse replied. Not far enough, he thought, but they had only the two horses and he knew better than anyone how easy it would be for one of them to take a misstep in the dark. And both she and the girl had to be near exhaustion.

"We'll stay here for the rest of the night, then continue at first light."

"What is this place?"

"A herder's hut that was abandoned when the owner died," he explained. Another casualty of the outlet, shepherds grazing their flocks in the outlet, the only place open to them. Until they were run off or killed. He'd stayed in one like this farther south when he'd come into the outlet alone all those years before.

"I'm so tired, I don't care if there are varmints in there," Lucy wearily said as she took the rolled bundle she'd brought with her and shoved open the sagging door.

Ranse unsaddled both horses and handed her the saddle blankets. Then he led the horses around to the back of the hut and hobbled them.

There was more open space than roof, but neither she or Lucy minded as they made make-shift beds out the saddle blankets. By the time Ranse joined them, dropping the canteen to the dirt floor and propping his rifle against the remaining stout wall, Lucy was already asleep and snorting softly, Rose's shotgun beside her.

"You'd best get some sleep too," Ranse told her.

"What about you?" she asked as she curled on her side on the blanket. Considering the past several nights as Newcomb had dragged her through the outlet sleeping on the ground or in a niche in the rocks, by comparison, the hut with holes in the roof and three standing walls might have been the finest hotel.

"I'll be awake for a while," he replied, removing his jacket and laying it over her.

It should have been easy to fall asleep after everything that had happened.

"What was it like when you came here alone all those years ago?" she asked.

He didn't answer right away and she thought he might not, the past, sometimes a place best forgotten. If one could remember.

A match flared in the dark of the hut as he lit a cigarette, the glow flashing across handsome features drawn taut by the last hours. And those memories?

"Long days, constantly watching for outlaws, renegade Indians, anyone looking to steal your horses, money, your clothes; places like this when the weather turns and everything runs to mud for days. Nothing prepares you for the beauty of it and how dangerous it is. You get to that place where you want to give up, just find a place in the shade, and never get back up again."

"But you did get back up."

There was another long moment of silence before he answered.

"Yeah, I got back up," he eventually replied. "I had to finish what I started."

She nodded. It was something she understood, she thought, as her eyelids grew heavy.

"Get some sleep," he told her. "It will be morning soon enough."

He stubbed out the cigarette, then set a rope across that sagging doorway, just in case anyone tried to enter the hut during the night. Then he laid down beside her with his revolver close at hand.

Her breathing didn't change even when he pulled her against him. Instead she curled toward him, her head resting on his shoulder.

.   .   .

LAINE WOKE as the first light of day streamed in through the roof. She glanced at the saddle blanket beside her. It was still warm beside her.

She rose, moving stiffly at first. She found Ranse with the horses and handed him the saddle blanket.

"Where's Lucy?"

He nodded a short distance away from the hut. "There's a creek down there. She decided she couldn't stand the way she smelled after her escape at Cherokee Springs."

Laine followed where a path had been cut through the tall grass. She found Lucy sitting on the bank of the stream shaking water from her hair. The ugly dress Rose had her wear had been replaced by a simple muslin gown, transforming her back into the young girl she had been before her father sold her to the woman.

Her teeth chattered slightly as she looked up with a smile. "I kept this dress, but it don't exactly fit so good anymore."

"It fits just fine, better than what you were wearing."

Lucy grinned. "Smells better too. I took a quick bath even though I near froze my ass off. First chance I get, I'm gonna burn that damn dress Rose had me wearin'."

Laine didn't blame her; she would have done the same. She washed her face and arms, drying her face with the sleeves of her shirt as best she could. They walked back to the hut together.

The horses were already saddled. Ranse helped them astride Laine's horse, then handed them each a strip of dried beef and the canteen of water. She was so hungry she was certain nothing had ever tasted so good.

"What about you?"

"I'll eat later," was all he said as he swung his horse about.

They were headed north again, the sun slowly rising off their right side as they rode out from the shepherd's hut.

Ranse set a relentless pace, refusing to stop even for the

shortest rest, his gaze constantly scanning the rolling grassland behind them. It was long past midday and they'd been in the saddle for hours when they crested a hill that looked down onto a farmhouse with a dozen or more cattle in an adjacent pasture and a field of corn waving in the afternoon breeze.

The farmhouse itself was white clapboard single story with a porch across the front. Two dogs announced their arrival, two children playing in the side yard. A young man slowly strode toward them from a smithy's anvil where he was shoeing a horse.

His greeting was cordial but cautious as he glanced from Ranse to Laine and Lucy.

"You look like you've come a ways," he commented.

"We left Cherokee Springs and rode a good part of the night." Ranse swung down from his horse and slowly approached the farmer.

"Marshal McCandliss out of Guthrie," he introduced himself and Laine noticed that he was once again wearing his badge.

"Cherokee Springs? That's sure enough a hell hole." The man had begun to relax after Ranse introduced himself.

"These women were there?"

"That's right and in need of some food if you can spare some."

"Name's Jessup," he introduced himself and his two oldest boys. "My wife is Sara," he introduced a slender woman who came out of the farmhouse. "You're more than welcome." He called to his boys to see to their horses.

Laine had almost forgotten what it was to have a full stomach of warm food. Sara Jessup was an incredible cook. Supper was potatoes and vegetables with chicken in a thick sauce and included biscuits and apple pie.

There were four Jessup children—the two older boys, and a younger boy and girl, Oliver and Emmy. They kept up a lively chatter, curious about Cherokee Springs and how she and Lucy came to be there.

"Enough," Sara Jessup finally told them. "Sara you may clear supper dishes and put them to soak in the tub. Anson and Michah, we will be needing hot water in the washhouse."

When the two older boys protested that it wasn't yet time for weekly baths, their mother gave them a look that almost had Laine burst out laughing.

"For our guests, boys. Now, don't make me ask again. And see to the animals before you come in."

There was a chorus of, "yessum," and they left the table to see the chore done.

Ranse went with Jake Jessup to the corral to see to the horses while Laine and Lucy attacked the pile of dishes that had been set to soaking.

"You're not expected to work for your supper," Sara Jessup pointed out.

"I've worked my whole life," Lucy pointed out. "I wouldn't know what to do with myself if I didn't."

They quickly formed a line, washing, rinsing, then drying the mountain of plates, cups, and utensils needed to feed several. Afterward, Sara untied the apron from around Laine's waist.

"You'll have to take turns in the washhouse, but there should be plenty of hot water and soap. It's nothing fancy," she added looking over at Laine. "But it will get the dirt off." She led the way to the adjacent washhouse.

For as long as she lived, Laine was certain nothing would ever feel as good as that bath, sitting up in a huge barrel with lines of laundry overhead that had been set to dry.

She scrubbed and rinsed her hair, then washed her shirt-waist and underclothes.

"This should fit you all right though you're a bit taller than me... " Sara announced when she returned with a nightgown draped over her arm.

Laine looked up when she heard the hesitation in Sara's voice as she stared at the newly healed wound at her shoulder.

"I can't take your clothes."

"Well, you can't very well go around naked as the day you were born, not that my oldest boys would object, mind you. They're gettin' to that age... And I'll leave this for the girl." She smiled gently.

"No need to worry. You and the girl are safe here."

That seemed an odd thing to say, Laine thought as she dried off and dressed in the simple gown. She left her hair down so that it could dry. She passed Lucy as she left the washhouse.

"You and Lucy can take the boys' room. They like sleeping out in the barn this time of year anyway," Sara announced as she returned to the house.

Ranse and her husband had not yet returned.

"It must get lonely out here," Laine commented as she helped put away the dishes they'd washed earlier.

"I never thought of it as lonely. With four youngins running around and everything that needs to be done just to keep this place going, there's no time to be lonely.

"Most days, you just fall in bed exhausted at the end of the day, but it's so much better than in a city where you can't even breathe for the smoke from the factories and everyone crowded into one small room. This land and what we make of it belongs to us, and we got the most amazing sunsets."

Laine couldn't remember ever seeing a sunset before coming to the Territory, as dangerous and wild as it was.

Sara showed her to the loft that served as a bedroom for the older boys. In spite of the fact that it looked down onto the main room of the farmhouse, along with all its noise and conversations, she fell asleep almost instantly. She didn't even waken when Lucy crawled into the bed with her.

"I understand," Jessup said as he stood with Ranse. "You have my word. I'll see that the girl has a place to stay until we can find her young man. I'll put the word out to my neighbors, it shouldn't be too hard to find out where he is. And as for the other young woman. There's a mail coach that comes through regular. He takes on passengers when need be. I'll see that she gets back to Guthrie. "

Ranse knew money was hard to come by on these outlying farms. Most goods were traded for, but with four children... He handed Jessup several folded bills.

"Buy your wife something pretty," he told him when he would have refused to accept payment.

Then he bedded down in the barn with the two boys, very near the same age he was when he went into the outlet for the first time.

He rose at first light and saddled his horse. Jessup had provided him food and water the night before to take with him. He led his horse from the corral and slid the rifle into the stock.

"You're leaving?"

She had heard Sara in the kitchen below the loft, setting the coffee and the batter for breakfast. She had looked out the ground floor window as she came downstairs, a quilt wrapped around her against the morning chill, and saw him lead his horse from the corral.

Ranse looked up as she slowly crossed the yard and something inside him tightened at the sight of her, dressed in a simple nightgown, barefoot, the quilt wrapped around her shoulders, her hair down in thick waves past her shoulders.

He had wanted to be gone before she rose, simpler that way. Easier. But there was nothing simple or easy about what he felt at the sight of her, the sun burning like fire on her hair, her eyes as deep a blue as any sky, making him want to stay, to hold her and never let go, to wipe away her tears and then taste morning at her mouth.

"There are things that need to be done," he said simply, because there was no easy way to say it, and he wouldn't lie.

"You're going after them, aren't you."

His silence was her answer.

"But what if... " The words caught. Everything she heard about the Daltons, their reputation, the men left dead behind them.

"What if you don't come back?"

Ranse reached out and touched her cheek. "You sure are pretty, Miss Dalton." He turned then and climbed into the saddle.

"Ranse...!"

But he was already out of the yard.

She shielded her eyes against the morning sun as she watched him disappear.

"Damn you, Ranse McCandliss."

"How far?" Laine asked.

The clothes that she'd washed the night before had dried. After she watched Ranse ride out, she had returned to the farmhouse and dressed.

"The marshal said I was to see that you got back to Guthrie," Jessup replied. "He was real clear about that."

He was determined to follow Ranse's instructions; she was equally determined that she was not going back. At least not until she had the answers she'd come for.

"You are not the marshal," she pointed out as she crossed the yard to the corral.

She'd asked one of the boys to saddle her horse. He stood at the corral with a sheepish expression at his face, her saddle on the top rail.

"Miss, I can't let you go alone." Jessup followed her across the yard. "It's too dangerous."

"He's right," Lucy had followed from the house and added her voice to the argument. "The marshal wouldn't want you puttin' yourself in danger."

She thought of Ranse, already well on his way.

"How far?" she asked insistently.

"Must be a good thirty miles up north to Coffeyville. You can't travel that alone on horseback."

Coffeyville. Thirty miles. There were a lot of things she couldn't do. But that was before, this was now. So close, yet still a good distance away, and something important that sent Ranse there, deliberately leaving her behind.

"Is there at train that goes there?"

"There's the water stop along the main line that goes straight into Coffeyville," his oldest boy spoke up and immediately received a reprimand from his father.

"How far is that from here?" she asked.

Jessup shook his head. "Just west of here, no more 'an three, four miles; train stops to take on water on the afternoon run."

She pulled her saddle—the one Addison had given her—from the top rail of the corral. Jake Jessup swore and took it from her.

"Can't have you goin' off on yer own." He yelled at one of his boys to saddle his horse.

"I understand the reason you gotta go," Lucy said, coming up beside her as she slipped the bridle over the gelding's head.

Laine smiled. They had more in common than anyone would have guessed. "I hope you find your farmer," she said, squeezing the girl's hand.

Lucy looked around at the Jessup farm, the younger children feeding chickens at the yard, one of the dogs chasing a rabbit while one of the older boys led a horse from the barn that he'd just saddled.

"It's not a bad life," the girl commented. "More than I ever had, and with the right man... " she didn't finish what she would have said as Sara Jessup joined them.

She handed Laine a wrapped bundle. "Some food in case you get hungry." Then, unexpectedly, she wrapped her arms around Laine and hugged her tight.

"You be careful out there, you hear."

Laine thanked her and tied the flour sack to the saddle horn. She gave Lucy a hug.

"Be happy," she told her, knowing how important that was. Then she climbed up into the saddle.

Jake gave instructions to his boys to see to the cattle, then squeezed Sara's hand.

"I'll be waitin' supper for you, Jake Jessup," she called after them.

A simple gesture, the touch of a hand that said so many things and just one thing that mattered. And Laine squeezed her eyes shut at the memory of Ranse's parting hours earlier.

The anger was there, that he would leave her and go on alone. Along with the fear that she might have come this far and never know the truth.

What would happen in Coffeyville?

18

It was late afternoon when Bob, Grat, and Emmett Dalton along with Bill Doolin and Pete Spence checked and re-checked their weapons. Then at a nod from Bob Dalton, they swung up into their saddles, and slowly rode out single file from their hiding place at the edge of town.

Two banks, two robberies. No one would be expecting it.

Just outside of town, Bill Doolin pulled his horse up, the animal lame. Cursing his damn, fool luck, he doubled up with Spence. He wasn't about to be left behind on this job. Finding a horse in town when it was over would be easy.

Released only a few weeks earlier from the jail in Tulsa, he had ridden hard to catch up with Bob and Grat Dalton. If they pulled this robbery off, it would be the greatest in history. Stories would be told about this robbery long after all the money had been spent.

Ranse McCandliss leaned against the trunk of a huge alder tree in the center of town. He reached inside a vest pocket and pulled out a cigarette. A match flared and was then quickly extinguished and tossed to the ground. Fragrant smoke filled the air as he glanced down first one street and then the next.

The town was quiet, almost too quiet, with only an occasional townsperson seen, then quickly disappearing. Further on down Eighth Street in front of the banks, the street had been torn up for repairs. The hitching posts had been torn down and lay in a heap along the length of the sidewalk.

Ranse glanced as four horses with one doubled up with two riders appeared at the end of Eighth Street and felt that warning tingle at the back of his neck.

He couldn't see their faces at that distance, but he didn't need to. He recognized three of the men as they continued around the corner. He tossed his cigarette down and ground it out under his boot, then crossed the street in front of the hardware store, his hand resting on the handle of his revolver. He knocked on the paned window of the store.

"Lock up, and don't come out."

The door was immediately shut and locked. Just down the way two armed deputies stepped back into the shadows between two buildings. Ranse tipped his hat casually in the direction of the bank across the street.

A window shade immediately lowered. Everywhere along the street, the signal was given and passed along, weapons readied.

The riders never left his sight as they rounded a corner and headed into the alley that ran behind the bank.

There was no one on the street as gunfire exploded.

Laine heard the first sound of gunfire as she stepped down from the train platform.

"There's trouble in town, miss," the stationmaster told her. "Best not go there."

She didn't hear the rest of it as she ran toward the center of town. She rounded the corner from the train station then suddenly stopped as the sounds of more gunfire reached her.

The main street was completely deserted except for an empty wagon in front of a mercantile store. Somewhere nearby a dog barked frantically, a child suddenly darted out from a shop, quickly grabbed by his mother and dragged back inside, the door slammed behind them.

"Miss!" someone called out to her from the saloon. "It's not safe. Get in here."

The man leaning through the door was armed with a rifle, another man stood beside him equally armed.

"Where?"

"It's the Dalton Gang! They're holed up in the alley behind the bank. Don't go down there, Miss...!"

She ignored the warning shouts that followed her and bolted across the street, lunging out of the way of a riderless horse that ran down the street.

Ranse saw her as she barely avoided being run down by a stray horse.

What the hell was she doing there? Damn stubborn...! He crouched low, running the length of the street towards the First National Bank.

He glanced along the second story of the building directly across the street from the bank. Three men moved along the roofline within an easy shot of the back alley.

Gunfire erupted from the alley where she disappeared a few seconds earlier, and at a sudden lull in the gunfire—let her be alive!

There were no sounds coming from inside the bank, where two of the Daltons had entered a few minutes earlier. He exhaled slowly as he pushed open the door of the bank, then dropped down low and crossed the floor, coming up against the teller's counter.

Behind the counter, the bank clerk lay dying, an unfired gun still clutched in his hand. Ranse bent down beside him.

"Out the back," he whispered.

Ranse was through the back office, past the large, gaping safe and out the back into the alley.

Several of Coffeyville's citizens had joined the fight. Two of them lay face-down behind the bank. One had been cut almost in half by the blast of a shotgun, the other had taken a bullet in the chest.

Ranse stepped over them with a feeling of dread that he was following a trail of bodies to get to her.

At the end of the street, he saw two heavily dressed figures steal around the corner onto Union Street. He followed, keeping to the near side of the alley where shadows offered some protection.

He suddenly stopped as he saw her. She stood at the side of a building. A body lay in the dirt at her feet.

"Grab her!" Someone shouted as a short man in a flowing overcoat scrambled up from the alley floor.

Blood soaked through the layers of the long coat, staining the sleeve. The arm hung useless at his side. A second man, lunged towards her.

"Who the hell is she?" The taller, dark-haired man growled, panic clearly marking his voice. Nothing had gone according to Bob Dalton's plans.

"Easy pickin's," Doolin replied.

So far, the only easy pickin's had been them. The whole town must have been waiting for them. It was like trying to get out of the middle of a battlefield. He had a bad feeling about this whole thing.

"The horses are just around the corner. We'll be damned lucky if any of us get out alive." The shorter man darted past Laine. He was dressed like the others, a revolver in his hand, another in a shoulder holster.

Laine turned and came face to face with Bob Dalton.

Behind them came the sounds of the sheriff shouting orders to his men. Bob Dalton cursed, moving towards the other three men at the opposite end of the alley, the only other way out.

An arm caught at Laine from the back, dragging her roughly.

"This ought to make gettin' outta here a little easier. We'll just see what that sheriff decides when he sees we got ourselves a hostage," a voice growled in her ear.

She stumbled as she was hauled backwards and cried out as the barrel of a pistol was jammed against her right temple.

"You cooperate and we just might all get out of here alive."

"Let her go, Doolin," Bob Dalton's shout filled the air, lost in a hail of gunfire as the sheriff's men filled the alley.

Ranse dropped to the ground in the alley. He took careful aim, waited, and then tried again, but couldn't get a straight shot at Doolin or Spence without the risk of hitting her.

Doolin moved, taking her with him, using her as a shield as he moved down the alley as the citizens of Coffeyville poured into the alley. Gun smoke filled the air. He fired over his shoulder as the alley erupted into a nightmare of blood and death.

Ranse rolled out of the direct line of fire that blazed through the alley, coming to his feet at the opposite side. He knew there was no hope of talking anyone down. Caught in the middle between Bill Doolin and Emmett Dalton, he turned and fired.

The first shots caught Spence. More gunfire exploded as the deputies dove for cover. Ranse turned back just as Bob Dalton reeled from a shot taken in the chest. He staggered against the far side of the alley.

Two shots from the sheriff's deputies tore through Emmett Dalton and he slumped against the far wall, a smear of blood staining the stone as he slid down the wall. At the far end of the alley, Grat Dalton took a blast from a shotgun.

Ranse ran across the alley as Bob Dalton moved along the wall, following Doolin. He was badly wounded, and he was now the most dangerous kind of outlaw—trapped and with nothing to lose.

"Let her go, Doolin. She ain't nothin' to you," Bob called.

"That's right," Doolin shouted back. "She ain't nothing to me." He whirled around as the sheriff's men blocked his escape and retreated into the street, holding Laine in front of him.

"Give it up," the sheriff shouted at him. "There are more than forty armed men just waiting for you to set foot out of this alley. You won't get out alive."

"Sorry to spoil your plan, sheriff." Doolin laughed, as his gun pressed against the side of Laine's head.

Ranse knew Doolin. If he was going to die, he was just crazy enough to take her with him. He moved quickly while the sheriff held Doolin's attention, coming to within six feet of where they stood.

"She's Bob's sister," Ranse shouted, the only way he might be able to get her out of this alive. "She's got no part in this. Let her go." He caught the sudden movement as Bob Dalton's head came up.

"McCandliss? What the hell are you talking about?"

"A little girl that Adeline sent east."

"Damn! That was almost twenty years ago."

"You knew about it?"

"Yeah, I heard about it... "

"You got yourself in one helluva mess, Bob."

"That's for sure."

Bob laughed. "You always were right there over my shoulder. You and Frank, trying to get us to go straight. I don't think we're going to get another chance at it. Grat's dead and Emmett is shot up. Strange isn't it, how it all comes down to this stinkin' alley in the middle of some lousy little town."

"You always knew it would end hard."

"I suppose we caused everyone a lot of grief, including Ginny." He paused. "Damn, I loved her. Can you understand?"

Bob Dalton winced as the pain in his chest spread. He shook his head.

"I don't want nobody else to die because of us."

Was there regret there? Ranse thought, now that it was all about to end in a way it didn't have to.

The sheriff held his men back. At the far end of the alley, Doolin leaned heavily against the wall, the barrel of his gun pressed against Laine's head.

Bob Dalton shouted at Doolin. "Let her go."

Ranse saw that flicker of defiance and regret as Bob raised his pistol and charged Doolin.

Smoke from his gun exploded in the alley. A volley of gunfire from the deputies tore through him and his body was thrown back.

"I'll kill her!" Doolin screamed.

Less than ten yards away, Ranse took the shot. Doolin's head snapped back. He collapsed to the ground dragging Laine with him.

Ranse pulled her into his arms when he reached her. She fought him, trying to push him away. Tears streaked her cheeks.

"Bob?"

Ranse held on to her. "You don't want to see him like this."

Over the next several days all the major newspapers across the country carried the sensational story of the massacre of the infamous Dalton gang at Coffeyville, Kansas.

In twenty short minutes, a daring, double bank robbery had ended with the deaths of all but one of the outlaws.

Four of the town's people died that morning, with another three seriously wounded. Of that shootout in a back alley that soon became known as Death Alley, only Emmett Dalton survived. Badly wounded, he was heavily guarded in the Farmer's Hotel.

Newspaper reporters poured into Coffeyville, eager to get the story for their newspapers. It was hardly a surprise that one very enterprising reporter had access to information recapping Laine's background, and the circumstances that had brought her to the Oklahoma Territory.

Everyone who had seen or heard anything of any of the robbery was given an interview, with accounts that varied wildly. The sheriff's office made a brief statement based on information supplied by Ranse.

He was unable to keep the press from sensationalizing Laine's relationship to the Dalton brothers once it was learned she had been there.

In the days following the shootout she took up a silent vigil beside Emmett Dalton's bed. There was nothing to prove that she was related to him or any of the Daltons, but she couldn't leave that room.

When the fever from his wounds came, she kept a cool cloth on his forehead and gave him water. On the fourth day after the attempted robbery, Ginny arrived from Kingfisher. Too ill to travel, Adeline Dalton had remained at the old farm with the girls. It was doubtful she even understood what had happened when Ginny received word.

In her room at the opposite end of the hall, Laine smoothed the coverlet on the bed. Ranse had left the hotel earlier, asking her to meet him in the dining room for supper. She hadn't slept or eaten much of anything the past days.

She let herself out of the room, and slowly exhaled at the sight of the sheriff's deputies who stood guard outside Emmett Dalton's room.

The doctor had informed her earlier that his condition remained unchanged. He was alive and that was the best anyone could say for now.

Ginny Morton had arrived earlier. She had spent the morning at the morgue, making the necessary arrangements for Grat and Bob Dalton.

Laine could only imagine how difficult that was; taking care of the details to bury the man Ginny had loved and hoped to marry—if only.

In the last days the hotel had taken on the atmosphere of an armed camp. She passed the deputies in the hallway. Their guns were vivid reminders of what had happened there. She ignored the deputy who followed her as she descended the stairway into the main lobby.

She braced herself at the sight of the reporters, faces were pressed against the glass windows in hopes of obtaining some new information for their newspapers. The hotel manager nodded to her as he came around the end of the desk.

"The dining room is through there."

Ranse was seated at a table in the far corner, away from any windows. He stood as she approached.

"I thought you might have decided to stay in your room and get some rest."

She nodded. She felt numb and empty with a sense of loss that was hard to understand with no way of knowing the truth.

Ranse reached across the table, his hand warm against hers. "I know it's hard, but don't hide. You've nothing to be afraid of from anyone."

His words were soothing. She needed them. God, how she needed them. But he couldn't take away the memory of what had happened. She almost wanted to laugh at the absurdity of it. How could she mourn something she'd never had?

Ranse's hand tightened over hers as he saw the emotions in her eyes. She was fighting the horror of the last days, and he couldn't be sure of the outcome.

"How do you do this? How do you get past it?"

He could give her some meaningless words meant to comfort, but the truth was that it was different for everyone.

"You don't," he gently told her. "It's always there, part of you. But you learn to hold on to other things." His hand had tightened over hers. He understood the sadness and the loss, and the not knowing.

"Tell me about them," she said. She didn't need to explain what she meant.

Ranse sat back in the chair. "The boys all used to come up here when they were younger. Frank told me they even hid out with one of their cousins up here for a while 'til things cooled off, after he was caught stealing cattle," he repeated.

Laine watched him. "Tell me about Frank Dalton."

That dark gaze met hers. "We were a lot alike in many ways. Frank left home early because there were so many mouths to feed. We were two of a kind, then. I hadn't gone east to school yet. We drifted together, worked odd jobs—legitimate jobs, and shared just about everything friends can share. That's how I got to know the family.

"Addison knew about it, and he liked Frank. But even then, I knew his brothers were involved in some bad things. It was like Frank had to prove that not all Daltons were bad.

"We both signed on as deputies. He took dangerous assignments, like there was something inside him that he had to prove. He went out alone that last time when he was ambushed. I followed him, but it was too late. The men he was after gunned him down simply because he wore a badge.

"When I found him, he was dying, and talking crazy about all sorts of things, his family, the times we'd shared. There wasn't time to get him to a doctor. I always thought that what was good in the boys, died with him."

"And Ginny?" she asked.

"She tagged along with the boys after her folks died. She's been in love with Bob for as long as I can remember."

"Even knowing what they did?"

He nodded. "Bob told her they were going to get married, settle down with a family. He was going to quit running from the law. He told her they'd find a place, maybe up in Canada, where no one ever heard of the Daltons. But there was never enough money, not when he split it up so many ways."

"And then you left to study law."

"It seemed a better choice."

Conversation drifted off as they ate their dinner. Laine responded vaguely to Ranse's casual comments. When a waiter overturned a tray very near their table, the contents crashing loudly to the floor, she jumped, her hand closing over his.

"It will take time," he said gently.

She was silently grateful the meal was very nearly at an end. She paid little attention as someone stopped beside their table.

"Laine, I would like to talk to you, if you don't mind."

Her startled gaze came up, locking with Ginny Morton's.

Ranse stood and gave Ginny a hug. "I'm sorry it had to be this way."

She nodded.

He brought a chair over from the adjacent table and motioned to the waiter to bring another cup of coffee. Except for their table, the dining room was now completely empty. The only patrons of the hotel for the last several days had been the sheriff's deputies. Other than that, the hotel was off limits to everyone else.

"How is Adeline?" Laine asked.

Ginny nodded. "I told her and the girls. But there's no way of knowing if she understood what I was saying. Maybe later when she has a better moment, although I don't know what good it does." She looked down at her folded hands. "I think we always knew it would end this way.

"It changes you. You learn to get on with living. Because that's the only choice you have. I think in some ways we all did our mourning for the boys a long time ago. Sometimes I think that's what Adeline did, then she just went away inside herself."

"After you left, one of the girls gave this to me. It's Adeline's bible. She wrote the dates each of her children were born in front. It might be helpful." She handed it to Laine.

She read the list of names that had been neatly written there, each with the date of birth, that included Frank Dalton's name and the date of his death—February 8, 1881.

The rest of the names were there— Robert, Grat, Emmett, the girls, and a last entry—Laine Dalton: born May 6, 1871, died September 4, 1875.

"I don't know if it helps. She had two other babies that didn't live," Ginny explained. "According to the date, that little girl was born before the girls."

But she had died September 4, 1975. What did it mean?

19

Laine paced the small room at the Farmer's Hotel. The last days had been exhausting with an endless round of questioning by the sheriff, making his reports of the events that had led up to the attempted dual bank robbery by the Daltons.

Ginny had boarded a train the day before that would take her back to Kingfisher with the bodies of Bob and Grat Dalton. They were to be buried at the old homestead in the side yard where other Daltons were buried.

There was still no certainty that Emmett Dalton would survive the bullet wounds he had received during the robbery attempt. If he did, he was looking at a long prison sentence.

She had seen little of Ranse. As far as the sheriff was concerned, he was in charge of the investigation into the attempted bank robbery. With a sudden wrenching feeling deep inside, the first emotion she had felt in days, Laine realized how badly she wanted to see him. He had been there during the endless rounds of questions, providing explanations for questions she couldn't answer.

Then, it was over. Now she could go home. Laine almost laughed at the thought. Home. Philadelphia. She hardly remembered what it had been like before Ranse had entered her life.

Love, warmth, security, happy memories, hope for the future-all the meaningful words that she associated with the word "home and family" somehow didn't describe what she had left behind in Philadelphia.

Her childhood hadn't been unhappy. Althea Ralston had made certain that she had all the material things she needed. And she had felt great affection for the woman who had been her guardian. But she was always aware that there was something missing from her life.

Her lack of family, of that connection and memories set her apart from other girls her entire life. In the few months she had been at the Oaks, she had glimpsed what might have been. The fragile bonds of family had been extended to her at the Oaks. And now?

With aching reality that brought tears to her eyes, Laine realized that Ranse considered the entire matter ended. At the knocking on the door, she carefully closed the envelope, sealing it over the letter she had written.

"Will you be needing fresh linens today, miss?"

"No. I'll be leaving on the afternoon train," Laine replied. The maid left, moving on down the hallway.

"May I come in?"

Laine whirled around at the sound of that voice.

The clothes Ranse had worn since their ride from Cherokee Springs had been replaced with black corded pants smoothed over the lean, hard line of his body, the light blue shirt, with a dark vest worn over.

His dark gaze was guarded, catching hers before glancing away. He carried his black, wide-brimmed hat with the silver headband loosely in his fingers. His hair was almost too long, sun-streaked, dark waves spilling over the collar of his shirt. A single revolver in the black holster.

Ranse moved across the room, idly lifting a sheet of paper from the small desk where Laine had sat a moment before. He felt her gaze, and for a moment allowed himself to meet those dark blue eyes.

"The sheriff wanted you to know that with the information Ginny gave him before she left, you've been cleared of all involvement with the Dalton gang."

He wanted to comfort her, to hold her but something in her eyes stopped him.

She nodded. "I've decided to return East, as soon as possible. There's a train leaving this afternoon that will connect in St. Louis."

She waited for him to say something. When he didn't, she continued, not trusting herself to meet his gaze just yet.

"Unfortunately, I don't have the fare. The funds I was expecting are in Guthrie."

"Maybe you should consider returning for a few days," he suggested. "You might want to say good-bye to Addison."

"I've written him a letter, explaining everything. I thought that would best. I didn't want to cause him any more embarrassment by returning to the ranch."

Ranse watched her. She was different now. She was no longer the young woman he first met all those weeks ago. She was changed.

Where was the stubbornness and determination? The grit that had sent her there, that had defied everyone to find the truth? Had that died in that alley along with the Daltons?

He settled his hat on his head. "I suppose that's easier for everyone. I'll make sure you have the train fare and make arrangements for the rest of your things to be sent to you when I get back."

He hesitated. "I'm sorry that it ended this way." There was more he wanted to say, but those things had never come easily. He'd spent a lot of years simply shutting things away.

The door closed behind him. When she would have gone after him, she caught herself, then tucked the letter inside the envelope for the clerk at the front desk.

Just as he promised, Ranse made certain she had sufficient fare for her ticket to Philadelphia, plus substantially more left in an envelope with the stationmaster. The accompanying note explained there had been a reward after the death of Newcomb and the Indian at Cherokee Springs.

"There won't be any sleeping accommodations until you get to St. Louis, miss," the ticket master reminded her. "They'll be puttin' on a sleeper car then, and I've marked your ticket accordingly," he said congenially.

"I'm sure this will be fine," Laine replied. "Could you please make certain this is sent right away?" she handed him the note she had written to Addison.

"Sure thing." Again, that smile. "Say, aren't you that Dalton gal?"

She didn't answer, instead she simply thanked him.

In the distance she heard the train whistle. She walked slowly to the edge of the platform. She was going to have several days to do nothing but sit and think on the trip back to Philadelphia.

Right now, she just wanted to look out across the rolling landscape, and not think. She stepped back as the train slowly rolled into the station and glanced down the platform at the other passengers who also waited.

"Ticket please, miss." The attendant reminded her again.

Laine smiled at him briefly as she cast one last glance down the length of the platform, then handed him the ticket.

Late afternoon sunlight spilled through the windows of the car as she moved past the seats to the rear of the car. Perhaps here she could travel undisturbed. She was going home.

Home. Somehow it seemed hollow and meaningless.

Ranse reined in hard, dust and dirt settling on the deserted platform. He crossed the platform towards the enclosed waiting area of the station and pulled the glass door open, causing several people to glance up.

"Is there something I can help you with?" the stationmaster asked.

"There was a young lady leaving on the two o'clock train.

"Yes, sir. Real pretty. She got on that train all right. But I don't think she was all that anxious to go, acted like she might have been waiting for someone."

"What's the first stop on the line?" Ranse leaned across the counter and seized a piece of paper and pencil.

"That would be Topeka. But they'll stop to take on water along the way." The stationmaster glanced past Ranse as someone entered the train station behind him.

"I'm glad I found you."

Ranse turned around at the familiar voice, a smile easing the frown on his face as he recognized Curry.

"What are you doing here?"

"Addison got worried about your getting back to the ranch. He asked me to give you this." Curry handed the thick envelope to Ranse, the familiar scrawl of Addison's handwriting on the outside.

Ranse opened the envelope and scanned the contents of the letter. "Anybody else know about this?"

"Only Addison, and now you. He didn't say what was in it. Just that I was to get it to you right away, or break my neck tryin'."

"I appreciate it." The smile had become almost hopeful.

"Say, Marshal. That lady you were askin' about?" the stationmaster reminded him. "She left a letter she wanted posted. I promised her I'd get it right out, but I recognize you, Marshal McCandliss. I thought you might want it instead. I knew right off she was that Dalton gal."

It had to be the letter she was going to send Addison. He

stuffed it into his coat pocket along with the envelope Curry had brought.

"How long ago did the train leave?"

"No more than ten minutes. It was on time today."

Ranse and Curry left the station. He handed several bills to Curry.

"Get some rest and something to eat, then head back to the ranch."

"Where you going?" Curry squinted into the afternoon sun.

Ranse smiled as he swung into the saddle.

"I've got a train to catch."

LAINE SHIFTED against the hard wooden seat. The heat inside the passenger car was stifling but it was preferable to the soot and cinders that filled the car when the windows were opened.

Across the aisle a young mother sat rocking her infant, while a toddler sat across from her. Further down from the young mother was an elderly couple, the woman dressed fashionably. She guessed the gentleman to be a banker or perhaps a lawyer by the cut of his clothes.

The sky had transformed to pale gray as the sun lingered like a brilliant, crimson ball suspended over the distant hills. The Flint Hills, Laine heard the elderly couple tell the young mother.

All across the rolling landscape was a riot of brilliant golds, oranges and amber as the sun slowly slipped from a purple sky.

This land was magnificent. It was massive, dangerous, and in many ways uncompromising, but it held such promise. Ranse had spoken of that promise, and she knew he loved the Territory in spite of its harshness, in spite of the toll it took. And for just a moment it had been part of her life.

She thought of Adeline Dalton—the hardships, the pain, and losses she had faced. In a way the land had beaten her, taken everything, until there was nothing left, not even hope. And Ginny, who had loved a man in spite of it all, in spite of the things he'd done, then accompanied those two plain caskets alone, back where it all began.

Then, she thought of the Jessups, raising a family in such a place, taking what came at them, fighting back, refusing to give up or give in, for a place to call their own—refusing to give up or give in...

There was a jerking motion as the train slowed around a bend. Surely they weren't stopping for water already. Then a new thought and fear tingled at the back of her neck. It had been a night just like this one that Black-faced Charley and his men had attacked the train she was on.

The train lurched and slowed and then continued to roll down the track for several hundred more yards before stopping. The attendant had gone ahead some time earlier. Mr. Roosevelt's private car was directly behind the car she was in.

Laine turned as the door at the far end of the car opened. Across from her, the young mother cradled her sleeping infant and protectively gathered the dozing toddler to her side. Laine's breath caught at the sight of the lean figure that slowly walked toward them.

Head bent, the wide brim of that hat shielding his face, it was impossible to see the man. He approached the first passenger. He then approached several other passengers. Each in turn rose and walked quickly down the aisle and left the car.

An elderly gentleman coughed nervously as he rose to assist his wife from the bench seat, casting a nervous glance in Laine's direction. He waited in the aisle as the stranger approached the young mother. When she also rose, the older man took the sleepy-eyed toddler from her, and escorted the women from the car. The door closed behind them. The stranger slowly walked towards her, the light from a lamp in the car gleaming off the badge he wore.

She rose from her seat.

"What are you doing here?" she demanded. "What did you tell those poor people to make them leave?"

"I told them you were a dangerous outlaw, and it would be safer for them in the next car."

Of all the... "Why?"

"Unfinished business."

"What unfinished business?"

"The reason you came out here. The answers you were looking for. You came for the truth. It's what you risked your life for. You can't walk away from it now."

"What are you talking about?"

He pulled out the envelope Curry had given him.

"I promised I would help you find the truth. It's there in that envelope."

Laine stared at it. Then, slowly opened it.

The uniquely cut, perfect teardrop crystal dropped into her hand. Tears filled her eyes. She thought she'd lost it when she left the ranch. She recognized Addison's signature at the bottom of the note.

"Hannah found it after you left the ranch. Addison wanted you to have it, he hoped it might change your mind about leaving."

She sat down. "I don't understand?"

Ranse sat across from her. A twenty-year-old tragedy, not so very different from his own loss and hundreds of others for those who came out here looking to build a life, only to lose it. And somewhere in the middle of it, a little girl who had survived, like others, in spite of all of it.

She sat across from him now, no longer a little girl but a young woman who had come to that wild and dangerous Territory to find answers.

He told her a story, about that little girl who arrived in Philadelphia with a note pinned to her dress clutching a pendant that was all she had from that night when her entire world turned upside down.

"Addison's son, John, met his wife in New York. They travelled to Europe right after they were married. John found a crystal lamp while on their travels similar to one his mother had a long time ago, that was broken when it was shipped out from St. Louis. He bought it to replace the one that was lost and had it sent back to New York.

"Their daughter was born after they returned. Addison never met his son's wife, but he had pictures of her. The only pictures he had of his granddaughter were taken when she was an infant. He was told that she had blue eyes like his wife. She would have been two years old would when John and his wife made plans to come to the Territory.

"As much as anyone knows, they were attacked outside of town. There was a bad storm that night, the carriage overturned as they tried to escape and cross the Cimarron. Addison and several of the men went out to search for them.

They found John down river from the carriage. He'd been shot, money taken. They found his wife inside the overturned carriage. Both were dead. There was no sign of the little girl."

She stared at him. "What are you saying?"

"You're that little girl who travelled with her parents from the East over twenty years ago and escaped the night they died." He reached out and took her hand in his.

"Addison is your grandfather. The truth was there in the crystal you had all along."

"But how?" her eyes filled with tears. She wanted to believe it.

"When the lamp arrived, it was missing one of the crystal pendants. It seems that even as a small child you were stubborn when you decided you wanted something. Your father removed one crystal and had it put on a chain for you."

"Addison tried for months to find you, but there was never any trace of what had happened to you."

She stared down at the pendant.

"I don't remember seeing a lamp with a missing pendant," she looked at him.

"Addison couldn't bear to look at it and had it put away after your parents were killed. It's all there in his note."

"And you rode all the way out here to bring me this...?"

She was trying to take it all in, to understand everything he was telling her. He had come there for Addison, to give her the note and the pendant that she thought she had lost.

"That's part of the reason." He stood then, paced a half dozen steps away and then back.

How did he explain it so that she would understand? How did he explain what it was like that long ride back alone with his father's body, all he would ever have of who he was, might have been, all those years before? How did he explain what those nights were like out there, alone? The fear, the emptiness inside, the loss, convincing himself that he didn't need anything or anyone?

He'd brought his father's body back and in doing so came back a different person, who didn't let anyone in, who learned to hide his emotions through the years that followed and became someone else.

Until that night at the Oaks when the storm hit and he saw the terror in her eyes, felt it in her and it pulled him back through the years. And as the storm broke around them, she was there... she needed him.

He turned and looked at her.

"It was you."

He slowly walked back to her until they were standing so close that he could feel her, breathe in that faint scent of her that he'd discovered that one night during the storm.

"I never needed anyone..." he said, almost angrily, as he

cradled her face in his hands and pressed his forehead against hers and let the words out, everything he hadn't said, hadn't even admitted to himself. Not that night, not later in the outlet when he didn't know if he would find her dead or alive, not even at the Jessup's before he rode off and left her there, or in that alley with blood and death all around them. But it was there.

"I need you," he whispered against her lips, tasting her, breathing her in, holding on to her.

"Your stubbornness, your strength, courage... I don't care what your name is—Dalton, Stanton, Ralston... I need *you*."

She touched his beard-roughened cheek with her fingers.

"When you walked away at the hotel... I didn't want you to leave."

"I'm not walking away now." He closed his eyes, fighting those old demons, prying open the past at little bit more, reaching for the future.

"Laine McCandliss."

A man of few words; but those few words said so much. His name. A name of her own.

They both looked around at a sound behind them. The attendant stood there, a stopwatch in his hand.

"You did say ten minutes, marshal?" the attendant reminded him.

Ranse looked at her.

A man of few words, who had walked into her life, turned it upside down, promised her nothing, and gave her everything. She touched his face. She saw the boy there inside the man.

"I think I'll take a lifetime..." she told him.

Ranse smiled. "That starts now..."

ALSO BY CARLA SIMPSON

Always My Love

Seductive Caress

Seduced

Deceived

ABOUT THE AUTHOR

"I want to write a book... " she said.

"Then do it," he said.

And she did, and received two offers for that first book proposal.

A dozen historical romances later, and a prophecy from a gifted psychic and the Legacy Series was created, expanding to seven additional titles.

Along the way, two film options, and numerous book awards.

But wait, there's more a voice whispered, after a trip to Scotland and a visit to the standing stones in the far north, and as old as Stonehenge, sign posts the voice told her, and the Clan Fraser books that have followed that told the beginnings of the clan and the family she was part of...

And now... murder and mystery set against the backdrop of Victorian London in the new Angus Brodie and Mikaela Forsythe series, with an assortment of conspirators and murderers in the brave new world after the Industrial Revolution where terrorists threaten and the world spins closer to war.

When she is not exploring the Darkness of the fantasy world, or pursuing ancestors in ancient Scotland, she lives in the mountains near Yosemite National Park with bears and mountain lions, and plots murder and revenge.

And did I mention fierce, beautiful women and dangerous, handsome men?

They're there, waiting...

Join Carla's Newsletter

www.ingramcontent.com/pod-product-compliance
Lightning Source LLC
Chambersburg PA
CBHW050029120726
47903CB00006B/1964